By Julie Garwood

Gentle Warrior

Rebellious Desire

Honor's Splendour

The Lion's Lady

The Bride

Guardian Angel

The Gift

The Prize

The Secret

Castles

Saving Grace

Prince Charming

For the Roses

The Wedding

The Clayborne Brides

Come the Spring

Ransom

Heartbreaker

Mercy

Killjoy

Murder List

Slow Burn

Shadow Dance

Shadow Music

FIRE AND ICE

BALLANTINE BOOKS
NEW YORK

FIRE
AND
ICE

A NOVEL

JULIE
GARWOOD

Copyright © 2008 by Julie Garwood

All rights reserved.

Published in the United States by Ballantine Books, an imprint of The Random House Publishing Group, a division of Random House, Inc., New York.

BALLANTINE and colophon are registered trademarks of Random House, Inc.

ISBN 978-0-345-50075-5

Printed in the United States of America on acid-free paper

www.ballantinebooks.com

2 4 6 8 9 7 5 3 1

First Edition

Book design by Susan Turner

For Sharon Felice Murphy, the bravest person I know,
and
for Elena O'Shea Nordstrom, my friend forever

FIRE AND ICE

JOURNAL ENTRY 1
CHICAGO

Today we celebrate. The foundation has finally approved the grant money to fund our study. There are four of us, all with doctorates, but we're acting like irresponsible teenagers laughing and carrying on. Later, we'll probably get as drunk as dropouts. We've worked hard to get here.

Our backgrounds are quite diverse. Kirk has come to us from St. Cloud, Minnesota, where he did extensive work with gray wolves in Camp Ripley. His expertise with the wolf pack's family dynamic will be invaluable to us.

Eric comes from the prestigious TNI research facility in Chicago. He is the youngest but has the most degrees. He calls himself a lab rat, as he has been isolated in the lab doing extensive research on two projects funded by the Kenton Pharmaceutical Company. He's a biologist and a chemist, and I think his background in immunology will compliment the other studies.

Brandon, our director, has been in North Dakota for eleven years. He observed and documented wolves traveling more than two thousand miles. He would like to put tracking devices, radio-controlled collars, on two separate pairs of alpha males and females so that we can record their movements. His focus is on behavioral habits.

I'm the only behavioral scientist here, but I'm a biologist as well. My personal quest is different from the others, but it's my hope that there won't be a conflict. We're all interested in the dynamic within the pack, but I'm also interested in the effects of stress on the individual . . . extreme stress.

ONE

A POLAR BEAR DID HIM IN. THE BIGGEST DAMNED POLAR bear anyone had ever seen in or around Prudhoe Bay in the last twenty-five years, or so it was reported.

Arrogance got him killed, though, and if William Emmett Harrington hadn't been such a narcissist, he might still be alive. But he was a narcissist, and he was also a braggart.

The only topic of conversation William was interested in was William, and since he hadn't accomplished much of anything significant in his twenty-eight years on earth, he was painfully boring.

William lived off his inheritance, a hefty trust fund set up by his grandfather, Henry Emmett Harrington, who must have had an inkling of the lazy-ass gene he was passing down, because his son, Morris Emmett Harrington, didn't work a day in his life. And William happily followed in his father's footsteps.

Like all the Harrington men before him, William was a handsome devil and knew it. He didn't have any trouble getting women into his bed, but he could never lure any of them back for a repeat performance. No wonder. William treated sex like a race he had to win in order to prove that he was the best, and because he really was a narcissist, he didn't care about satisfying his partner. What *he* wanted was all that mattered.

His past conquests had come up with various nicknames for him. Pig was one. Quick Trip was another. But the one that was uttered most behind his back was The Minute Man. All the women who had gone to bed with him knew exactly what that meant.

Besides self-gratification, William's other passion was running. He'd made it a full-time job because, as with sex, he was shockingly fast. In the past year he had accumulated twenty-four first-place prizes within a six-state area, and he was about to enter a 5K race in his hometown of Chicago to collect his twenty-fifth. Since he believed crossing the finish line first was going to be a momentous event that everyone in Chicago would want to read about, he called the *Chicago Tribune* and suggested they do a feature article about him in the Sunday paper. Harrington also mentioned more than once how photogenic he was and how a full-color photo of him would enhance the article.

One of the local news editors at the *Tribune* took the call and patiently listened to William's pitch, then bounced him to one of the entertainment editors, who quickly bounced him to one of the sports columnists, who bounced him to one of the health and fitness editors, who wrote an entire article on the top-five allergens plaguing Chicago while he listened to the spiel. None of them was impressed or interested. The last editor to speak to William suggested that he give him a call back when he had ninety-nine wins under his belt and was going for one hundred.

William wasn't discouraged. He immediately called the *Chicago Sun Times* and explained his idea for a story. He was rejected yet again.

William realized he was going to have to lower his expectations if he wanted to see his name in print, and so he contacted the *Illinois Chronicle*, a small but popular neighborhood newspaper that focused primarily on local issues and entertainment.

The editor in chief, Herman Anthony Bitterman, was an antacid-popping seasoned veteran of the press with a pronounced Brooklyn accent. For thirty years he had been on the foreign desk of *The New York Times* and had garnered several prestigious honors including the RFK Journalism Award and the Polk Award, but when his good-for-nothing son-in-law ran off with another woman—his daughter's yoga instructor, for the love of God—Herman retired from the *Times* and moved with his wife, Marissa, to Chicago where she had grown up and where their daughter now lived with her four little girls.

A newsman at heart, Herman couldn't stay retired long. When the opportunity presented itself, he took the job at the *Chronicle* as a distraction from boredom and an escape from the horde of meddling in-laws.

He liked Chicago. He'd gone to Northwestern University, where he'd met Marissa. After graduation, they had returned to his hometown, New York, so he could take a job at the *Times*. Coming back to Chicago after decades in New York was a real adjustment. He had lived in a cramped two-bedroom Manhattan apartment for so long that a two-story brownstone took some getting used to. His only real complaint was the lack of noise. He missed falling asleep to the soothing sounds of cars screeching, horns blaring, and sirens shrieking.

With so much quiet, even at the office, Herman found it difficult to get any work done. To compensate, he brought in an old television set from home, plopped it on top of his mini refrigerator, and left it on all day with the volume turned up.

When the call came in from William Harrington, Herman hit the mute button before picking up the phone. While he ate his lunch—an Italian sausage and green pepper sandwich drenched in ketchup and washed down with an icy cold Kelly's Root Beer—he listened to Harrington pitch his story idea.

It took Bitterman all of half a minute to sum up William Harrington. The man was an egomaniac.

"Red, huh? You always wear red socks and a red T-shirt for every race. And white shorts. Yeah, that's interesting. Even when you run in the winter? Still wear the shorts?"

His question encouraged Harrington to ramble more, allowing Bitterman time to finish his sandwich. He took a long swig of his root beer, then interrupted Harrington's grandiose opinion of himself and said, "Yeah, sure. We'll do the story. Why not?"

After scribbling down the particulars, Bitterman disconnected the call, then wadded up his brown lunch sack and tossed it into the trash can.

He crossed the office to get to the door—a no small feat considering nearly every inch of the room was filled with crates of Kelly's Old-Fashioned Root Beer stacked halfway to the ceiling. Since his door wasn't blocked, his office hadn't been deemed a fire hazard, at least not yet. He was hoarding what was left of Kelly's Root Beer because, in his estimation, it was the best damned root beer he had ever tasted, and when he'd heard the company had been forced to close its doors and was going out of business, he had done what any root beer addict would do and rushed out to buy as many bottles of the stuff as he could get his hands on.

"Blond Girl!" he shouted. "I've got another story for you. This one's a humdinger."

Sophie Summerfield Rose tried to ignore Bitterman's bellow as she put the finishing touches on an article she was about to e-mail him.

"Hey, Sophie, I think Bitterman's calling you."

Gary Warner, a brute of a man and the office snitch, leaned over her cubicle. His smile reminded Sophie of a cartoon fox with his teeth bared. He looked a bit like a fox, too. His nose was long and pointy, and his complexion was as dull as his long straggly hair. Mullets had never really been in style, but Gary loved his and used so much hair spray on it, it looked starched.

"Since you're the only female here today and since you're the only blonde in the entire office, I'm pretty sure 'Blond Girl' means you." He had a good laugh over what he considered a hilarious observation.

Sophie didn't respond. No matter how obnoxious Gary became, and he had cornered the market on obnoxious a long time ago, she refused to let him rile her. She carefully pushed her chair back so she wouldn't hit the file cabinet again. It already had so many dents, it looked like someone had taken a baseball bat to it.

The *Chronicle* was housed in an old warehouse. It was a huge, gray stone building with gray cement floors, gray brick walls, and a dingy gray ceiling that Sophie suspected had once been white. The fluorescent lighting was nearly as old as the building. The presses were in the basement. Circulation and the other departments were on the first floor, and the editorial offices were on the second floor. It was a huge space, yet each gray-paneled cubicle, including hers, was the size of a refrigerator. A side-by-side, but still a refrigerator.

The *Chronicle* could have been a depressing place to work, but it wasn't. Colorful posters hung above the gray file cabinets that lined the far wall, and each cubicle was brightly decorated. Some were more creative than others, but each gave a hint of the occupant's personality.

Gary's cubicle was decorated with half-eaten sandwiches and pastries, some at least a week old. He wouldn't let the cleaning crew touch his desk, and Sophie didn't think it had ever been cleared of the clutter. She wouldn't have been surprised to find roaches skittering under all the garbage, but Gary probably wouldn't have minded. He was most likely related to some of them.

Still hanging over her cubicle wall, his frame was so large she thought he might just snap the panels. When Sophie stood, Gary was entirely too close, his rancid aftershave overwhelming.

So that he couldn't snoop while she was in Bitterman's office, Sophie turned her computer off and made sure he saw her do it. She wasn't being paranoid. Just last week she had caught him sitting at her desk trying to get around her password to access her e-mail. He had already rifled through her desk. Two drawers were open, and he hadn't bothered to put the stack of papers back where she had left them. When she demanded to know what he was doing at her desk, he stammered lamely about his computer being down and how he was checking to see if hers was down, too.

Bitterman roared again, and Sophie, feeling somewhat like a mouse navigating a maze, hurriedly zigzagged her way around the cubicles to reach his office at the end of the long room. She pictured a piece of yellow cheese dangling from a string in front of her boss's door. Wasn't that the reward for the little mouse at the end of the maze?

"Hey, Sophie, heard from your father lately?" Gary shouted from behind.

He had asked her that same question about ten minutes after she had started working at the *Chronicle*, which was probably why she had taken such a quick dislike to him. Not only was Gary a snoop, but at times he could be downright antagonistic. Usually, people skirted around the subject of her dad, Bobby Rose, when they first met Sophie, but not Gary. She had just started writing her first article when Gary had called over the cubicle wall, "Hey, Sophie Rose . . . oops, it's Sophie Summerfield, isn't it? I forgot, you're not using your daddy's name. Guess you don't want the world to know who you are, huh? I wouldn't either if my old man was a crook. Who's he scammed lately? Heard he's made off with a butt-load of money. If you ever see him again, tell him ol' Gary could sure use a loan. Tell him a couple of million would do just fine. . . ."

She hadn't answered him then or the hundred or so other times he'd asked about her father, and she wasn't about to answer him now.

Gary wasn't the only one interested in finding her father. She received regular visits from the FBI, the IRS, the CIA, and just about every other government agency with initials. All of them wanted to know where Bobby Rose was; all of them wanted a pound of his flesh.

She heard Gary call out his question again, but she continued to ignore him as she rounded the last cubicle and reached Bitterman's office.

"Shut the door, will you," Bitterman ordered. He didn't bother looking up.

The urge to slam the door was strong, and though it would have given her enormous satisfaction for a fleeting second, with her luck these days she'd break the glass and Bitterman would make her pay to replace it. Besides, if truth be told, she actually liked her boss. For all his bluster and bellowing, he was a good man. He loved his wife and family, and he cared about his employees, too, at least most of them.

One of her conditions for accepting her job at the *Chronicle* was that Bitterman wouldn't pressure her to talk or write about her father, which was the reason she had left her last job. Bitterman had given her his word, and so far he'd kept it. He'd taken his promise a step further, too. He shielded her as much as he could from what he called those blasted, sleazy, rag mag, bottom-feeders—he absolutely refused to call them journalists—who continually hounded her for an interview. Bitterman also attempted, but failed miserably, to protect her from the FBI, citing every amendment and law he could think of that would give her the right to be left alone.

No, she wouldn't be slamming any doors today. No matter how much he aggravated her, Sophie would treat Mr. Bitterman with the respect he deserved. She gently pushed the door shut, stepped around a crate of root beer, and waited for him to look up from the stack of papers he was bent over.

"Sir, you really have to stop calling me Blond Girl. It's sexist, rude, and demeaning. I've worked here long enough for you to know my name, but just for fun, let's go over it one more time. Sophie Summerfield Rose. There. Not so difficult to remember, is it?"

"No, it's not," he agreed. "And you're using your mother's maiden name on your bylines. Summerfield, right?"

Since she had just reminded him of her full name, she didn't feel it necessary to answer.

Bitterman couldn't help but notice she was still frowning. "All right. No more Blond Girl. I promise."

"Thank you."

He considered her for a long minute and then said, "Sophie, everyone in Chicago knows who you are. You're Bobby Rose's daughter."

"Yes, I am his daughter," she agreed. "However, I don't believe *everyone* in Chicago knows, which is why I use my mother's maiden name on my articles."

He tried to lean back in his chair, but the crates of root beer stopped him.

Not wanting to continue the conversation about her father, she hastily said, "I finished that piece on termite infestation you wanted. It's riveting. I e-mailed it to you a minute ago. Do you have anything else disgusting for me to research and write about? Sewage? Vermin? The mating habits of beetles?"

He laughed. "Why, Sophie Rose, are you giving me attitude? I think maybe you are. I know it when I hear it. I get enough sass from my eight granddaughters. I don't need to hear it from my employees, not even from my favorite one."

She smiled. "Sir, you have four granddaughters, not eight."

He reached for his root beer. "When they're all chattering away at me, it seems like eight. And yes, I do happen to have something else for you. A man named William Harrington called and pitched a story idea. You ever run a 5K?"

He explained the human interest story, told her how long he thought the copy should be, handed her his notes, and said, "Call him and set up a time to meet before the race. Maybe you could get a couple of photos of him, too. Yeah, do some before and after shots. You know, get a good one of him starting off and one of him crossing the finish line. Harrington swore to me that he's photogenic. He seemed to think being good-looking was important."

"Shouldn't Matt take the photos? He's always telling everyone here that he's the official photographer for the *Chronicle*; I'd hate to upset him. You know how he can be." She didn't say the word "neurotic," but she thought it. "The more excited he gets, the higher his voice goes. He could break glass if he tried. With all these root beer bottles, it would be a disaster."

Bitterman nodded. "You're right. Matt should take the photos . . . if he were still working here. He quit on me. Gave me his notice last night and told me he didn't want to stick around this dump—his words, not mine—for two more weeks. He said it was a waste of his valuable time. That's right . . . *his* valuable time. He cleared out his cubicle lickety split." Bitterman waved his hands, one over the other, like a professional card dealer signaling to the ceiling cameras in a casino. "I don't know if he has another job lined up. He told me he wanted to take *important* photos for *important* articles."

Sophie hadn't known Matt well. She'd only worked with him on a couple of stories, and both times he'd thrown a territorial tantrum.

"To be honest, he was a lousy photographer anyway," Bitterman said. "Always cutting off the top of people's heads, and besides, you've got a better camera than the *Chronicle*'s ancient one. I think Jimmy Olsen used one like it in that Superman movie. And those photos you took last month of the kitchen makeover were good, real good."

"I'll give it my best try," she said. She was looking at his notes, trying to decipher his chicken scratches. "Sir, I can't tell . . . when is the race?"

"Saturday." He put a hand up to ward off any argument she wanted to give. "I know what you're going to say. It's short notice."

She laughed. "Short notice? Tomorrow's Saturday."

He shrugged. "What can I tell you? It's obvious we weren't Harrington's first choice . . . or second or third, I'm guessing. The guy just called."

"I won't have time to do much of a background check."

"We've already got this Sunday locked in, so we won't run it until next Sunday, and if Harrington turns out to be a wacko, it might even make for a more interesting article. You're not going for the Pulitzer here. Do what you can, and if it doesn't work out, if the guy really is a flake, we'll run something else. Time's a-wasting. Better get going."

She was pulling the door closed behind her when he said, "You know the drill. Meet him in a public place, and better yet, take a friend with you. Be safe, not sorry."

He always said those exact words to her whenever she left on an assignment. Be safe, not sorry. The ritual was actually comforting. Bitterman, she decided, had a duel personality. One minute he was barking orders like a mad Doberman, and the next he was playing the part of an overly protective mother hen. At least she thought that was how a mother would act. She didn't have enough experience to know.

In her cubicle, Sophie typed "William Harrington" into a search engine and within seconds all sorts of information about him popped up on screen. The man had his own website, a blog, and would soon, according to his entry, have a video of himself on MySpace, YouTube, and Facebook. He'd written long essays on his childhood, his summers in Europe—which should have been interesting but weren't—and on his fitness campaign.

Sophie wouldn't have any trouble recognizing Harrington. There were dozens of photos of him on his website.

After making a few notes about his other 5K wins, she called him. He must have been waiting to hear from her because he answered on the first ring. Sophie thought it would take only a few minutes to set up a time and place to meet, but Harrington was a talker and kept her on the line for a good fifteen minutes before he finally got around to scheduling their interview.

"Of course you know the race is tomorrow, so we'll have to meet tonight. I hope you're a morning person because the 5K starts early, and you'll want to be there, right? With a photographer," he added in a rush. "The race is in Lincoln Park, so how about tonight we meet someplace around there?"

"How about Cosmo's Pub?" she asked and gave him the address.

"I've never been to Cosmo's. I go to more upscale restaurants. But that's just a few blocks from where the race will start tomorrow. We could meet at seven. No, better make it six-thirty to give us more time. Does six-thirty work for you? I need to get to bed early. I want to be in top form tomorrow, especially since I'm going to be filmed."

"Someone's filming the race?"

"No, they're going to film *me* running the race," he corrected. "They'll stay with me the whole way."

"Do you plan to put the video on your website?"

"Of course."

The man sounded serious. Who besides William Harrington would watch it? she wondered.

"So you're paying someone to film the entire race?" she asked, still doubting.

He spoke at the same time. "Twenty-five wins is more than impressive, at least to some very important people it is. After the trial, there will be another video on my website, and that one will, no doubt, be just as impressive. Twenty-five wins is a huge accomplishment. Don't you agree?"

Running the Boston marathon was impressive, and finishing that race was definitely an accomplishment. But a 5K? Not so much. Sophie kept her opinion to herself, though, because she didn't want to squelch his enthusiasm or antagonize him. Harrington had an ego the size of Illinois, but he was polite and eager and seemed harmless enough.

Getting him to stop talking about himself proved to be a challenge, and time was slipping away. It was already after three.

"What did you mean when you said there will be another video after the trial? What trial?"

"I've been invited to join the Alpha Project. It's very exclusive," he boasted. "Only the fittest are asked, and I plan to break a record with this race. I'm going to shave off a couple of minutes. Bring a stopwatch if you don't believe me."

When he finally took a breath, she blurted, "So much to talk about tonight. I'll see you at six-thirty. Bye now."

He was still talking as she disconnected the call. She quickly gathered her things and raced around the cubicles to get to the elevator. In her hurry she nearly ran headfirst into a delivery man wheeling a dolly with yet more crates of Kelly's Root Beer. She pointed the way to Bitterman's office.

We're ready to head north. After years of studying the arctic wolves in captivity, Brandon and Kirk will finally be able to observe these glorious animals in their natural habitat. Eric and I are novices, but our excitement matches theirs. If everything goes as planned, we'll know much more about the socialization of this subspecies as well as their adaptation to their environment, which is what I'm most interested in.

Not looking forward to the cold, but the information we'll be able to contribute to the scientific community about these mysterious creatures will be worth any personal sacrifices we may have to make.

Who knows? We might become famous.

TWO

ALL HE WANTED WAS A CHEESEBURGER.

Agent Jack MacAlister had just completed a grueling two-day undercover assignment in one of Chicago's toughest neighborhoods, and he was tired and dirty and hungry. The last thing he needed as he walked into the burger joint was to interrupt an armed robbery.

With a single shot through the center of the heart, Jack's bullet propelled the man backward, away from the teenage girl he was holding hostage, and slammed him into the wall. A single stream of blood oozed down the perp's dirty T-shirt.

Jack didn't have to kill the other one. A couple of swift moves, and he was able to disarm the guy and get him facedown on the floor. He held him there with a foot on the back of his neck.

Outside, Jack's partner, Alec Buchanan, heard the gunshot. Drawing his weapon as he deftly slid over the hood of his car, Alec raced to the door. Inside the restaurant, bedlam had erupted. The teenage girl was screaming at the top of her lungs and backing away from Jack. When she turned and saw Alec—though it didn't seem humanly possible—her screams got even louder. It was apparent that she was as terrified of them as she had been of the men who would have killed her.

Jack held up his badge. "FBI!" he shouted. "You're okay now. You can stop screaming. You too, ma'am," he added to the nearly hysterical woman fanning herself with a limp napkin and bouncing up and down as though she were doing some sort of manic jumping jacks.

Alec dug his badge out of his pocket and held it up as he made his way over to his partner. He squatted down next to the dead body. "Nice shot," he remarked when he saw where the bullet had penetrated.

"Didn't have a choice," Jack replied quietly, so only Alec would hear. The man he was holding down started squirming. "You get up, and I'm just gonna mow you down again."

Alec put his foot down hard on the base of the man's spine to get him to stop moving.

Three police cars, sirens blaring, screeched to a stop in the parking lot. To keep from getting riddled with bullets, Jack and Alec continued to hold up their badges. Since the two of them had just been doing undercover work, with their greasy long hair and scraggly beards, they looked more like deranged killers than agents of the FBI.

"Don't you want to know what happened?" Jack asked Alec as he tilted his head toward the man he'd killed.

"I figured he didn't get your order right."

"He was hopped up on something. God only knows what. He was gonna kill the girl, no question." He glanced down and shifted his stance so that more of his weight pressed on the captive. "This guy's eyes are so dilated they look like saucers."

Alec noticed another teenager holding up his cell phone. He wondered how long the kid had been taking video. Muttering an expletive, he turned his back on the teenager and said, "We just blew our cover. How much you want to bet we're on the Internet within the hour?"

Jack shrugged. "The job was done today anyway."

Jack and Alec stepped aside as the police swarmed through the door.

The first officer knelt beside the body. "It's Jessup," he called to the others.

A couple of policemen came closer to take a look. "Son of a gun," one of them said. "Never thought he'd be taken down."

"Who's Jessup?" Jack asked.

The officer kneeling on the floor looked up. "A major drug supplier. We've been trying to stop him for years. Looks like he started sampling some of his own stuff."

Paramedics walked in with stretchers, and soon the tiny burger joint was crowded.

Jack leaned against the counter and turned to Alec. "You still hungry?"

Alec picked up a laminated menu. "I could eat."

Three hours later, after filing reports and turning the case over to the police, they were finally on their way back to headquarters. The second they walked inside, they were told to report to the office of the special agent in charge. No surprise there. She had already texted them. Three little words that spoke volumes: My office. Now.

Margaret Don't-Ever-Call-Me-Maggie Pittman sat behind her massive desk. A group of agents had formed a semicircle behind her, all of them intently watching her computer screen.

"Look who's decided to join us," she drawled in her Arkansas twang. "Agent Hot Stuff and his sidekick Agent Hot Shot."

"YouTube?" Alec asked.

In unison every agent in the room nodded.

"That's enough now," Pittman dismissed the crowd around her desk. "You've all had your fun. Get back to work while I talk to the movie stars." Had she been smiling, her comment would have been funny. "Gentlemen, step over here. Agent MacAlister, perhaps you can tell me what's happening here." She pointed to the monitor.

Damn. The kid had gotten it all. Jack winced when he saw himself leaning against the hood of Alec's car. One ankle was crossed
over the other, and he was devouring his cheeseburger while the
paramedics were rolling the body bag past him.

"Do you know what this looks like, Agent? I'll tell you. You kill
a man, karate chop and tae kwon do the hell out of another man to
put him down, and then you enjoy a nice cheeseburger while you
take in the afternoon sun, acting like none of it affects you one little
bit. That's what it looks like."

Jack thought she was finished. "In my defense—"

"Now we know it's all in a day's work, and we can't let it get
to us, but the public doesn't necessarily understand that, Agent,
and they expect us to be . . . sensitive. Yes, I said sensitive, Agent
Buchanan. They don't want us to be cavalier or blasé after we gun
down someone."

Sensitive? Jack thought. Was she serious? She couldn't be, could
she? Since Alec had worked with Special Agent in Charge Pittman
longer than he had, Jack looked at him to see his reaction. No help
there. Alec was stone-faced.

"What would you consider appropriate behavior, ma'am?" Jack
asked.

She squinted at him. "I'll tell you what *isn't* appropriate. Eating
a damned cheeseburger while they're carting a corpse past you."

He had a feeling she wasn't finished. He was right.

"Sit down, both of you. I'm tired of cranking my neck back."

She waited until both men were seated facing her from across
the desk, then said, "Now today is an interesting exception. The
higher-ups aren't going to be happy when they see this video." She
sighed and then said, "They've probably already seen it. However,
the public, at least the public looking at this video, have turned you
two into rock stars."

"Rock stars?" Alec said

"That's crazy," Jack said at the same time.

"That's right, rock stars. So far, this little video has had over two thousand visitors and counting. Hopefully, once you two clean up and get rid of the long hair and beards, you won't be recognizable to your fan club."

Jack groaned. "Fan club? You've got to be kidding."

Pittman glared at him. "Do I look like I'm kidding, Agent MacAlister?"

Having caught on that she liked to answer her own questions, Jack didn't respond.

"No, I don't kid," she snapped. "The media are another story. They'll try to interview you, and we don't want that, do we?"

She hesitated a good ten seconds before answering. "No, we don't. Fortunately, you had already finished your last assignment, and of course there won't be any more undercover work for a long, long time. Until this situation blows over and the public finds something else to get all worked up about, you two are going to keep a low profile. Got that? A low, *low* profile. In fact, I think it would be a good idea if you both took some vacation time."

"I wasn't planning—" Alec began.

"Agent Buchanan, did you think I was making a suggestion? Let me clear up that misconception right now. You *are* taking time off. You too, Agent MacAlister. This isn't a choice. Oh, and you will stay in Chicago during your vacation."

"Why aren't you calling this what it is?" Alec asked.

"And what might that be?"

"A suspension."

She shook her head. "A suspension would indicate that I believe you've done something wrong."

"How long are we on vacation?" Jack asked. He folded his arms across his chest while he waited for a response.

She didn't answer the question. Instead she said, "While you are enjoying your vacation *in Chicago*," she stressed, "you will report in by e-mail or phone every morning. You will avoid talking to the media, and that includes telling them where you think they should put their microphones, Agent MacAlister. You will be ready to go back to work twenty-four hours after you're notified, which is why you will stay close in case I need you."

Jack was going to argue, but Alec spoke first. "When does our vacation begin?"

"Now."

Jack was following Alec out the doorway when Pittman called out, "Agent MacAlister?"

"Ma'am?"

"Good work today."

What the . . . He didn't say what he was thinking. He simply nodded to his superior and continued on, but once he and Alec were in the elevator, he repeated her remark.

"*Good work today?* What'd she mean by that? You've worked for her longer than I have, so tell me, was she being sarcastic, or was that her attempt at humor?"

"Neither," Alec said. "You did good work today, and she's acknowledging it. You watched the video. The kid got it all, from the minute those drugged-out bastards walked inside, until it was over. You prevented a bloodbath."

"One of us should have grabbed the kid's phone before we ordered the cheeseburgers."

Alec laughed. "Yeah, that's what screwed both of us. They weren't even good cheeseburgers."

The elevator doors opened on garage level B. Alec headed one way and Jack the other.

"What time tomorrow night?" Jack shouted.

"Try to get there by nine, and bring money, Jack. Lots of it. I want to win back what I lost."

Jack laughed. "Yeah, like that's gonna happen."

Arrived in Fairbanks this afternoon. It's spring, but it's still chilly.

We've all brought extra equipment with us. Brandon has assured us that everything we'll need is already in our shelter waiting to be unpacked. We'll fly into Barrow tomorrow, and from there we'll have quite a trek to our research facility. Brandon has shown us photos. The lab is quite spacious by most standards and connects to two temporary structures where we'll live.

Besides our scientific work, each of us has other duties. Eric is our designated medic. There will be times in the winter months when it will be impossible to get help, should there be an emergency. He's stocked the lab with supplies and medicines, but we all know the dangers we'll be facing, living such an isolated life while we do our work.

Kirk is in charge of weapons. We have no desire to hurt any animal. We are the intruders, after all, not they, but should we run into a grizzly, the sound of our rifle will hopefully chase him away. None of us will leave the safety of our shelter without protection. The arctic fox is known to carry rabies, and we will kill any rabid ones we encounter.

Yes, there will be challenges. We will meet them head on.

THREE

SOPHIE KNEW SHE'D BE CUTTING IT CLOSE, BUT SHE'D spilled salad dressing on her blouse at lunch and needed to go home first to change clothes before she met William Harrington at Cosmo's. She also needed to grab her recorder.

Times like today, when she was rushing around like a crazy woman, Sophie wished she still owned a car. She would have to run in high heels three blocks—three long blocks—to get to the El, and at this time of day the train was going to be packed with the surly going-home-from-work crowd.

She squeezed into the train just as the doors closed. The air inside was stuffy and smelled of old disinfectant. Sophie slowly made her way to the back of the car. Two teenage boys tried to engage her in conversation, but other than giving them a quick smile, she ignored them and continued on. She passed a middle-aged man who reeked of whiskey and who obviously hadn't touched a bar of soap in a long time. She thought herself fortunate to find an empty bench behind him and sat down. The drunk turned to face her. His eyelids were at half mast and he began to list to the left, but he jerked himself upright and moved toward her. He held on to the bar above his head and kept trying to get her attention by making weird sounds as he leered at her. He embodied the expression "dirty old man." Sophie thought he might be a relative of Gary's: his repellent leer was nearly identical.

The two teenage boys turned out to be quite chivalrous. Like everyone else on the train, they noticed the man's behavior. Jumping to their feet, they squeezed their way around him and blocked him from getting closer to Sophie. They also blocked him from getting off the El when she did.

She gave the boys an appreciative smile, though their sweet gesture hadn't really been necessary. She was quite capable of taking care of herself. The husband of her best friend was an FBI agent, and he'd taught Sophie all the moves she needed to protect herself. She also carried pepper spray. And as she stepped off the train, she released the grip she had around the canister.

She had a half hour before her appointment. Fortunately, her one-bedroom Lincoln Park condominium was just a couple of blocks from Cosmo's, a fact she deliberately hadn't mentioned to Harrington. Few people outside of law enforcement knew where she lived, or so she liked to believe, and she was determined to keep her private life just that: private.

Her father had given her the condo for her sixteenth birthday, and as soon as she was of age, he had transferred the title to her. With conditions. She couldn't sell it, which to her meant she didn't really own it. Still, there wasn't a mortgage, and she was thankful for that. Her father had paid cash for it, and back when she was a teen, Sophie didn't ask or care where his money came from. She had been too busy worrying about Social Services taking her away after his arrest, which she had thought was inevitable. At the time, there simply had not been room in her mind to think about cash problems or how her father, without any noticeable job, was able to live such an extravagant life. Back then, extravagant seemed ordinary. Sophie had never known anything different.

The morality of her situation didn't register until after she had graduated from the university. Due to the prodding of her two closest friends, she finally stopped taking money from her father, and that meant drastically modifying her lifestyle. When her car was in need of costly repairs, she sold it and began to walk or take the El to get around the city. Her life had become more strenuous, but it was definitely simpler now, and she liked that. She was proud that she had become a strong, independent woman who could succeed on her own.

Today was her personal best, she decided. She had a history of being late, but she was making a real effort to change that bad habit. After a quick stop home, she reached the bar and grill five minutes early.

Cosmo's drew a diverse crowd. There were always the junior executives networking while they sipped white wine or martinis, construction workers unwinding after a hard day's work while they snacked on appetizers and drank icy cold beer, and couples and singles from the neighborhood stopping by for a cold one and catching up on the latest news.

The bar was known for its bottled beer served just two degrees above freezing. Cosmo, like his father before him, was a fanatic about the temperature. There was also a small but adequate selection of wine from the vineyards of California, and draft beer that was brewed right there in Chicago. The grill was popular for its jalapeño hamburgers that seemed to get hotter every year. There wasn't anything pretentious about Cosmo's, which was probably why Sophie liked it so much. It was comfortable and inviting, a place where all the locals could come dressed in evening attire or jeans and feel right at home.

The decor was as eclectic as the owner. The furniture was sleek and contemporary with polished chrome tables and chairs with thick, black, padded cushions. Booths with plush, tufted benches lined two walls. The ceiling was the eye-catcher, though. Cosmo loved astronomy, and since he tended the bar nearly every night, he had decided to bring the sky inside. He had painted the arched ceiling a deep blue, dappled it with yellow circles that were supposed to look like planets, and strung tiny white Christmas lights along the beams. When the lights were on, the ceiling became his own dazzling, star-filled night.

Cosmo spotted Sophie the second she stepped through the door. He shouted her name to get her attention, blew her a kiss, then patted his chest a couple of times to indicate a heart beating wildly for her. He had developed a special fondness for her after she had written a rave review about his bar. Cosmo had been so pleased he'd had it blown up and framed. He kept it propped behind the bar where everyone could see it. She noticed a sign leaning next to her article tonight. In big bold letters Cosmo had printed "No more Kelly's Root Beer."

Sophie wound her way through the crowd looking for William Harrington. She found him in the back, sitting in a booth. He looked anxious.

"Mr. Harrington?"

He jumped to his feet and thrust his hand out. "You're Sophie Summerfield?" he asked. He sounded shocked and looked astonished.

She couldn't understand his reaction. "Yes, I am," she answered. "You did say six-thirty."

"Yes, yes, I did." He continued to stand, looking perplexed.

"Shall we sit down and get started?" she suggested.

She slid into the booth, waited until he'd taken his seat across from her, then reached for her digital tape recorder. "This is the first time I've used this, so please be patient," she said. Normally, such a small, sleek recorder would have been horribly expensive, but this particular model had been discontinued, so she had been able to buy it at a huge discount. Since it was a company expense, she was sure Mr. Bitterman would reimburse her. She checked the charge before placing the recorder on the table between them.

Harrington stared at her intently.

"Is something wrong?" she asked.

"I knew you were young," he said. "I could tell from your voice over the phone, but I didn't expect you to be so pretty."

When she didn't respond, he asked, "Were you surprised when you saw me?"

Did he expect her to return the compliment? "I saw your photos on your website," she replied, "so no, I wasn't surprised. I knew what you looked like. Why don't we get started?"

"Wouldn't you like something to drink first?"

He insisted she order, and so she asked for an iced tea. He ordered a sparkling water.

"I make it a rule never to drink alcohol or caffeine the night before a race. You know how long a 5K is, don't you? It's over three miles. I can't be sluggish, or it will affect my time, which is why I stick to water."

"Why don't you tell me about your first race?"

She didn't ask another question or say another word for the next hour. Once he started talking, he didn't stop. He was agonizingly boring, but whether she liked it or not, he was determined to go through all twenty-four races, from start to finish—and he had them all memorized.

Had her recorder been the old-fashioned kind, she would have gone through at least two cassettes. A good reporter would cut him off and take control of the interview, she thought. Or at least might bother to listen to what he was saying. In her defense, she did try several times to interrupt him. And she also tried to pay attention, but his monotonous voice could put an insomniac to sleep. He was on his tenth race when she completely zoned out and started thinking about all the mundane errands she needed to do over the weekend.

Once she had organized her schedule in her mind, she began to daydream about traveling through Europe again. She'd gone once before, after she'd graduated from the university, but she had missed some of Western Europe. Next time she'd love to see Spain and Portugal. A nice river cruise might be a relaxing way to see the beauty of these countries. She could certainly use a quiet vacation. Or perhaps she could book a stay in the posh spa she had read about in *Vogue* that had just opened on St. Barts . . .

Reality was quick to step in. At the moment she didn't have enough money in her account to buy an airline ticket to anywhere, unless she decided she could go without food for a month or two.

"I've made it a tradition to wear bright red socks."

Her attention bounced back to Harrington. "Yes, you mentioned that. Red socks, white shorts, and a red T-shirt."

"Did I mention my socks are a special kind? Each one has a tiny white band around the top. Only one store carries them, and I've bought over a hundred pairs. I don't dare run out," he added. Then with a shrug he said, "I guess I'm superstitious. Are you getting all this?"

"Yes." Sophie pointed to the recorder.

"Okay, good. Let's take a minute to talk about blisters. Readers will probably want to know all about them. Some have been real bad. There was this one . . ."

I hate my job, at least right at this moment I do. And I really hate being poor. But who doesn't hate being poor? she asked herself. Maybe Gandhi and Mother Teresa hadn't minded, but they were both considered saints, and Sophie certainly wasn't a saint.

Harrington ended his dissertation on foot ointments and, without stopping for breath, said, "Let's get back to the races, shall we? Now the morning of my eleventh race . . ."

Dear God, just kill me now.

Had she groaned out loud? Harrington either didn't notice or care that her eyes had glazed over.

She took a deep cleansing breath and pretended that she was in her yoga class. She would remove all negative energy from her thoughts and think only positive thoughts. Tomorrow night she was having dinner with Regan Buchanan and Cordie Kane, her two best friends since kindergarten. She couldn't wait to see them. Regan had been traveling for business but was returning to Chicago late tonight. Cordie had been working on her thesis for a PhD in chemistry, and Sophie hadn't seen her in over two weeks. She was wondering where they would eat when she realized that Harrington had stopped talking and was looking at her expectantly.

"I'm sorry. Would you repeat that last—"

"I asked if you were seeing anyone."

"Oh . . . no, I'm not," she answered. And then, before he could ask another personal question, she dug through her purse, pulled out her notebook, and flipped it open. "On the phone you mentioned being invited to join some kind of exclusive project, and you also mentioned something about a trial. I believe you called it the Alpha Project. What exactly were you talking about?"

"I don't remember saying anything about a project or a trial." He looked down at the table when he answered, a sure sign that he wasn't telling the truth.

She wasn't interested enough to pursue it. "Okay then, I guess that's it."

She was putting her notebook away when he reached across the table and picked up her recorder.

"How do I turn this off?"

"I'll do it."

"No, here it is." He pushed one button, then another. "There, now it's not recording. I don't want what I'm going to tell you on any kind of recorder. This is strictly 'off the record.' Isn't that what reporters say?"

"Actually—" she began, but he cut her off with a wave of his hand.

"I trust you won't tell anyone. This is very hush-hush." He leaned forward and in a near whisper said, "It's like the Olympics. At least that's how it was explained to me."

She put her purse back on the seat beside her and gave him her full attention.

"What is like the Olympics?"

He nervously looked around to make certain no one was listening, then said, "I'm in excellent condition and that's why I qualified."

He was maddening. "Qualified for what?"

"The trial," he explained. "Just like the Olympic trials . . . you know, the qualifications. The physical exam took three long days, and I swear they took half my blood to test. Oh, and I had a full body scan and an MRI, too. They didn't tell me why all those tests were necessary, but I think they were making certain I didn't have any big problems, like an aneurysm or a blockage, anything that might inhibit my peak performance or disqualify me." He smiled as he added, "It's really something to be invited to participate. Only a select few are chosen."

His eyes swept the room as he took a quick drink of his water and said, "I hope I'm not giving you the wrong impression. I don't want you to think I'm bragging, but you can see why I was chosen, can't you? I mean, just look at me."

She swore that if he flexed his biceps, she was going to get up and leave, story or no story. Fortunately, he didn't.

"You were chosen for what, Mr. Harrington?"

"William," he corrected. "Please, no formalities. I can already tell you and I are going to be close."

Wanna bet? Sophie impatiently brushed her bangs out of her eyes and let her frustration sound in her voice when she repeated her question for what seemed like the umpteenth time. "You were chosen for what, William?"

Mr. Talkative suddenly became evasive. "I really shouldn't be discussing this."

"You're the one who brought it up."

"I know I did, but I'm not supposed to talk about it. Not until it's over."

She decided not to press him. She checked the time instead. It was already close to nine o'clock. Harrington had been talking non-stop about himself and his twenty-four races and his blisters for over two hours, and now that the subject had become interesting, he turned reticent. It all sounded so bizarre, she thought he might be making it up to keep her there.

"I understand, William," she said. "If you can't talk about it—"

"It's confidential," he blurted.

She nodded. "Confidential. Then I guess we're finished here. Thank you for the interview."

"Would you like another drink?" he asked as he held up his hand to get the waiter's attention.

"No, thank you."

The poor waiter, his eyes shooting daggers, had been watching them for about an hour now. He looked hostile as he dropped their bill on the table. An iced tea and a sparkling water—not much of a tip there.

Sophie was hungry, but she didn't want to eat with Harrington. She would wait until she got home and could kick off her shoes. She'd relax while she zapped a frozen dinner in the microwave.

"I'll tell you what I'll do," he said in a conspiratorial whisper. "If you will go out to dinner with me tomorrow night, I'll explain everything to you then. I guarantee you'll be happy you did."

"Happy I went to dinner with you, or happy I heard what you had to say?"

He smiled. "Hopefully, both. Interested?"

"I'm sorry. I already have dinner plans tomorrow night . . . and Sunday."

"Monday night then?"

Sophie weighed the bad against the possible good. On the one hand, she'd have to suffer through another night listening to him drone on and on about himself, but on the other hand, what if he was telling her the truth? What if there was some kind of a secret club that only a select few were invited to join? What would be the purpose of such a club? And if they all had to be super athletes, was it some kind of a superman club? What would be the point?

Crazy. It had to be crazy. Still . . .

"Yes, all right, I'll have dinner with you, but . . ."

"Yes?" he asked eagerly.

"We'll have dinner here at Cosmo's. Seven-thirty, Monday night."

"No, no, I don't want to eat here. I want to take you to a five-star restaurant. Perhaps Nuvay or J'Adore. They're both excellent. Give me your address and I'll have a driver pick you up at seven. Don't you worry," he added with a wave of his finger, "I can afford to take you to dinner anywhere in the world."

She remained unimpressed. "As enticing as that sounds, I still prefer eating here at seven-thirty or not at all, William. Take it or leave it."

"I don't like bar food," he pouted.

While Sophie would have loved to dine in a great restaurant, she felt safe at Cosmo's, and she didn't know much about William Harrington except that he seemed totally into himself.

He must have figured from her silence that she wasn't going to budge.

"Oh, all right. We'll eat here," he conceded. "If you weren't so pretty, I wouldn't bother with you, but I'm a sucker for curvy blondes, and those gorgeous blue eyes of yours . . ." He looked away as he said almost offhandedly, "You're stunning." He shrugged. "I guess you've heard that before." His glance shifted to her feet and slowly moved up her body. "You know, Sophie, women don't usually play hard to get with me."

She decided to ignore his lascivious smirk. "Where would you like to meet tomorrow before the race?" she asked impatiently.

It took another ten minutes for him to settle on a time and place, and then she was finally free to head home. He stood and offered his hand as she slipped out of the booth.

"Until tomorrow then," he said.

She shook his hand. "Good night."

Glancing at her watch, she walked toward the door. Almost three hours now. Unbelievable, she thought. If there wasn't the possibility of another story here, there was no way she would spend another second with this man. He was insufferable. And what did he mean by "curvy"? Was he telling her he thought she looked healthy? Wholesome? Chubby? Or overly endowed? He'd been glancing at her chest every other minute since they'd sat down. And the comment that he wouldn't bother with her if he didn't think she was pretty? Was that supposed to be a compliment? The man was unbelievably rude, and his ego was somewhere in the stratosphere.

Sophie had calmed down by the time she'd reached home and was bolting the door behind her. It was rare for her to be home on a Friday night. The truth was, she couldn't remember the last time she had stayed in, and she planned to take advantage of her down time. She would catch up on her e-mails and go to bed early.

But time always seemed to get away from Sophie, and tonight was no exception. She didn't get to bed until well after one a.m., which would have been fine if she didn't have to get up at the crack of dawn for her second round with William Harrington.

JOURNAL ENTRY 22
ARCTIC CAMP

Brandon and I headed out again. It was a bitterly cold day, but we took every precaution against frostbite. Last week, Eric and Kirk had spotted a pack of wolves crossing this plateau, and they tracked them to see where they would settle. Brandon and I won't set up our monitoring equipment until we are certain we have found a stable sampling.

FOUR

HARRINGTON HAD BEEN INSISTENT THAT THEY MEET TWO hours before the race. He was waiting for her at the designated spot in front of a fountain that was one of Sophie's favorites. It was shaped like a weeping willow with water gently cascading down from the top branches.

He was doing stretching exercises as she approached. True to his word, he wore his uniform: white running shorts, which she thought were a little too form-fitting; a red T-shirt; black running shoes; and red socks with a thin white band around the top. She snapped quite a few photos while he chatted away and made suggestions for poses. Sophie wasn't much of a morning person, but Mr. Self-Involved seemed not to notice or care that she wasn't saying much. How could he possibly notice? He never stopped talking . . . or giving directions.

"Are you sure you'll have your camera ready at the finish line? Do you know where you'll wait? I think the steps across the street from the finish line would be the best spot. It's important that you get a good picture, don't you think? Especially since it's going to be on the front page." His tone sharpened as he asked, "It is, isn't it?"

"I don't know. I'll have to check—"

He interrupted. "I was promised the front page."

"You were? Then I guess—"

Again he interrupted. "It was implied."

"I see." She didn't, but it was all she could think to say. Oddly enough, her response seemed to placate him.

"Now about the photos," he began. "You have to be ready. A professional photographer would know that. I honestly don't understand why *you're* taking the pictures. You should have brought one of the photographers from the paper with you. Do you even know what you're doing? Be sure to snap at least one of me at the starting line, and you have to get just the right angle with the sun behind me when I cross the finish line. Not exactly right behind me, mind you, or you'll get a glare, and we don't want that, do we? But you need to be ready or you'll miss the shot."

She swore that if he told her she needed to be ready one more time, she was going to start screaming. "Yes, you mentioned that." *About twenty times now*, she silently added. "And I assure you, I'll be ready."

He acted as though she hadn't spoken. "I know what we can do. Do you have any of your business cards with you?"

She found one in the bottom of her purse and handed it to him. She didn't have a logo or a business address on her cards, just her name and her cell phone number. She'd had them printed after she had left her old job. Trying to stretch every dollar, she was determined to use all of them before she had more made.

Harrington unzipped a pocket in the back of his running shorts and pulled out a thin leather wallet. He opened it to slip her card in but stopped as though he'd just had a second thought. Stuffing the wallet back into his pocket, he said, "I think I'll give this to someone on the film crew." He knelt down on one knee and tucked her card in his right sock. "He can call you when I get close to the last hill. You know, so you can be ready."

Ready for what? She was dying to ask that question just to see how he would react. Not well, she guessed. He didn't seem to have much of a sense of humor, and normally this early in the morning, neither did she.

He stretched his arms over his head, rolled his shoulders as though he were trying to get rid of a crick in his neck, then said, "Okay, I'd better get going. I like to be the first to sign in, and I'll need to limber up even more. I allow thirty minutes for stretching."

"Exactly thirty minutes?"

"Yes, of course. I don't like to be surprised, so I plan down to the last detail. I believe it's important to be precise. You might want to mention that in your article about me."

"You'd better get going then . . . if you want to keep on schedule."

"Yes, you're right."

He was jogging down the path when she called out, "Good luck."

He glanced back at her. "I don't need luck. See you soon."

Sophie was happy to be rid of him for a little while. She backtracked to a coffee shop three short blocks away, drank two cups of hot tea, and, feeling human again, headed to the starting line to watch the race.

Runners were milling around the street with numbers safety-pinned to their shirts. She had her camera ready to take the photo of Harrington as he started out, assuming that he would be in the front of the pack, but she couldn't find him anywhere. She circled to the other side of the starting line, found an empty park bench, and stepped up on it, craning her neck to find Harrington in the throng. Still no sign of him. His red T-shirt should have made it easier for her to pick him out of the crowd, but who knew that so many people would be wearing red today?

The loud pop of the starting gun sent the runners scurrying for position. A sea of faces streamed before her, but none of them belonged to William Harrington. She had missed him.

Irritated, Sophie slumped down on the bench with her camera

in her lap. If Harrington was so adamant that she get a shot of him at the beginning of the race, why wasn't he in front? He had been one of the first runners to arrive at the park, even before the organizers had set up their tables, so he'd had ample time to get a good spot. Why would he let others take off ahead of him? With thousands of runners swarming down the street like some massive colony of ants, there was no way for her to see every one.

She looked around the crowd of spectators for some sign of a film crew and couldn't see any.

There was nothing to do now but wait. The course of the race wound through the streets and ended half a block from where she was standing. She made her way to the finish line to watch for the winner to appear.

Minutes later she saw a figure rounding a corner a couple of blocks away. The crowd cheered him as he drew closer.

Okay, here we go, Sophie thought. She raised her camera, ready for the shot at the finish line.

The runner came closer and closer, and was within a hundred yards of the line as the other competitors came into view far behind him.

Sophie lowered the camera slightly to get a better look. Uh-oh. The winner wasn't William Harrington. It was a man she'd never seen before. She quickly glanced back at those now approaching. Harrington wasn't among them either.

Runner after runner came across the line, but still no Harrington. He wasn't first—nor last—nor anywhere in between.

The man had simply disappeared.

Eureka! We have identified the pack. Six adults and three pups. We were able to pick out the alpha male right away. He's quite easy to identify because of his thick white coat tinged with a small dark patch across his back. He is also physically larger than the others. Brandon is thrilled with this new family we will study.

The alpha male is magnificent.

FIVE

I T WAS SOPHIE'S TURN TO PAY FOR DINNER.
  Regan insisted on eating at The Hamilton, the flagship of
her family's five-star hotel chain. She reserved one of the private
dining rooms adjacent to the atrium. The two-story windows
looked out over Lake Michigan.

As Regan led the way to the table with Cordie and Sophie trail-
ing behind, Sophie said, "I don't understand why you insisted on
eating here."

"I told you. I was in the mood for scallops, and I love the way
Chef Eduardo prepares them," Regan declared.

Sophie wasn't buying it. While it was true that Eduardo's scallops were outstanding, she knew the real reason Regan wanted to
eat there. If they ate at her family's hotel, a bill wouldn't be presented. Convenient, since it was Sophie's turn to pay.

"You're just doing this because you know I'm poor," she said.

A waiter pulled out a chair for her. Sophie flashed him a smile,
thanked him for the menu he offered her, then turned to Regan
again.

"Admit it."

"You don't like dining here?" Cordie asked. She was looking at Sophie over the top of her menu.

"I love dining here, but that isn't the issue. I simply want Regan to admit—"

"That you're poor? Okay. You're poor," Regan said cheerfully.

Cordie nodded. "Yes, you are. Very poor. I'd say you were dirt poor, but you know, that expression doesn't make any sense to me. What's dirt poor?"

Sophie frowned. "Not being helpful, Cordie. Regan, I want you to admit that my being poor is the reason we're eating here."

"Of course it's the reason," Cordie said.

"Yes, it is," Regan agreed amiably.

Cordie put her menu down. "You aren't going to get huffy, are you, Soph?" Her smile indicated she wasn't too concerned about the possibility.

"My being poor is all your fault, Regan, and yours, too, Cordie. I was perfectly happy going along with my life, buying whatever I wanted. I had a beautiful car, credit cards without limits, amazing clothes, and I didn't have a single worry line."

"You weren't happy," Regan countered. "Yes, you had to give up your car, but walking is better for you than driving. You still have beautiful clothes even if they're last season's. You don't need credit cards, and you still don't have a single worry line."

"Poverty agrees with you," Cordie said without laughing.

"You asked us to help you wean yourself off your father's money," Regan reminded her.

"Yes, but did you have to be so . . . enthusiastic about it? So rigid? What's wrong with buying an occasional Prada blouse?"

"The clothes are gorgeous, but taking the money from your father to pay for the blouse is wrong," Cordie said.

"The money your father gave you was gotten by illegal means," Regan said.

Sophie reached for her water glass. "How do you know that for certain? He's never been convicted of any crime, and aren't you supposed to be innocent until proven guilty?"

"I don't know it for certain," Regan said. "That's what you told us, which is why Cordie and I agreed to help you."

"Help me be poor?"

"Help you do the right thing."

Sophie impatiently brushed her bangs out of her eyes and sat back. "I really hate being poor."

"It's not so bad," Cordie said. "You'll learn to budget like I do."

"Oh please, you're not poor. You have a huge trust fund your father set up for you, and Kane Automotive is now nationwide. You know what your problem is? You don't care about money because you have it. I want to buy . . . stuff. Oh, God, I sound shallow."

Before Cordie could argue, Sophie said, "Let's not talk about money anymore. I'm starving. I want to order dinner."

Although the room was quite elegant with candlelight and crystal, none of the three had champagne appetites. Sophie ordered salad and soup. Cordie wanted grilled chicken, and Regan ordered a grilled cheese instead of the scallops. None of them wanted to drink anything stronger than iced tea.

"Do you realize it was on this very day a million years ago that the three of us met in kindergarten at the Briarwood School?" Regan asked.

"You two became my sisters that day," Cordie said.

"I remember you arrived in a limo," Regan told Sophie. "I thought you were a princess with your white-blond hair and blue eyes."

"You arrived in a limo, too," Sophie said.

"My father drove me in his old pickup truck," Cordie laughed.

"Sophie, you got us into so much trouble with your schemes," Regan said. "You were always the champion for anyone you thought was being treated unfairly."

"You're still that way," Cordie told her.

"Do you remember the time we got locked inside the coat closet?" Regan asked.

Cordie chimed in. "We were positive no one would ever find us. When we discovered a candy bar in the pocket of Billy Miller's jacket, we were so relieved because we figured we could ration it among the three of us and survive for days."

One memory led to another and another as the three reminisced about their childhood antics. Dinner was served and devoured while each of them told her favorite stories.

"I wondered why you reserved a private dining room, but now I know why. We make a lot of noise laughing and carrying on," Cordie said.

"Aiden suggested this room," Regan said. "He says we get rowdy."

"Your brother's right."

"When did you talk to Aiden?" Cordie asked. "Is he coming home soon?" She realized how eager she sounded and quickly added, "I'm just curious. That's all. I lead a very dull life. I do," she insisted when she thought her friends were going to protest. "Think about it. I teach high school chemistry to kids who just want to blow up stuff, and when I'm not teaching or preparing lesson plans, I'm working on my thesis. I don't even know anymore why I'm doing it. If one more student brings Mentos to my lab with bottles of Coke, I won't be responsible for my actions. I need to know that there are people out there doing exciting things. All three of your brothers travel the world building hotels. They lead glamorous and fascinating lives, and I love hearing about them."

"Not them, him," Sophie said. "You love hearing about Aiden."

"Why wouldn't I? He's the oldest and the most sophisticated. He's probably on a jet flying around Australia this weekend. You know what I did yesterday afternoon and all day today? Research. I was stuck in a library doing research."

"Oh, please. I've so got you beat," Sophie said. "I gave up my Friday night to sit and listen to the most obnoxious, self-centered, narcissistic man talk about himself. I also had to get up before dawn today to meet him in the park and listen to him yet again. His name is William Harrington. My boss wanted me to write an article on him, but Harrington bailed on me."

She then told them about the 5K and how Harrington had disappeared.

"Do you think he got sick?" Cordie asked.

"Maybe he was hurt warming up," Regan offered.

"No, I think I know what happened," Sophie said. "I talked to a couple of the event coordinators after the race. They told me they knew Harrington and that he'd never checked in. The winner of the race was a newcomer named Brett Mason, and everyone was talking about how fast he was. I think Harrington heard all the talk before the race and was afraid of the competition. He wasn't about to take the chance that he might lose his twenty-fifth race, so he took off. I can't believe I wasted all that time on him and ended up without a story. I don't know what happened to him, but I'm determined to find out and make him apologize."

Regan shook her head at her two friends and their frustrations. "Do you know what both of you need?" she asked.

Sophie groaned.

Cordie sighed and said, "Let me guess. You think we need to fall in love and get married. That's easy for you to say, you found the perfect man."

Regan's lips curled upward in a dreamy smile. "Yes, that's true. Alec is perfect." She quickly switched back to being serious. "But we're not talking about Alec and me. We're talking about the two of you. I don't think you have to get married necessarily. Just fall in love. Make room for a relationship, that's all I'm suggesting. I know both of you could go out with a different man every night of the week if you wanted to . . ."

"You're not going to tell us we're too particular, are you?" Cordie asked.

"No, no, of course not. But I think you're doing what I used to do before Alec came along. You're dating the wrong kind of men. They're all . . . I don't know . . . country club. You know what I mean?"

Ignoring their dismissive frowns, she continued, "I want to fix both of you up with real men."

"Real men as opposed to . . . ?" Sophie asked.

"I don't do blind dates," Cordie said at the same time.

Regan ignored their protests. "Alec has lots of friends. He has a partner now. He's really good-looking, and he's unattached. Sophie, I think you should go out with him."

For a second or two Sophie thought Regan was joking. When she realized she was serious, she said, "He's FBI. You can't honestly think I would be interested in him, and he certainly wouldn't be interested in me. You do remember who my father is?"

Regan shrugged. "I didn't forget, but I think going out with an FBI agent might help you get over your aversion to anyone associated with law enforcement."

"What is this? Behavior modification? I don't have an aversion," she protested. "You know I love Alec, and I like his friends Gil and John, and they're both in law enforcement."

"Gil's retired, and you've known both John and him for a long time. You've gotten used to them, and they don't work with the agents who have been investigating your father. It's not the same thing. You still have the aversion. I really think you ought to give it a shot. His name is Jack MacAlister, and I'm sure Alec could talk him into a blind date."

"You're joking, right? You have to be joking. You are, aren't you?"

Regan didn't answer. "I have news. Alec and I are going to be looking for a place to live here in Chicago."

"You're staying permanently?" Sophie asked excitedly.

Everyone started talking at once. Sophie couldn't stop smiling. Regan and Alec had moved a couple of times since he'd joined the FBI.

Cordie was also thrilled. "How did this happen? Did Alec put in for a transfer? I knew he was tired of undercover work, but how—"

"No, he didn't have to ask. The last year and a half, he's had cases in Chicago, so the agency has decided to assign him here permanently. His new partner had something to do with it, too. Sort of, anyway."

"Then I already love him," Cordie said.

"How was he responsible?"

"When you get home, get on the Internet and go to YouTube. Type in Jack MacAlister's name. You'll see."

"Just tell us," Sophie said.

"Oh, no. You have to see it."

"It?" Cordie repeated.

"A video. That's all I'm going to tell you, and since you just said you already love his partner, I think you should go out with him."

"Oh, no you don't," Sophie said. "You're not taking Cordie to the dark side. One FBI agent in this family is enough."

Regan beamed. "So you've accepted Alec into our family?"

"I guess I have."

Regan held up her glass. "Time for a toast. To family."

Kirk named the alpha male Ricky. The alpha female that Ricky has selected as his mate we call Lucy. Ricky is very partial to her. Lucy appears to be mischievous and playful, while Ricky seems a bit put out by her antics.

The adults head out in the morning and bring their prey back to Lucy and her pups.

This morning we waited until they were far enough away, then Brandon and I used dart guns to sedate the adults. We had to work quickly to attach the tracking monitors. I wanted to take blood samples, but he convinced me there wasn't enough time.

We hunkered down a far distance away and used our binoculars to observe. We were too far away for any of them to see us, though we know they had our scent. Ricky was the first to wake. When he finally was able to stand, he appeared to look directly at us. Did he know what we had done? His unwavering stare made me think he did.

He bared his teeth at us, and the wind carried his growl.

I got a cold feeling inside.

SIX

WHILE SOPHIE AND HER FRIENDS WERE CHATTING IN the dining room, another gathering was taking place on the other side of the hotel lobby.

Once a month Alec's poker club met at the Hamilton.

There were a dozen players in the club, and most of them were in law enforcement, but because of their complicated work schedules, never more than half that number could make it each month. During the summer when the weather cooperated, they met on the rooftop garden, and when it didn't, they met in a private room connected to the bar on the first floor of the hotel.

John Wincott, a sleep-deprived detective with the Chicago Police Department, was a regular, and so was Gil Hutton, a retired policeman who always seemed to know the latest news before anyone else did. Gil didn't like to drink alcohol these days, and so he was always John's designated driver because, after one and a half beers, John was usually half asleep.

Since it was unseasonably hot and humid that night, they met in the room off the bar. Gil and John were already at the table when Jack walked in.

"I hate this frickin' heat," Gil remarked. "I hate the rain, too."

"I'll take hot over cold anytime," Jack said. His shirt was covered with wet spots, and his dark hair was damp.

There was a small bar in the corner, and it was always fully stocked. Jack grabbed a Diet Pepsi and was opening it when John called out, "Get me a beer, will you?"

"I barely recognized you, Jack," Gil said. "Without the matted, snarly, long hair and the beard, you look kind of human."

"Kind of human?" John repeated. "I think he looks like a movie star. Wait, did I say movie star? I meant Internet star."

The two men shared a good laugh. Jack handed John his beer, took a sip of his Pepsi, then dropped into a chair across from the two men. "I take it you've seen the video on YouTube."

"About ten times now," John said, grinning. "I don't think it's ever going to get old."

"I found the cinematography visually stunning as well as suspenseful," Gil said with a straight face. "The way you held the perp down while you discussed the menu with Alec. Priceless."

John nodded. "I hear they're going to show it at the IMAX."

Alec, carrying a tray stacked with sandwiches, walked in just in time to hear John's comment. "YouTube?" he asked Jack.

All three men nodded. Since Gil had a knack for knowing what was going to happen before it happened, Alec asked him how long he thought it would take for this to blow over.

Gil scratched his bald head while he thought about it. "I'd give it a couple of days at the most before another video takes center stage. You shouldn't be on 'vacation' long."

"You know about the forced vacation?" Jack's surprise was evident in his voice.

"Of course. I've always got my finger on the pulse, Jack." He tapped his wrist. "On the pulse."

"So we'll be back at work in a week at the most," Alec said, nodding.

"Unless Jack needs to shoot someone else while he's ordering a taco or something," John said cheerfully. "Or . . ."

Jack sighed. "Or what?"

"Or unless the networks pick it up."

"Ah, damn," Jack groaned.

John thought Jack's reaction was humorous and laughed until tears came into his eyes.

"Are we through talking about this yet?" Jack demanded.

"Probably not," Gil said.

"We're here to play poker, aren't we?" Jack asked. "Who are we waiting for?"

"Vice," Gil answered.

"All of them?" Alec asked. He ducked down behind the bar to get a soft drink from the refrigerator.

"No, just Woods and Zahner." Gil smiled as he said their names. Most of the guys from vice were good card players, but Woods and Zahner were the exception. They were both terrible. The funny thing was, neither seemed to realize it. They always thought their losses were due to bad luck, and none of the other players felt the need to enlighten them.

"What about Aiden?" John asked.

"He can't make it tonight," Alec said. "He's still in Sydney on hotel business."

A collective sigh of relief went around the table, for Alec's brother-in-law was the reigning champion. When he played, he usually won, and when he was on a hot streak, he won damn near every hand.

Jack's cell phone rang. He smiled when he saw who was calling, got up from the table before he answered, then walked to the window and looked out at the rain while he listened.

"Must be a woman," John commented.

"Ah . . ." Gil sighed. "I remember those days."

There was a knock at the door, and Regan opened it and stuck her head into the room. "May I interrupt you for a moment?"

Gil and John stood as she hurried to her husband's side. They watched as Alec leaned down and whispered something into her ear that caused her to blush. Gil rolled his eyes heavenward. Alec and Regan had been married for well over a year, but they still acted like newlyweds. He couldn't fault Alec for his lovesick behavior. Regan was quite a catch: dark hair, pretty eyes, long shapely legs. Gil understood why Alec had been drawn to her—any man would be—and he also understood why Alec had stayed. She was a smart businesswoman; she had a kind heart and gentle spirit, and her sense of humor was almost as warped as Alec's. They were meant for each other.

Regan chatted with Gil and John for a couple of minutes to catch up. She had known both of them for as long as she had known Alec and considered them good friends. She would have spoken to Jack, but he was on the phone and had his back to her. She had met him once at a dinner party and had been impressed. He was better than good at what he did—Alec had told her so. He also assured her that he could not have a better partner, so she didn't have to worry as much. She had seen the video on YouTube, and that had impressed her as well. In a crisis, Jack had shown amazing strength, speed, and accuracy. It was a bit scary how nonchalant he had been about it all, but then he was used to undercover work. Jack and Alec, she decided, were perfect partners. They were so much alike.

Jack finished his call and turned around just as Regan said, "Sophie needs a favor."

He walked forward. "Hi, Regan. It's good to see you again. Who's Sophie?"

"You haven't told him about Sophie?" John asked Alec the question and started to laugh.

"No one told *me*," Alec said.

"John, what's so amusing?" Regan gave him the very same look his own wife used whenever she was irritated with him.

"It's just that . . . you know . . . her . . ." John began, then looked to Gil for help. John had started to say something about Sophie's infamous father but stopped in time. Regan was extremely protective of Sophie.

"Her what?" Regan said.

"What's going on?" Jack asked.

"You've missed out," Gil said. "Not meeting Sophie. She's something else. If I were thirty years younger and thirty pounds lighter . . ."

"You still wouldn't have a shot in hell," John said. He looked at Jack as he explained, "Sophie doesn't particularly like the police or the FBI—"

"Or any law enforcement agency. We're the exceptions," Gil said. "She loves us."

"You really never mentioned Sophie to your partner, Alec?" John was having difficulty wrapping his mind around the fact.

"It never came up," Alec said. "And by the way, when you found out, you didn't tell me."

"We're getting off track here. Let's get back to Regan, shall we?" Gil said.

"Yeah, okay," John agreed. "You said Sophie needs a favor? What kind of favor? Is it legal or illegal?" he asked Regan.

She leaned into her husband's side. "It depends on how you look at it. She needs Gil's help."

John nodded. "Say no more. I get it."

Jack kept waiting for someone to fill him in. He knew he'd missed something vital in the conversation. He hadn't known Gil or John long at all, and he'd only been Alec's partner on the last three assignments, so he figured this had to be an inside joke.

They all heard laughter coming from the main bar, and a second later the door opened and Sophie walked in.

Whoa. Jack felt as though he'd just taken a hard hit to his midsection. The sight of her knocked the air out of him. Long blond hair swayed against her shoulders with each step she took, and her body—my God! her body—was sheer perfection. She was wearing ridiculously high heels that made her legs look a mile long, and the fluid drape of her silk dress revealed every curve. If there were any flaws, Jack couldn't find them, but then he was distracted by the sexy way her hips moved as she walked toward Regan.

Sophie greeted Alec first with a kiss on his cheek, then turned to smile at John and Gil who were both grinning at her like boys with raging hormones.

Regan introduced her to Jack. "This is my best friend, Sophie Rose."

Sophie smiled at Jack and said hello, but other than that, she pretty much dismissed him. That pricked his interest all the more. Jack wasn't used to being ignored by women. He loved them and they loved him. Alec called him a player, but Jack didn't think he was. He just didn't believe in committed relationships, and while marriage might work for his friends, it wasn't for him. He liked being free to do what he wanted when he wanted, and he made certain the women he dated understood that. The truth lessened complications. There were as many women as men who felt exactly the way he did.

He watched with a connoisseur's appreciation as Sophie sat down at the table next to Gil.

"Gil, I hate to ask . . ." Sophie began.

"What is it you need, love?"

"Would you mind cleaning my apartment again?"

"Of course I wouldn't mind. You know I'd do anything for you. What about your office? Do you think it needs a good cleaning, too?"

She thought about it for a few seconds and was about to say no, that it would be too much of an imposition, but Regan nudged her and whispered, "It couldn't hurt, could it?"

"Yes, all right. I would appreciate it if you could clean my cubicle, too. What time is good for you?"

"How about tomorrow afternoon around four? I'll start with your apartment," he explained. "And if you can wait, I'll clean your office after five Monday evening. Does that work?"

She nodded. "Yes," she said. "And thank you so much. I don't know how I'll ever repay you."

He wobbled his eyebrows comically. "We'll think of something."

Sophie laughed. "Come on, Regan. Cordie's trapped in the bar with two guys from vice. They're scaring the other customers."

Alec held the door open for his wife and her friend, smiling over something Regan said as she passed him, but as Sophie was walking out the doorway, she looked back over her shoulder at Jack. "It was lovely to meet you."

Damn. Her sultry smile had just the impact Jack thought she intended. She left him gaping.

She was gone before he could think of a response. He stared at the door for several seconds while he tried to remember how to swallow. He finally got it together and turned to Gil to ask if Sophie was involved with anyone.

Sprawled in their chairs, John and Gill were watching him, grinning like idiots.

"What?" Jack demanded.

"She's pretty, isn't she?" Gil said.

"Yes, she is," Jack agreed.

At this point Woods and Zahner followed Alec into the room. The two vice cops looked like they owned a tattoo parlor. Their arms and necks were covered in faded designs. Woods had two bottled beers in his hands, and Zahner was carrying a bowl of cashews.

"What's going on?" Zahner asked as John started laughing.

"Jack just met Sophie," Gil explained.

"Yeah? Just now?" Zahner asked, breaking into a wide smile.

"She's not married," John volunteered.

"And Regan says she isn't dating anyone at the moment. Are you interested?"

Jack pulled out a chair but didn't sit. "What's wrong with her?"

"He doesn't know?" Zahner asked.

"Apparently not," Woods said.

"What's wrong with her?" Jack repeated. "Has she been married three or four times? Is she out on bail for murder? What?"

"She's never been arrested," Alec volunteered.

"She's an upstanding citizen," John added.

"She's a real sweetheart," Woods said.

"And?" Jack prodded, waiting for the zinger.

"And she's hot, man, really hot," Zahner said.

"And her name is Sophie Rose," Alec said.

He was about to explain that Rose wasn't Sophie's middle name, but John shook his head and held his hand up. "Wait for it . . . wait for it . . ."

Jack suddenly flinched.

John burst into laughter as he leaned back and put both hands up. "And there it is."

Jack frowned. "Son of a . . . she's Bobby Rose's daughter?"

"He's not an FBI agent for nothing," Woods drawled.

"Jack figured it out quicker than you did," Zahner reminded him.

"If you could see your face, Jack, you'd think you were having a stroke," Gil told him.

Jack dropped into his chair. He looked dumbfounded. "What's the cleaning her apartment all about? You looking for bugs?"

"That's right," John answered for Gil.

"And every time I look, I find them."

"Who plants them?" Jack asked.

"I've tried to find out," Alec said. He wasn't smiling now. "No agency will own up to it, but if I had to guess . . ."

"FBI?" Zahner suggested.

"No, definitely not FBI." Alec was emphatic.

"I'm thinking CIA," Wood said, nodding.

"No way. It's IRS," John said. "Yeah, definitely IRS."

"ATF," Gil said. "Absolutely ATF."

"FDA," Woods said.

"That's food and drugs, you idiot," Zahner said, laughing.

"My guess is none of the above. Are we playing cards or what?" Alec asked.

John dealt the first hand. He looked up at Jack and asked, "You still want her phone number?"

Jack didn't answer.

Eric and I managed to collect several blood samples.

Arctic wolves haven't been hunted by men, so they've been relatively trusting. They stare, but they don't retreat or attack. They're curious creatures, and our scent must be strange to them.

Yesterday was a sad day. One of Lucy's pups died. Though we were curious to know the cause, Brandon is insisting that we not interfere. He wants to watch the dynamic of the pack as it deals with the loss, so we won't do an autopsy. Ricky was quite stoic about it and left the camp to gather food as if nothing had happened.

The blood Eric and I have studied thus far has indicated a hormone I have not been able to identify yet, and Ricky appears to have high levels of it. I'm anxious to delve into this further.

Brandon isn't interested in our discovery. He seems a bit threatened by any activity he hasn't approved of in advance. Kirk is indifferent to it all. Each evening he writes copious notes about each member of the pack.

I also write in my journal as often as I can. I can't wait to begin my own experiments, but I must wait until the dead of winter to begin.

SEVEN

SOPHIE COULDN'T GET BACK THE HOURS SHE'D SPENT WITH William Harrington, but she felt she was owed, at the very least, an apology. She had taken more than an hour after the race to look for him.

As she had walked back to her apartment that morning, she had tried to call Harrington at his home. His answering machine had clicked on, and she'd left a message for him to please call her. She had tried to sound concerned, not irritated. But she *was* irritated. How could anyone be so rude? And what about dinner Monday night? That, she assumed, was off.

By Sunday morning there was still no word from him. She called his home number again. After two rings, a mechanical voice clicked on, announcing that the phone number was no longer in service. She thought she must have punched in the wrong numbers, but when she entered them a second time, she got the same message. She called his cell phone number next and got another mechanical message. No longer in service.

That left Harrington's website. When she had looked at it during her research on him, she had discovered that he provided visi-tors a place to leave comments. She decided to pull up the site and leave a written message. She typed in the address. His website was no longer there. She did a quick search and couldn't find a trace. The website, like Harrington, was gone.

Okay, now it was getting really weird. She decided to make one last effort to get hold of him before dropping the matter. She had his home address—he'd given it to her during their interview Friday night—and since he didn't live all that far from her, she decided to walk to his building, knock on his door, and demand some answers.

Harrington's condominium was much farther than she had esti-mated. It actually took her forty-five minutes and a twenty-dollar cab ride after her feet started screaming because she had forgotten to change out of her three-inch heels.

Harrington lived in an exclusive neighborhood. His building was sleek and modern with reflective, tinted windows. The door-man wearing an impeccable gray uniform let her inside. A short cor-ridor led to a palatial lobby with marble floors and walls covered in white linen. A thirty-something man with a buzz haircut and an ex-tremely muscular frame was adjusting his tie as he rushed behind the granite counter to wait for her to approach.

He was either ex-military, she thought, or a bodybuilder. He re-minded her of Bluto in the Popeye cartoons. His eyes seemed too small for his head, and his head seemed too small for his huge shoul-ders and arms. Receptionists were supposed to be friendly, but Bluto must not have read the job description. Stone-faced, he stared at her and waited for her to speak. He was neatly dressed in dark pants and a striped shirt. Sophie decided to give him the benefit of the doubt. Perhaps he was part of the building's security team and was just fill-ing in for the actual receptionist.

The security was impressive. She saw cameras tucked into the crown molding at every corner of the fourteen-foot-high ceiling. Somewhere, maybe through the door behind the reception counter, there was a security center where computers recorded every person who came into the building.

"Can I help you?" he asked, his voice surprisingly pleasant and at great odds with his frown.

"Yes, thank you. Could you please call William Harrington's apartment and tell him that Sophie Summerfield would like to speak to him?"

"He isn't here," he said, glancing over her shoulder to the hall-way leading to the street.

Sophie couldn't tell if the impatient man just didn't want to be bothered or if Harrington really wasn't home.

"Please call just to be certain."

"He's not home." His voice was no longer pleasant.

His scowl didn't faze her. "Do you know when he'll be back?"

"No." He looked toward the entrance again.

Was he worried the doorman would catch him being rude? He didn't look the sort to worry about people's impressions.

"Would you like to leave a message?"

"No, I think I'll wait here until Mr. Harrington returns."

"That's out of the question."

"Why?"

"Mr. Harrington won't be home for a long time. He packed up and left for Europe. He didn't say when he would return."

"Why didn't you tell me when I first—"

"We guard our tenants' privacy."

"Is there a way I could get in touch with Mr. Harrington? Do you happen to have his schedule or know where he's staying in Europe?"

"No, I don't. And if I did, I couldn't give that information to you or anyone else. Like I said, we guard out tenants' privacy." Without pausing he added, "Would you like me to show you the way out?"

Sophie got the message. She didn't answer him but simply turned around and left. She thought about telling the doorman how rude the man at the desk was, but what could he do? Surely he already knew the man was rude.

Sophie felt she had gone the extra mile. She was now officially finished with William Harrington.

She rummaged through her purse for cash. She had enough to take a cab back to her apartment, but if she spent it, she'd be short for the rest of the week, and she certainly didn't want to have to borrow later from the "purse fund" she kept hidden in her closet. She decided walking would do her good. Plus, she could window-shop along the way.

Although it wasn't yet three o'clock when she walked through the doors of her building, Gil was already waiting. Her condo didn't have quite the security Harrington's building had, but it was still safe in Sophie's opinion. There weren't cameras at every corner, but there was a doorman and good locks and buzzers that worked.

The doorman knew Gil and had let him wait in the lobby. He was reading *The New York Times* when she walked inside.

Finding bugs wasn't as easy as it looked in the movies. It took time and expertise. Fortunately, Gil was a pro and knew where to look, but he wasn't complacent. He always checked and rechecked every possible hiding place. Their routine was simple. She turned on the television, plopped down on the sofa, and stayed there until he gave her the all clear. While he was searching, neither of them spoke.

Gil found three devices this time. Two were what he called standard issue, but he had never seen anything like the third device before. Alec would be interested in seeing this one, he told her.

It was past six by the time Gil finished, and Sophie rushed to dress for her date. He was picking her up at seven. She had promised to attend a charity function with Jeffrey Oakley, a friend and her go-with guy when she wasn't dating anyone and needed an escort. Jeffrey was as sweet and as bland as a marshmallow, and for years he had been carrying a torch for Regan, but now that she was married to Alec, the torch had been passed to Cordie. He professed his love for Cordie on a regular basis, and Sophie listened sympathetically.

Sophie's own love life was a barren wasteland, but that was okay with her. She didn't need the complication of a romance in her life right now.

THE CRANK CALLS STARTED early Monday morning. Sophie didn't even have time to put her purse in her cubicle desk drawer before the first call came in.

"Sophie Rose?" A muffled voice hissed her name.

"Sophie Summerfield," she corrected. "Who is this?"

"You can't hide from me."

"Who is this?" she repeated forcefully.

"Your father took my money, and he's not going to get away with it."

"Tell it to the police," she suggested.

She was about to hang up when he said, "I've come up with a better idea."

Don't ask, she told herself. *Don't ask.* "What could that be?"

"I'm going to hurt you. Soon, Sophie. Real soon. And then your daddy will know what it's like to lose."

Slamming down the receiver in its cradle, she dropped into her chair. That was a new twist, she thought. Whenever her father was being blamed for something, the callers threatened to get even, and she was supposed to pass the message on to dear old dad. This call had sounded more sinister, and she wasn't sure what she was going to do about it.

She decided to concentrate on work until her nerves settled. This creepy caller had scared her, and that hadn't happened in a long time. Work would help her put things in perspective.

The first order of business was William Harrington. She headed to Bitterman's office to report what had happened. But what could have been explained in five minutes took fifteen because, once she started, she couldn't stop. The longer she talked, the angrier she got. Bitterman let her rant about her wasting her time while he enjoyed a frosty Kelly's Root Beer, then gave her two more ideas to replace the Harrington story.

Bitterman wanted to discuss each one at length, so by the time she got back to her cubicle, there were three messages from the switchboard operator waiting for her. Two were from Regan, and one was from Cordie. All three were marked urgent.

Her friends had left messages on her cell phone as well, but she didn't get a chance to listen to them because she was summoned to the production room to answer some questions. When she returned to her desk, Bitterman was shouting at her. This time he used her name, and that could mean only one thing: whatever he wanted was bad.

Gary tried to follow her, but Bitterman waved him back, pulled Sophie into his office, and shut the door in Gary's face.

The television was blaring. He turned the volume down and said, "It just hit the noon news."

"It?" she questioned.

Nodding to the television, he said, "There's a press conference going on."

Sophie knew what he was going to say before the next words were out of his mouth.

"The FBI has just named your father as a person of interest."

Again.

Ricky has become quite predictable. He sets out on foraging trips with the other males at the same time each day and returns at approximately the same time. Today, however, he was gone only an hour. When he returned to the den, he was agitated and roused the pups out of their naps. The other males circled the den in confusion. They knew something was wrong.

Ricky moved to stand in front of the den, his back to the pups, and stared off to the north. We could see nothing in the distance, but with binoculars we spotted a bear about half a mile away. As the bear drew closer, Ricky began to growl. The other males followed his lead. A hundred feet or so from the den, the bear stopped and raised up on his hind legs.

Ricky didn't back down. The bear paced back and forth several times, but finally turned and headed to the east. Facing a formidable adversary like Ricky and his small army was probably not in his plans.

EIGHT

DADDY WAS ON THE LAM AGAIN.

Bobby Rose would never make the FBI's Most Wanted List. He loved his country; he loved his hometown, Chicago; and he loved his fellow man. He had never raised a hand against anyone; he didn't own a firearm, and he didn't believe violence ever solved a problem. He certainly wasn't a threat to any law-abiding citizen. He had style and charisma and was always a gentleman. And oh, yes, he was a thief.

As much as the authorities wanted to put him behind bars for various thefts they were convinced he had committed, they had yet to come up with a single shred of proof.

One disgruntled investigator was quoted saying Bobby Rose was nothing but a common criminal. Chicago disagreed. There wasn't anything common about the man. He did steal, but he had his standards. He only took from those men and women who had accumulated wealth through illegal or immoral means. Bobby knew, before any law enforcement agency, who those men and women were and, more important, where they hid their money. The law had been outsmarted time and again by Bobby Rose, and they didn't like it.

To most of the public, he was a modern-day Robin Hood. When times were tough, they needed to believe in him. And times were tough now. Families were finding it harder and harder to stretch the dollar. Prices for necessities were up, and salaries were either frozen or down. Home foreclosures were at an all-time high; outsourcing had become a hot-button topic, and it seemed that every other week another company closed its doors, putting more and more men and women out of work while greedy CEOs pocketed millions.

Fear, frustration, and anger were the staples these days, and the "get-even" stories about Bobby Rose gave them hope.

Sophie stood next to Bitterman with her arms folded across her chest, her stance rigid as she watched the live press conference. She didn't recognize the man standing in front of the microphones, but that really didn't matter. Her father's accusers all looked the same to her. Dressed like senators in their designer suits, their hair as perfect as the knot in their ties, their speech as polished as fool's gold, their expressions always righteous and indignant—they had to practice in front of a mirror to be perfect—they pounded on the podium with their fists vowing to bring Bobby Rose to justice.

Her father got blamed for everything but the weather. And whenever the finger-pointing started, Sophie received invitations from the Chicago Police Department or the FBI, and sometimes the IRS, to sit down and have a chat about him. These weren't invitations she could decline. If she didn't cooperate, she would be dragged out of her office chair and taken into custody for obstructing an investigation.

In other words: same old, same old.

Bitterman awkwardly patted her shoulder, then squeezed past the crates and banged his already bruised elbow as he dropped into his chair.

"Move those papers off that chair and take a seat," he suggested.

Too anxious to sit, Sophie turned her back on the television, leaned against the side of the desk, and said, "I don't want to listen to another pompous speech about how terrible my father is. Please, just tell me what he's been accused of now."

Bitterman hit the remote's mute button and began to absent-mindedly rub the sting out of his elbow while he explained.

"Kelly's Root Beer. That's what this is all about."

"Root beer?"

He nodded. "The man doing all the yapping is Darren Ellis of Ellis, Ellis and Cooper, Attorneys at Law. Their firm represents Kevin Devoe."

Sophie glanced over her shoulder to look at the attorney. "And who is Kevin Devoe?"

He didn't immediately answer her question. "Do you remember how you wanted to write about Kelly's closing, and I pointed out that every other newspaper in the city was already writing about it?"

"Yes," she replied. "And you were right."

"A company everyone in Chicago loves as much as they love the Bears shuts down after sixty-some years in operation, and people want to know why."

"I read the company wasn't making any money. Costs were up and profits were down."

"Yes, I read that, too, but that isn't much of an explanation, now is it? No details were given. No, closing didn't make any sense to me. The best damned root beer in the United States isn't making a profit? Hogwash. Why didn't the company simply hike the price per bottle? I would have paid double, even triple, and most of Chicago would have done the same. Can't get root beer like Kelly's anywhere else, can you?"

Sophie doubted everyone in Chicago loved Kelly's Root Beer as much as Bitterman did, but she might hurt his feelings if she told him so. For some reason, he was sensitive about his soft drink.

"No, sir, you can't get root beer like Kelly's anywhere else," she said.

He smiled because she had agreed with him. "Turns out there's a whole lot more to the story. The retirement fund for all those loyal employees is gone. Gone," he repeated, snapping his fingers for emphasis.

"How is that possible?" she asked. "A pension fund is closely monitored by . . ."

He shook his head, stopping her. "It wasn't a pension fund. It was a retirement fund. Big difference. Kelly was a shrewd businessman, and he wanted to do right by his employees. He hired an investment manager and told his employees that if they wanted to, they could put as much as a third of their monthly paycheck into a retirement fund, and he would match their contribution. An employee puts in a hundred bucks a month; Kelly kicks in a hundred. It was a generous retirement plan and, over the years, had great tax advantages. The investment manager Kelly chose was good, real good, and the fund showed strong growth."

"What went wrong?" she asked. A feeling of dread was twisting her stomach into knots.

"People get old and tired," he said matter-of-factly. "The investment manager was the first to retire, and Kelly chose a man named Kevin Devoe to replace him. He was a conservative investor, and the fund continued to grow under his supervision. Initially, that is.

"Kevin met Tom Kelly's only child, a daughter named Meredith, at one of the company functions, and they took a shine to each other. Six months later they married. Tom was ill and finally retired. He named Meredith president and left her husband in charge of investments. Don't know that that was legal, but no one objected at the time.

"Now here's where it gets dicey. Two years after Kevin took over as investment manager, he moved the money into another fund. There were three companies in the fund, and all of them were showing remarkable growth. On paper, that is. The numbers were inflated, and Kevin now says the money was invested in what he thought was a reputable stock fund, but now he realizes he was scammed. He also says no one but Bobby Rose could have pulled this off, and as Kevin's attorney just stated on television, they have discovered that Bobby owned an interest in one of the companies. He didn't say what that interest was."

"My father is a convenient scapegoat these days."

Bitterman didn't disagree. "Kevin's wife filed for divorce a few weeks ago, just before all this came to light."

Sophie shook her head. "Don't tell me they're blaming my father for that, too."

"For the divorce? No, no, of course not." He picked up a pencil and began to roll it between his fingers. "I mention it because Kevin was eager to turn over his financials to his wife's attorney, and made sure the press got copies. And guess what? On paper he looks like a pauper. He wants everyone to know that he put most of his own money into the stock fund and that he is as much a victim as the employees."

"That's ridiculous. He chose the fund, didn't he?"

"He sure did, but he insists the numbers were grossly inflated."

"Besides the possibility that my father had an interest in one of the companies, is there any actual proof that he took the money?"

"No, but the FBI is looking for it."

"They won't find any. My father didn't do this."

Her loyalty was admirable. In this case, Bitterman thought it was also justified.

"Yeah. I don't see this as something your dad would do. However, there are a lot of people who think he used the classic pump-and-dump ploy. You know, the stock gets talked up until a huge amount is sold, then the guys who did the talking sell and, boom, the stock crashes. There are a lot of people who think he did take the money. They're angry, very angry."

She nodded. "I understand. I read that some of those employees had worked for Kelly for over thirty years. Now they have nothing."

"I'm just letting you know that microphones are going to be shoved in your face the second you step outside. Security already called to say a couple of reporters for those rag mags have tried sneaking up here."

"Thank you for the warning," she said. "There's nothing worse than being blindsided."

"You might want to think about some time off until this blows over."

"If I did that every time my father was in the news, I'd never get anything done."

Bitterman stood and looked past her into the main office. "Here comes the FBI."

"They're early this time," she said without turning. They usually didn't take her in for the chat until at least a day or two after her father hit the news. "I wonder why the hurry."

Bitterman looked sympathetic as he answered her. "Because I called them."

Today we observed the pack take down a caribou. It was amazing to watch the wolves work together to cut a straggler from the herd and attack from all sides, as though they communicated by mental telepathy.

Ricky orchestrated it all, and the others followed his lead. He made the kill. His powerful jaws clamped down on the caribou's throat, and he would not release his hold until the animal had fallen to the ground. The other wolves pounced then, and with Ricky's permission, enjoyed a feast.

I cannot feel sympathy for the caribou. His purpose was obviously to feed Ricky and his family.

Survival of the fittest.

When he returned to our facility, Eric and I talked about Ricky's amazing strength and the abundance of the mysterious hormone in his blood. Eric is calling it K-74. He's asked for my help in isolating Ricky so that we can take another blood sample. Since Brandon and Kirk have shown little interest in Eric's findings, he has asked me not to mention what we're doing.

I have become Eric's willing assistant, for my curiosity as a scientist is the reason I have traveled this far. I believe we must be flexible and willing to try new methods. Since Brandon is old school and would not agree with my opinions, it's best he not know what we're doing.

NINE

DECISION TIME. SOPHIE COULDN'T QUITE MAKE UP HER mind if she wanted to play the dumb blonde or the bitchy blonde during the questioning. Over the years, she'd perfected both roles. Maybe for a change of pace she'd be flirty this time. Her friends said she knew how to work a room. Flirting with an FBI agent, though? Sophie doubted she could pull that off.

She knew there would be two agents. They always seemed to travel in pairs. For safety's sake, she supposed.

She squared her shoulders and turned around. All thoughts of playing any games flew out the window as soon as she saw Alec approaching. She relaxed her guard and took a deep breath.

Bitterman edged his way around the desk and went to the door to open it. Sophie was smiling until she saw another agent turn the corner and follow Alec. Uh oh. He was the man she had met at the hotel the night of the poker game. Jack MacAlister.

It had taken a considerable amount of discipline on Sophie's part to dismiss him then, but she wasn't sure she could pull it off again. No harm looking, was there? He was awfully handsome. What woman wouldn't look? But Jack was also in the FBI, and she was the daughter of a man they considered a career criminal. That reminder helped her control the attraction. She barely glanced at him again and kept her focus on Alec.

Her boss had met Alec several months ago when he had given her a ride to work. He shook Alec's hand and said, "Come on inside."

Alec introduced Jack to Bitterman and smiled as he watched Sophie's boss squeeze his way around the root beer to get to his chair.

"Have a seat, all of you," Bitterman said.

Jack looked around the office in astonishment. "There must be a hundred crates in here."

"I only wish I had that many," Bitterman said. "If you want a cold one, there's some in the fridge behind Sophie."

Neither one of the feds took him up on his offer. "You do know this is a fire hazard, right?" Jack asked.

"The way I see it, the root beer would put any fires out."

Jack laughed. "It probably would."

"Before I forget, Regan wants you to call her," Alec told Sophie.

"I will."

"Do you remember meeting Jack?"

She finally looked at the agent. "I remember. I would say it was nice seeing you again, but it might not be. I guess it all depends on why you're here." Turning to Alec, she asked, "Why did Mr. Bitterman call you?"

"You didn't tell her?"

Bitterman shook his head. "I figured she would just shrug it off. I thought I'd leave it to one of you to tell her and hopefully make her understand how serious this is."

Alec was pretty sure she would shrug him off, too, so he nodded to Jack to let him know he wanted him to break it to her. Maybe hearing the news from someone who wasn't a friend would have a greater impact.

Jack didn't bother to be diplomatic or ease into the announcement.

"Someone wants you dead."

"Okay." She nodded, nonplussed.

"Okay? That's all you've got?" Jack asked.

As far as Jack could tell, the news didn't affect her at all. God love her, she shrugged. She was good. He couldn't help but be impressed.

"Do you hear this kind of stuff often?"

"My father is Bobby Rose. What do you think, Agent MacAlister?"

He resisted the urge to smile. Yeah, she was good all right, but he still wasn't buying the blasé attitude.

Alec was much more gentle in his approach to get through to her. "There have been some threats."

Still no visible reaction. "Okay."

"We're not taking this lightly, Sophie," Alec said, his voice firmer now. He was trying the no-nonsense method even though he knew it was pointless. Sophie was as stubborn as his wife. No wonder they were such great friends.

"Thank you for telling me. If you'll excuse me, I'll go call Regan. You didn't tell her about the threats, did you?"

"No, I didn't tell her, but she saw the press conference. She knows your father's back in the news."

Jack noticed something protruding ever so slightly on the wall next to the refrigerator. He moved closer, then glanced over his shoulder at Alec and said, "There's a bug in here."

Bitterman planted his hands on his desktop, half stood, and looked around the room. "Where? What kind of bug? I hate roaches, and I hate spiders." He sat down again and was rolling up a newspaper as he anxiously waited.

"It's not that kind of bug, sir." Jack leaned close to Sophie, his arm brushing against her shoulder as he reached past her and pulled the listening device from the wall next to the refrigerator. To a novice, the barely visible bug would look like it was part of the dark wall socket. It was dusty, which meant it had been there for some time.

Jack tossed the device to Alec. "Look familiar?"

With Jack standing so close, Sophie was trapped. Pressed up against the refrigerator, she could feel it humming behind her back. She thought about trying to squeeze past him or nudge him aside, but he wasn't the type to be nudged. His body looked solid as a rock. She doubted she could nudge him anywhere. Besides, if she squirmed or moved at all, he might notice her discomfort, and she didn't want him to notice anything about her. FBI agents other than Alec weren't to be trusted, and she wasn't about to let Agent MacAlister know he made her nervous.

When it came to her father and his "issues," no one was going to push her around.

Jack glanced down at Sophie and held her gaze for only a second or two, but it was long enough to look into her gorgeous eyes, time enough to take in the scent of her subtle, feminine perfume. Very nice.

He quickly moved away. The last thing he needed was to get close to Bobby Rose's daughter.

Sputtering and red-faced, Bitterman drew his attention. "Are you saying . . . Are you telling me someone's bugging my office? Someone is listening in on my private conversations?" He was outraged. "Who's doing it?" he demanded in the next breath. "It's not FBI, is it? Is it FBI, Alec?"

Alec shook his head. "It's the same kind Gil found in Sophie's apartment," he told Jack. To Bitterman, he said, "Nothing we would use."

Bitterman realized he was still clutching the rolled-up newspaper. He tossed it into the trash can. "You're certain?"

"One hundred percent."

"It looks like something you could buy over the Internet," Jack remarked. "Amateur stuff."

"Hold on a minute. Someone bugged your apartment, Sophie?" Now Bitterman was outraged on her behalf.

"It's all right," she said to calm him. "I'm used to it. I don't want you to worry about this."

"You're used to having your privacy invaded?" Jack asked.

Exasperated, she said, "Again, Agent MacAlister. My father . . . Bobby Rose . . . ?"

The way she drew her father's name out made Jack want to laugh. If she were a man, he'd probably call her a smart-ass, but she wasn't a man. She was an outrageously sexy woman. With spunk. Ah, man, he should get away from her as soon as possible. He should have waited outside in the car. But he'd been curious. First impressions were often wrong, and he wanted to find out if she was as provocative as he'd remembered.

She was. Definitely.

His voice was abrupt when he said, "Show me where you work."

Sophie assumed that Jack was going to sweep her cubicle, and as she was walking toward the door, she asked Alec to please call Gil and let him know she didn't need him to come to her office.

"All right," he agreed. "And while I'm doing that, I want you to pack up whatever you'll need from your office for the next week or two. You're going to be working from home. You know the drill."

"I am not going to stay home."

"Yeah, you are," Jack told her. He gave her a gentle push to get her moving.

His abruptness bordered on rudeness. Sophie thought about telling him to stay out of the discussion, but because he was Alec's new partner, she kept silent. There was also the possibility that he might not take criticism well and decide to take her in for one of those lovely interviews.

Alec wouldn't let him do that, but even so, why cause friction?

Bitterman stopped any further protests. "You have two articles to research, and you can do that from home. You've got a computer there and an Internet connection. You don't need anything else."

Sophie wished she could get Alec alone and ask him why he was wasting his time over a couple of heat-of-the-moment threats. He wasn't a rookie, so why was he given this assignment?

Or had he even been given this assignment?

"Mr. Bitterman, did you call the FBI, or did you call Alec?"

"Alec is FBI," he pointed out.

"Yes, but—"

"I did some snooping," her boss admitted sheepishly. "I looked through your address book and found his number."

"Get moving, Sophie," Alec said.

"Yes, all right. In a second. Was there more than one threat?" she asked her boss. "Whenever my father is in the news, there are always two or three threats at the very least. Agent MacAlister, if you push me one more time, I'm going to have to push you right back."

She didn't turn around when she made the threat. Jack grinned. Sophie was turning out to be far more stubborn than he'd been told. He decided he would leave it to Alec to get her to cooperate.

"Yes, there's been more than one threat," Bitterman said. "So far I've gotten three. The message was always the same. Your father took something of value from them, so they're going to take something of value from him. Meaning you," he added. He looked at Alec as he continued. "A couple of the callers used the same word: retribution. That was kind of odd, I thought. Real muffled voices, too, and all of them used the words 'we' and 'them.' That was odd, too, don't you think?"

"Why would they call you?" Sophie asked.

"I guess the callers figured I'd make you give up your father."

"Sounds like the threats came from the same men," Alec remarked.

"A buddy at the phone company checked the source of the incoming calls," Bitterman said. "They were made from public phones around town."

"How long has there been a price on Bobby Rose's head?" Jack asked.

Sophie whirled around. "What? There's a price . . ."

"The attorneys at the press conference said they'd put up a reward for information leading to an arrest and conviction of your father."

"Conviction for what?"

"Stealing Kelly's company retirement fund?" Bitterman suggested.

"So he's guilty until proven innocent? Is that how the system works?" Sophie blurted.

"Do you think the reward is why the office was bugged?" Bitterman asked.

"Sure," Jack said. "Think about it. This is a small neighborhood newspaper. How many enemies can you make writing articles about the pollen count? I know that sounds insulting, and I don't mean it that way, sir. I'm just saying, you don't tackle heavy political issues or—"

Bitterman waved his hand. "I get what you're saying, and I'm not taking offense. We are a small paper."

"But growing," Sophie said defensively. "And some people want to read about the pollen count."

"A lot of people know Bobby's daughter works here," Alec pointed out. "Maybe they're thinking she'll talk to him on the phone or talk about him to you, sir."

"I want to find out exactly who's listening in on my conversations," Bitterman said. "There could be more of those things, couldn't there?" he added, pointing to the bug Alec held in his hand. "And what about the phones? Do you think the phones are tapped? Damn it all, I want to know who's behind this."

"We'll get some techs in here—" Jack began.

"No, no," Bitterman interrupted. "I don't want this to get out yet, not until we find out who the culprit is."

Before Alec could point out the obvious, that bugging an office was an illegal activity, Sophie said, "What about Gil? He's a retired police officer, Mr. Bitterman, and he does consulting work now. His specialty is security and finding bugs. He'd be perfect for this job."

"Sure, Gil could help," Alec agreed. "You'll have to pay him, but his fee is reasonable."

"I'll pay anything," Bitterman said. "Wait, I didn't mean that. Don't tell Gil I'll pay anything. Could you get him on the phone now and ask him to get over here as soon as possible?"

"Come on, Sophie, let's get going," Jack said.

She led the way to her cubicle, then stood in the narrow corridor to wait while Jack searched for listening devices. He found one identical to the one in Bitterman's office. It had also been attached next to the electrical plate.

Gary came out of the lunch room eating a jam-filled croissant. He spotted Sophie and scurried over to her.

"Why are you standing in the hall?"

He didn't give her time to answer. He saw Jack sitting at her desk going through the drawers. "What's that man doing?" he asked with a mouth full of food. He saw the gun holstered to Jack's side. "Hey, he's got a gun."

"He's FBI," she said.

"He's not dressed like FBI."

Jack was wearing a pair of worn jeans and a faded burgundy T-shirt.

"It's casual Friday," she said with a straight face.

Gary went into his cubicle and continued to watch Jack. "Wait a minute. It's Monday."

"It's casual Monday," she said without missing a beat.

"What's he doing?"

"He's searching my office."

"He better not try to search my cubicle. My space is private, and no one is coming in here without a search warrant," he blustered. "You're supposed to be a reporter, Sophie. You should feel the same way I do. If I were you, I'd tell him to go—"

Jack suddenly stood, towering over Gary. His gaze was piercing. "What would you tell me?"

Gary shrunk before her eyes. He backed into the corner of his cubicle as he said, "Nothing. I didn't mean . . . never mind."

Jack stepped into the corridor so Sophie could get to her desk. It only took her a few minutes to transfer several files by e-mail to her home computer. She turned off her computer and stuffed two fat folders into her tote bag along with a book and a stack of papers she needed to go through. She pulled her purse from the bottom desk drawer, picked up her cell phone and charger, then looked around to make certain she had everything she needed.

Gary's curiosity overrode his fear of Jack. "Are you under arrest?" he asked Sophie. "What did you do? Did you help your father? That's it, isn't it? Is it Kelly's? Did you help your father rip off the retirement fund?"

Sophie was used to Gary's stupidity, but she couldn't resist feeding his frenzy.

"I'm ready, Agent. Are you going to put the handcuffs on me now or when we're in the elevator?"

"In the elevator," he answered without hesitation. "Just don't try anything funny."

She kept her head down, pretending shame. Jack motioned to Alec as he followed her to the elevator.

The farther away Jack got, the bolder Gary became. "She knows where her father is," he shouted. "She just won't tell. That's why you're taking her in, isn't it?"

"He's got it all figured out, doesn't he?" Jack shook his head as he lowered his voice. "How can you stomach working with him?"

"I don't have a choice," she answered. "Hopefully, someone will quit, and I can move away from him."

"He's a reporter?"

"He thinks he is. But he's not very observant. He didn't even notice you weren't carrying handcuffs. How come you aren't?"

"It's casual Monday. No ties. No cuffs. Do you want me to carry that?" he asked, reaching for her tote bag. It looked heavy.

The elevator doors opened just as Alec joined them. All three stepped inside.

"All right." Sophie handed him the bag. "But be careful with it. It's Louis Vuitton."

"Can Lou breathe in there?"

She smiled. "It's Louis, not Lou."

"Expensive, huh?"

"Yes, very expensive. It was a gift, and I'm trying not to get any scratches on it."

"A gift from your father?"

The smile vanished. "No," she answered abruptly.

She was glad he had asked the annoying question. She was starting to like him, and she was certainly attracted to him. Who wouldn't be? The man was sexy as hell. But fortunately his nosy question reminded her that he was FBI.

She stood between the two men facing the doors. She felt awkward and uncomfortable. If Jack hadn't been there, she would have been fine. She loved Alec because he loved Regan, and Sophie felt safe and relaxed around him. Alec didn't judge; Jack apparently did.

"Why don't you ride with Sophie, and I'll follow in my car?" Jack suggested.

She didn't look at him when she answered, "I don't own a car."

"Really? Huh. I figured you for a BMW or a Mercedes. Guess I was wrong."

"Really. Huh. I figured you for an arrogant, judgmental jerk." She didn't add, "Guess I was wrong."

She glanced at him to see how he was reacting to her comment and was taken aback when she saw the laughter in his eyes.

They reached the bottom floor. Jack had parked his car in the garage below the warehouse. When the elevator doors parted, he held his hand up to stop her. He checked to see that the coast was clear before he let her step out. There were no reporters lurking, waiting to ambush her. She thought Bitterman had overreacted when he'd said microphones would be thrust in her face. She climbed into the backseat of Jack's car. They drove down the ramp, and as Jack was waiting to make a left turn onto the street, a swarm of reporters suddenly appeared. They crowded both sides of the car, but they seemed to be as interested in Jack and Alec as they were in her, even calling them by name.

"How do those reporters know you two?" she asked.

"They don't actually know us," Alec hedged.

"They're shouting your names and taking your photos."

"She hasn't seen it?" Jack asked.

"Apparently not. Talk to Regan or Cordie," Alec told her. "They'll be happy to explain."

"Explain what? Alec, what are you talking about?"

He didn't answer. A cameraman pounded his fist on the hood of the car to get Jack's attention. He was obviously going for the deer-in-the-headlight shot. Jack didn't oblige.

"What can I tell you? It must be a slow week."

"FBI agents don't give interviews," she said. "And those reporters know that. Why are they hounding you two?"

"Not now, Sophie. When you get home, call my wife."

She decided not to wait. She pulled out her cell phone and sent a text to Regan and Cordie.

"How much do you think I'll get if I run over a couple of them?" Jack asked.

"I don't know. I'd give you ten, twenty bucks," Alec answered.

Jack laughed. "I meant years. How many years would I get?"

Traffic opened just as one reporter cleared the bumper, sliding toward Alec's window. Jack drove away before the man could get a clear shot.

"I hate reporters," Jack muttered. "Most of them don't ever write the truth."

"That isn't so," Sophie said.

He ignored her protest. "It's all about sensationalism. Anything for a story."

"I'm a reporter," she reminded him.

"My point exactly," Jack said.

"Agent MacAlister?"

"Yeah?"

"Bite me."

It's hard to believe we've been with the wolves for months now. We've gathered reams of data about their habits and have studied tissue samples to understand their physical adaptation, but there is so much more to learn. If our plans succeed, the foundation will extend our grant, and we'll be able to return to continue our study next year.

There haven't been any questions about losing the male that Kirk had named Jasper. They know I was the last to observe him, and they have accepted my report about the grizzly. I told them Jasper put up a good fight but succumbed to the strength of the bear.

The truth is a bit more gruesome. Eric and I had sedated Jasper to draw another vial of blood to see if his hormone level had fluctuated. When the grizzly approached, he was too woozy to fight. The bear tore Jasper apart as though he were some limp rag doll.

The violent scene was difficult to watch, but at least Eric was able to gather a sample of blood to compare with Ricky's.

TEN

SOPHIE USUALLY LIKED WORKING FROM HOME. THERE weren't interruptions; Gary wasn't hanging over her partition drooling like a St. Bernard while he pestered her for information about her father. Also, in her apartment, all of Sophie's forbidden snack foods were within reach. She didn't even have to answer the phone if she didn't feel like it. And if she were so inclined, she could work in her pajamas.

What she didn't like was being forced to work from home. She felt like a prisoner, and she didn't like the idea of anyone else making choices for her. Mr. Bitterman, however, was her boss, and he had her best interests at heart. Unlike the creep threatening to do her bodily harm. Now she was going to have to reschedule all of her appointments, which included apologizing ad nauseam and begging Raul to change her haircut appointment.

And all of this disruption because of a few crank phone calls. It could be worse, she supposed. She should be thankful she hadn't been dragged downtown by the authorities. Not yet anyway.

It didn't matter which agency called on her. They all asked the same questions over and over again. *Have you spoken to your father lately?* Like she would ever tell them if she had. *Has he ever told you how he made his money?* She had a lot of sarcastic answers for that one, but she kept silent because even at an early age she had learned never to alienate men with badges, especially if she wanted to go home rather than sit in a smelly interrogation room for hours and hours.

They all wanted to know about a safe, too. Did her father have one hidden somewhere? And where did he keep his important papers? Did he ever tell her secrets?

Nowadays, Sophie took the questions in stride, but that had not always been the case. The worst experience she had was when she was nine years old. A cranky old detective told her that if she didn't spill the beans—she had no idea what that meant—and tell him where her father was, he would call child protective services and have her taken away permanently and put in foster care. No one would know where she was, and she would never see her daddy or her friends again.

To this day, Sophie wasn't certain how Regan's brother Aiden found out about that interrogation. She thought perhaps her housekeeper had called him, but the woman never owned up to it.

Like a knight in shining armor, Aiden showed up at the police station with three attorneys to save her from the detective's terror tactics. Sophie remembered she cried when she saw him and ran into his arms. Aiden had seemed terribly old to her, but he was barely twenty at the time. He was outraged on her behalf and made quite a few threats of his own, including lawsuits for illegal detention, public humiliation, and heaven only knows what else. He got in the detective's face and told him that if the words "foster care" were ever spoken again, he would have his badge. Aiden's attorneys insisted he could do it, too.

Aiden drove her home, gave her the law firm's private phone number, and made her memorize it. He told her that she could reach them day or night. To this day she remembered that number, and occasionally she used it.

She never told Regan or Cordie what had happened the night Aiden rescued her, and she had asked Aiden to keep the secret, too, to never let anyone know, not ever, that she had cried. She was a worrier, and Aiden recognized that. He somehow tracked her father down as he was flitting from place to place and got him to agree to let Aiden become her guardian in his absence. Sophie was eternally grateful.

Sophie wondered if she was going to have to call Aiden's attorneys because of this latest round of threats. Her hope was that it would all die down and be forgotten in a couple of days.

When she arrived at her apartment, Alec and Jack went up with her. They stood by as she played the day's messages, all thirteen of them. None were threatening, but the last one perplexed Jack. The caller identified himself by the name Muffin, and the readout on Sophie's caller ID indicated he was making the call from the Southside Reserve Soup Kitchen. The deep timbre of his voice was a contradiction to his name.

"Sophie, honey, I wanted to thank you for the beautiful Fendi special edition purse and wallet. I'm looking at them right now, and they're spectacular, honey, just spectacular. Once again, you've outdone yourself. You know how much we appreciate it, don't you? And hey, rumor has it you're going for a Birkin next. That's awfully ambitious, but I know you can do it. You take care now. You know I love you."

Jack asked the obvious. "You gave a purse and a wallet to a soup kitchen? Did I hear that right?"

"Yes, that's right. Alec, are you going to look in all the corners and make sure no one's hiding?"

"I'll do that now."

"Hold on," Jack said. "You aren't at all curious about Muffin's phone call?"

"Not really," Alec replied, smiling as he walked into Sophie's bedroom.

Jack didn't want to let it go. "Explain why you would give a soup kitchen a purse and wallet."

"Because I wanted to," she answered. "Don't look so worried, Agent MacAlister, the purse and wallet aren't code words for anything illegal."

Sophie left Jack looking bewildered and went to the kitchen to get a bottle of water from the refrigerator.

Alec finished his inspection, got a bottle for himself, and tossed one to Jack. "Promise me you'll stay in tonight and tomorrow," he said to Sophie. "I'm not leaving until you give me your word."

"I promise. Don't forget that you already gave me your word you wouldn't tell Regan about the threatening calls."

"I won't tell her."

"Thank you. You know what a worrier she is."

"You're not worried?"

"Not at all."

"Regan might stop by later."

"No," she blurted before she realized it was a trap.

"But you're not worried," Alec said dryly.

"I just don't want to take any chances with my friend's life, that's all. I'm being cautious. Besides, I've got a lot of work to do."

He kissed her on the cheek. "Lock the door behind us."

Jack waited until he and Alec were in the elevator and then asked, "You're just gonna leave it at that?"

"She has protection. She just doesn't know it. Whenever her dad's in the news, I hire Gil, and he gets a couple of his friends, all retired cops, to help watch round the clock. No one will get to her. She'll be okay."

"The threats . . . these happen a lot?"

Alec nodded. "Yes, but this is the first time Bitterman has gotten any calls about her. That's new. But like I said, she'll be okay."

Sophie really wasn't worried. As soon as Alec and Jack left, she changed her clothes and went to work on her computer. Time got away from her, and it was almost seven when Cordie called. "It's on," she said. "Start watching."

Sophie didn't waste any time. She ran to the television to make certain she was recording the reality show. It was one of her favorites. The truth was, she and Cordie watched and loved almost all the reality shows. Regan called her friends reality junkies. Neither Cordie nor Sophie was offended.

Ten minutes later, Sophie called Cordie. "How can John and Sara think they're in the desert? There isn't any sand."

"They'll be the first to go," Cordie predicted.

Five phone calls later, the show was over and real life resumed. Sophie stretched her arms above her head and yawned. Deciding to turn in early, she switched off her computer and headed toward her bedroom. There weren't any sheets on her bed. She had only one set of king bedding, and they were in the washer. While she waited for the sheets to dry, she ate half of a cold pizza, then went to the bathroom to brush her teeth.

The phone rang. Seeing that it was Cordie, she picked up.

"Oh my God, Soph," Cordie laughed, "have you looked at YouTube yet?"

"What for?" Sophie mumbled through the toothpaste.

"Jack MacAlister. You've got to see the video."

"Okay, I will." She hung up the phone and went back to the bathroom to gargle.

The phone rang yet again. "Oh good grief, Cordie . . ." She plodded back to her bedside table. Caller ID displayed an unfamiliar area code. She hesitated for two rings, then decided to answer.

"Is this Sophie Summerfield?" Summerfield. Good. He wasn't calling for Sophie Rose, and he had a friendly voice.

"Yes."

"My name is Joe Rooney and I'm a police officer here at Prudhoe Bay. You know where that is?"

She knew it was somewhere in Alaska, but she didn't know which part. Fortunately, she didn't have to admit it.

"We're in Alaska, way up at the tip."

"Must be cold" was all she could think to say.

"Yes. It's already chilly here," he replied. "Unusually so, this early in the season. The reason I've called . . ."

His hesitation made her all the more curious. "Yes?"

"We found your card. Your business card. It's the only identification, so I thought I'd call and ask if you knew the man we found."

"He can't tell you who he is?"

"No, he can't say anything, ma'am. No easy way to tell you. He's dead. We found your card inside his red sock."

It couldn't be, could it? Sophie needed to sit. "Did you say a red sock?"

"Yes, it is," he answered, sounding relieved.

Harrington. Oh my God. William Harrington. She remembered he had taken her card and tucked it in his sock. He'd shoved it way down to his ankle and then pulled the sock halfway to his knee. Who else could it be? But it didn't make sense. Prudhoe Bay? What would William be doing in Prudhoe Bay? He was in Europe.

"I'm sorry to be calling with such terrible news," Rooney said.

Sophie needed to be sure before she gave the caller William Harrington's name. "Tell me what he looks like."

A long sigh came through the phone. "I'm afraid I can't do that, ma'am."

"Why not?"

"The problem is . . . we only found a piece of him. We found a foot and part of his leg."

"A leg and a foot?" She couldn't take in what he was telling her.

"A foot and *part* of a leg, not all of it," he said. "It was his right foot. Would that help you identify him for us?"

"Are you saying . . . my God . . . how did he die? And where's the rest of him?"

Another sigh came through the phone. "No easy way to say this," Rooney said. A slight hesitation and then he blurted, "We've got polar bears up here."

"Oh my . . ."

"A polar bear did him in."

It's great to be back in Chicago. We spent eight months together in Alaska, survived a bitter winter cooped up in our housing, and I accumulated enough data on the behavior of my coworkers to begin my paper.

The pecking order in our little family shifted over the course of our stay. Brandon could not handle disagreement of any kind, and Kirk became passive in every argument. Eric and I became the alphas, though admittedly Eric is too busy to lead anyone.

The foundation was impressed with our reports and has agreed to fund another two years. In three months we will head back north.

Eric is spending his time off in his lab. I brought with me a few early blood samples from each member of the pack—all but Lucy and her pups, that is—so I've also taken time in the lab to see if I can isolate the hormone Eric found in Ricky's blood. So far I've come up with some amazing and startling conclusions. I will have to wait until I return north to show Eric my discovery. I'm anxious to hear what he has to say.

ELEVEN

HOLY CRAP!
A foot and part of a leg were all that was left? Could it be William Harrington? Her business card had been tucked in his sock, his *red* sock. It had to be him.

Sophie's mind raced. She was so rattled by what she was hearing, she couldn't think of a single question to ask.

Rooney broke the silence. "It was a male."

"I'm sorry?"

"The polar bear was male," he explained. "Had to weigh in around twelve hundred pounds, give or take a hundred."

"Did anyone witness the attack?" she asked, mentally cringing at the possibility.

"No, but there were telltale signs. Can you identify the victim for us?"

"It must be William Harrington," she said. "I gave him my business card, and I saw him tuck it in his sock." She gave him Harrington's home address and said, "He lived alone. His phone has been disconnected, and I was told that he had left for Europe."

"He evidently changed his mind," Rooney said. "How did you know this Mr. Harrington?"

"I didn't know him really. I just met him a couple of days ago. I'm afraid I can't tell you much about him. I'm sorry."

"You've been a real help just giving us a name," he assured her.

"You will find a way to verify that it is Harrington before you notify his relatives, won't you?"

"Oh, yes. They'll send the remains to the morgue, probably in Anchorage. I'm new here, so I don't know the exact procedures they'll follow, but I can tell you the body parts will be kept in the morgue until positive identification has been made and instructions are given for the disposal."

Disposal. What a horrible word to use.

After promising Rooney she would call if she had any information that could help him, Sophie hung up the phone. The shock from the news about William Harrington's demise quickly evolved into puzzlement. Why was he in Alaska and not in Europe like she was told? She thought back to the events of the last couple of days, replaying what Harrington had said as well as what she'd found out at his condo. None of this made any sense.

Within an hour of receiving the call from Joe Rooney, the phone rang again. The second call also came from Alaska, and this time the caller identified himself as Paul Larson.

"I work for a security company up here," Larson said. "We're primarily responsible for the population at the oil fields, but the police are pretty shorthanded in these parts, so we help them out when we can. Joe Rooney told me about the death of your friend." Larson's voice became sympathetic. "I'm very sorry for your loss. I told Joe I'd do a little investigating to learn the circumstances surrounding the bear attack, so I hope you won't mind answering a few questions."

"I appreciate your condolences, Mr. Larson," Sophie said, "but I'm afraid I didn't know William Harrington well."

"Please, call me Paul," he replied. His demeanor turned professional again. "What was your relationship to Mr. Harrington?"

"We didn't actually have a relationship. I work for a small newspaper, and I was going to write a story about his running a 5K." She wondered if her explanation sounded as lame to him as it did to her. "It was a human interest story," she added, almost as an excuse. "I met with him for a couple of hours and interviewed him, but he only talked about running. He was very proud of his accomplishments and of his physical prowess. In fact, he mentioned that he'd been chosen for some hush-hush project because he was so superior to other men. Other than that, I'm afraid I can't give you any personal information about him. He didn't mention any family."

"Don't worry. We'll contact the Chicago police and track down the next of kin. You've been very helpful. Thanks."

"Paul, Joe said he was sure a polar bear killed Harrington because there were telltale signs. What were those signs?"

Larson hesitated a second before answering. "One of the pilots here saw the polar bear. There was . . . there was blood, a lot of blood, and the bear was cleaning himself. They do that, you know. They're kind of obsessive about cleaning themselves. Sometimes they'll stop in the middle of a meal just to clean up. It's an instinctive thing. If a polar bear's coat gets dirty and matted, it can't do the job nature intended and protect him from the harsh elements.

"The bear in question was dragging the sleeve of a ski jacket, and the remains, the victim's foot and leg, weren't that far away from him, and there was a blood trail, so you can see why we're assuming that's the bear that killed the man."

"What happens to the polar bear?"

"Nothing happens to him. This is his domain, not ours. Listen, how about I give you my private phone number? If you think of anything else that might help us, or if you have any questions, call me."

After she had written down his number, she asked, "Will you please call me when they get positive identification?"

"Sure. Hey, have you ever been to Alaska? I'll bet there are at least a hundred human interest stories here."

"Are you inviting me?"

"I am," he admitted. "It will be an adventure for you," he said. "I'd love to take you to dinner. Can't serve you wine. No alcohol allowed here, but I could dig up a couple of candles."

"How do you know I'm not married with six children?"

"I'm looking at you right now."

"You're what?"

"I'm looking at your bio. We have computers up here," he added. "I Googled you. Unless someone airbrushed the hell out of your photo, you're very attractive."

"Let's think about your invitation, Paul. I've just been told a polar bear ate a man, and now you're suggesting I come up there for a candlelight dinner?"

He laughed. "That was a rare occurrence. Besides, we've got a whole lot more grizzlies than polar bears around here this time of year."

"No worries then."

"I'll leave the invitation open. Call me, Sophie."

She hung up the phone but didn't move from the bed for a long while. Her mind jumped from one thought to another. Polar bears often stop in the middle of a meal to clean themselves. That's what Larson had said. Poor William Harrington was the meal. What a horrible way to die. A bear's snack.

Her thoughts moved back to Paul Larson. He had actually been hitting on her. Not real appropriate, she thought, given the circumstances of his phone call.

Restless, she went into the kitchen and grabbed a bag of forbidden potato chips to nibble on while she thought. They weren't good for her; she shouldn't eat them, but she didn't want to throw them out because that would be wasteful. It was a sin to waste food. The key to not eating potato chips was to stop buying them, but Sophie was honest enough to admit that wasn't going to happen. Every time she went to the grocery story she ended up with a big, fat bag of chips. Kettle-fried were her favorites. She couldn't make herself buy the baked ones.

She leaned against the counter and munched while she pondered more important things. Why had Harrington told the staff at his apartment building that he'd gone to Europe? And what was he doing in Prudhoe Bay?

Sophie didn't know all that much about the area, and feeling somewhat like a dumb blonde in all those jokes about dumb blondes, she put the chips away and went to her computer to look up Prudhoe Bay.

The largest oil field in North America, it was located on the coast of the Arctic Ocean. The Arctic Ocean? She shivered just thinking about how bitterly cold it could get, and though she had no plans to ever go there, she was curious to know all she could about Prudhoe Bay and any nearby towns. There had to be towns around there, right? And would those towns have accommodations for travelers? Surely they would. Not everyone who ventured that far north worked on oil rigs, did they?

Once she started reading, time quickly passed. A lot of what she already knew but had filed away in the recesses of her mind came flooding back. She now recalled the argument for and against the expansion of the pipeline. Both sides were passionate about the subject.

Reading about Prudhoe Bay led to reading about tundra and permafrost. She read well into the night, until her eyes blurred from staring at the computer screen. It was three in the morning by the time she collapsed into bed. She didn't think she would be able to sleep, what with all the facts and figures about the number of barrels of oil pumped from the icy water and sent down the pipeline swimming around in her brain, but as soon as her head hit the pillow, she was out.

She dreamed of polar bears. She was in a blizzard surrounded by the huge white animals, and then the scene changed to the street outside her apartment and the polar bears were coming after her with cameras. Finally, one of the bears morphed into Jack MacAlister, and the FBI agent moved toward her, more ferocious than any of the bears.

A bell saved her. The phone rang at 6:45. Her boss was on the line.

"Did I wake you?"

"No, of course not." She doubted he believed her lie since her voice sounded like a croaking frog.

"Have you gotten any more threats?"

"No, not one."

"They've stopped here, too," he said. "I still want you to stay home, though."

"I will."

"You should already be at the computer then," he said. His tone became all business. "Have you done any work on the cell phone piece I gave you?"

"Not yet."

"I'm going to need it as soon as you can e-mail it to me. The piece on bone density testing didn't get done. I assigned it to Bernie, and he couldn't get the interview with the specialist, so I've moved it to next week. How soon can you get your article to me?"

"How soon do you need it?"

"No later than noon tomorrow."

She relaxed. "No problem. Noon tomorrow."

"That's good. Now today I need the piece on the Southside Soup Kitchen you wanted to feature. They need donations, and I need the article. Get that to me by four and I'll put it on the front page. Have a good day, Sophie, and stay inside."

"But Mr. Bitterman . . ."

He had already hung up.

Sophie threw off the covers and staggered to the bathroom. She was going to be drinking gallons of tea with caffeine in order to concentrate on work. She needed a solid eight hours of sleep to function at her maximum capacity, but she could get by on six. Functioning on four hours was a definite stretch of brain power. Anything less than that and she'd turn into a blithering idiot.

She worked all day, got a solid eight hours of rest, then plunged into the next day of work, managing to get both articles with interviews completed by Bitterman's deadlines. By early afternoon, she was ready for a break. She should have wanted to get away from the computer screen, but not all of her questions about Prudhoe Bay had been answered. She wanted to learn all she could about the place. Maybe some piece of information might help explain why Harrington had gone there.

She pulled out her notebook and the digital recorder she'd used during her initial interview with Harrington at Cosmo's. Listening to him talk about his twenty-four races and his endless, disgustingly graphic descriptions of each and every blister wasn't something she was looking forward to, but had to be done, and probably more than once. No other way to try to solve this mystery, she thought.

After she put the recorder and notebook on her bed, she sat down at her computer again. There was a town close to Prudhoe Bay called Deadhorse. Cool name, she thought. Depending on what website she went to, the population varied. The optimistic number was twenty; the pessimistic number was seven.

A couple of personal accounts repeated a popular joke about the place. Men who were being recruited to come and work there were told they'd find a naked woman behind every tree. No wonder Larson had flirted with her. He probably hadn't seen a woman in ages in the treeless Arctic.

She stood and twisted her torso to stretch her muscles. She hadn't been to the gym for almost an entire week now. Her apartment was spacious, but she felt as though it were closing in on her. She walked past the digital recorder and groaned. She didn't want to listen to Harrington alone. Misery really did like company, she de-

cided, and in this instance she wanted Regan and Cordie to listen
along with her. She was dying to tell them about this latest develop-
ment with Harrington anyway, and perhaps one of them would pick
up on something she'd missed when she played back the interview.

How to get to The Hamilton without everyone going ballistic
was Sophie's real dilemma. She considered various possibilities
while she showered.

Getting around Bitterman was going to be the trick. She'd given
him her word she wouldn't leave her apartment; he'd pitch a fit if he
found out after the fact. But she wasn't a child. She didn't need his
permission to go outside, even if a promise was a promise, and her
boss had her best interests at heart. Sad as it was to admit, she was
used to hearing threats, but Bitterman had been shaken.

She had also given her word to Alec. Maybe if she called him, he
could pick her up and take her to the hotel. No, that wouldn't work.
Asking Alec to shuttle her back and forth would be an inconve-
nience for him. Besides, it seemed that wherever Alec went these
days, his arrogant, judgmental partner tagged along.

Sophie had to think of another way.

No one could complain if a former policeman drove her. Now
there was a plan! Gil could drive her to the hotel. He was most likely
downstairs in the lobby right now. She knew that each time her father was in the news or threats were made, Alec asked Gil and his
team to watch over her, but since neither Alec nor Gil ever mentioned it, she assumed they didn't want her to know what they were
doing, and so she had always kept silent. Yes, Gil was the solution to
her problem.

She decided to set her plan in motion by starting with Bitterman.

Bitterman wasn't in his office. Lucy, the receptionist, told Sophie he was taking a late lunch with his wife at the Pavillion, one of
his favorite restaurants. It was within walking distance of the newspaper.

Sophie called him on his cell phone.

"Yes, Sophie?"

"You ordered the grilled salmon, right? You always order the salmon at the Pavillion."

"How do you know where I am?"

"I'm a reporter . . . and Lucy was happy to tell me."

"I haven't even looked at the menu yet, but you're right, I'll probably order the salmon. I'm still waiting for my wife to get here. Why are you calling me? What do you want?"

"No more threats."

"Yes?"

"I kept my promise to stay in, but now that the threats have stopped, I'm going over to The Hamilton."

"Now listen here. You gave me your word, and I—"

"Two FBI agents will be with me." She was going to burn in purgatory for that lie.

"Alec and Jack?"

Don't make me say it. "Yes, sir."

"Okay then. I'll let you off the hook. I expect you in the office tomorrow."

He disconnected the call before she could say anything more. It was odd. She felt a pang of guilt over the lie she'd just told Bitterman, but she didn't feel any guilt at all about breaking her promise to Alec. She adored him, but he was an agent of the FBI . . . and he didn't sign her paycheck.

She called down to the doorman and found out Gil was in the lobby, taking his shift. When she got off the elevator, he'd have to go with her to the hotel.

Blindside him. The perfect strategy.

She grabbed her purse, dropped her notebook and keys inside, then reached for the recorder. It wouldn't turn on or off. Needed new batteries, she decided. Triple A, which she didn't have. The hotel would have some in the gift shop, or Regan would definitely have a supply on hand. She threw the recorder in her purse with the rest of her things and went to her closet. She reached for her favorite Dolce & Gabbana blouse and skirt. Whenever she wore them, she felt better. Clothing shouldn't affect her mood, but come on, it was Dolce & Gabbana, and she didn't know anyone who wouldn't feel happier wearing the designers' exquisite clothes.

She slipped on the skirt and then the blouse. She hadn't yet buttoned it when the phone rang.

"Hello," she answered hurriedly.

"Why are you home?" Regan asked. "Are you sick?"

"No," she answered. "I'm working. Doing some research."

"Why at home?"

"I felt like it."

Before Sophie could tell her she was on her way over to the hotel, her friend blurted, "Have you seen it yet? I was sure you'd call once you had, but when you didn't—"

"See what?"

"That answers my question. Just watch it and call me back."

"Regan, watch what?"

"The YouTube video. Just type in Jack MacAlister's name, and it will take you right to it."

"I don't like Agent MacAlister, so why would I want to watch his video?"

"Because you love my husband, and he's also in the video. Just watch it, okay? And why don't you like Jack? Yes, I know, he's FBI, and I know all about your aversion but—"

"Hold that thought. My cell phone's ringing."

Sophie cradled the home phone in the crook of her shoulder and fumbled through her giant purse searching for her cell phone.

"Just call me back," Regan said.

"No, wait," Sophie replied. "I want to tell you something."

The cell phone was, of course, at the bottom of her purse. "Ah, found it. Hello?"

"Hi, Sophie."

The male voice was cheerful and familiar, but she couldn't place where she'd heard it.

"Who is this?"

"I'll tell you in a second. I don't want to ruin the surprise."

"What surprise?"

"Look out the living room window, and you'll see."

Even though she knew it was a silly request, she was walking into the living room as she asked, "Can't you just tell me? I'm busy."

"Be a sport. You have to look, or I can't do it."

She was still trying to put a face to the voice. She reached the window and looked out. "Or you can't do what?"

"This."

She didn't hear his last whispered words. The bullet shattered the double-paned glass and struck her chest. The velocity threw her backward, and she crashed to the floor.

It's been three months since we left our arctic home in March, and now Kirk and I have returned. Brandon and Eric should arrive in a few more weeks.

The wolves mate in March, and the gestation period is a short sixty-three days. To our delight, Lucy has three new pups and is once again being fed by the males who hunt for her.

One of the older males, the one we called Lester, is no longer with the pack. Our tracking device didn't indicate a separation, so we can only speculate what happened to him.

Ricky is still definitely in charge. We've estimated his age to be six years, and since the average lifespan of the arctic wolf is about seven years, we would expect to see him slowing down, but he seems more vigorous than ever.

Eric and Brandon will arrive within days of each other. As soon as I have the opportunity to get Eric alone, I will confront him.

I know what he's been doing. The question is: will he admit it?

TWELVE

S HE JUST *HAD* TO LOOK.

Sophie was furious, mostly because of her own stupidity, though she would take that admission to her grave.

She was lucky to be alive. The bullet had struck her dead center, just below the front clasp of her bra. But the distance of the shooter on the roof of the apartment building across the street and the rising north wind slowed the bullet's velocity, as did the double-paned window and the thick metal clasp of her purse. Still, the bullet cut through her skin, leaving behind a small, perfectly round hole.

All things considered, it was really just a minor wound—at least according to the emergency room physician who gave his diagnosis even as he was backing away from the curtained-off cubicle to distance himself from Sophie's wrath. The doctor's nurse had already called security.

Sophie understood their reaction. After all, she had threatened to kill an aide, a woman wearing the name tag "Trainee Louanne," and if Sophie had been the one holding the scissors, she just might have followed through on her threat. Trainee Scissor-Happy hadn't gently removed Sophie's beautiful blouse. Oh, no. She'd used her scissors to cut it off her, and Sophie had been too woozy to stop her. When Sophie had tried to protest, the aide gave her a contemptuous grin and continued to shred the delicate silk.

The blouse, being unbuttoned during the shooting, had escaped the ravages of the bullet, but now it was in tatters. Her beautiful, beautiful Dolce & Gabbana blouse was ruined. Sophie knew she was being foolish, even a little crazy maybe, to love something as much as she loved that blouse, but she also knew it wasn't actually the blouse she loved as much as what it represented. It was the last thing she had bought with the birthday money her father had given her. She had worn the blouse several times before she'd developed scruples, and because it wasn't a new purchase, she didn't have any qualms about continuing to wear it. Since she would not allow herself to accept money from her father to buy such an extravagant gift, she doubted she'd ever buy anything that luxurious again. Any extra money she saved on her paltry salary went to charity. It was just the way things had to be. She wasn't sure why she was so obsessive about it. Perhaps she was doing penance for her father's supposed sins, or maybe it was her own pathetic attempt at damage control.

As soon as the nurse and the trainee left Sophie alone, she sat up and swung her legs over the side of the bed. Even though they'd given her a shot to ease her discomfort, she felt a jolt of pain. She winced, grabbing hold of the sheets on either side of her to keep from pitching forward. She heard raised voices coming from the nurse's station down the hall. Men were arguing. Probably doctors and security officers bickering about who was going to have to deal with her.

She felt a little embarrassed by the scene she'd caused, and she knew she had been a pain in the backside. But then she looked down, saw the tattered remains of her blouse, remembered the smug look on the trainee's face, and was once again furious.

Trainee Louanne pulled the curtain aside and returned to pick up the remnants. Her expression was downright ugly. It took Sophie about ten seconds to figure out what Louanne was all about. She was a bitter woman who felt she deserved better. There was a hard, mean look about her. She was in her forties, Sophie estimated, but her bloodshot eyes and red-veined nose suggested a liver that was pushing eighty. Her heavy, nauseatingly sweet perfume was, no doubt, poured on liberally to hide the smell of the alcohol she added to her drinks during breaks.

"I know who you are," Louanne said with a contemptuous snort.

"Good for you. Now go away."

"Your last name isn't Summerfield. It's Rose." Trainee Louanne all but spit out the name as though it was the most foul of words. She looked over her shoulder to make certain no one was listening before continuing. "You can't threaten me and get away with it. You're nothing but trash. You know what? Your daddy's a money whore, and you're his daughter, so you have to be a whore, too." When she didn't get any reaction, Louanne's anger intensified. "The police are going to arrest you. I'll file a complaint," she added. "They'll have to arrest you." Still no reaction. Louanne became incensed. "You better apologize."

That got a reaction.

"Apologize? That was a Dolce & Gabbana," Sophie railed. "Ga . . . bbana."

"Fine. I'll tell the police you struck me. That's called battery."

"No, that's called lying."

The one good thing about FBI agents was that they could be quiet when they needed to be. Louanne turned around and found Jack MacAlister standing just a foot behind her.

She looked back at Sophie. "It's my word against yours."

Jack didn't have the patience for stupidity. "Alec, you getting this?"

Only then did Louanne notice the badges and guns. "I didn't mean nothing by— That crazy woman yelled at me, and I didn't think that was right, and she threatened to kill me with scissors!" she added, bobbing her head frantically. "She'll probably deny it, but she did."

"I won't deny it. I did threaten to kill you. Hand me those scissors, and I'll do it."

"Sophie, for God's sake . . ." Alec began.

"See?" Louanne shouted. "Do you see? And she was screaming at me about a stupid blouse."

"It was a Dolce & Gabbana. Have a little respect."

"She's crazy."

Jack and Alec didn't say a word. They simply stared at the woman.

Louanne swallowed and stammered. "I wasn't really going to lie to the police. But she was terrible to me. Just terrible. And I was just trying to do my job. I'm behind on my work, so I better get to it. There are other patients more appreciative."

She pulled the privacy curtain closed and was sniffling as she hurried down the hall. Both men waited until she had disappeared around the corner.

Alec said, "I'm going to go get Regan. You keep Sophie company."

Jack took a step back. "I'm not going in there. I'll go get your wife."

Alec slid the curtain back and walked over to Sophie's bed. "Are you in much pain?"

"No, not really."

"Sophie, I'm so sorry this happened to you."

The sympathy in his voice made her feel weepy. She put her hand up and said, "Don't be nice to me, not yet anyway. I'm on the edge, Alec, right on the edge."

He smiled at her dramatic warning. "You should be ashamed of yourself. You made that trainee cry."

"I guess I'll have to find a way to live with that."

"I think my partner's afraid of you."

Now that cheered her up. "You always know just the right thing to say."

"I'd hug you and pat your back and tell you it's going to be all right, but I don't want to get blood all over me."

"You can show your love by shooting someone for me."

"Sure, why not?"

"How much longer do I have to wait? I've been X-rayed, CAT-scanned, prodded and poked. I lost some blood, and I think they may have taken the rest."

She felt nauseated again. The adrenaline rush from her anger had ebbed, and pain was now radiating up her chest.

"The surgeon's looking at the films now. Then he'll come in to talk to you."

"Why aren't you asking me what happened?"

"I know what happened. Someone shot you. I also know you couldn't have seen the shooter. He was too far away. There are some details you could clear up for me, but that can wait until you're sewed back together."

"Does Agent MacAlister go everywhere with you?"

"Actually, it's the other way around. I've been assigned to him. I go wherever he goes. That might change soon, though. Jack might be taking a leave of absence."

She didn't bother asking why. "Both of you should go home. This isn't a federal matter. I'll give my statement to the police."

"I'm not going anywhere, and it hasn't been decided yet if this will stay local or be a federal investigation. Besides, I want that bullet as soon as they pry it out of you."

She shuddered at the thought. "I'll mail it to you." She sighed and added, "I want to go home."

"You won't be here long."

Sophie didn't remember much after that. The surgeon came in with a nurse who gave her another shot, and sleep was almost instantaneous. She didn't know how long she was out, but when she next opened her eyes, she was in a hospital bed with an IV drip. Regan and Cordie stood together by the window whispering. Sophie knew they were worried.

"Did you see it?" Sophie asked.

Jack was in the doorway. He had heard what she asked and

thought the question odd. Why would she think her friends had seen her injury? Or maybe she was asking them if they had seen the bullet that had done the damage.

Apparently Cordie and Regan knew exactly what she was asking.

"Who would deliberately destroy a Dolce & Gabbana?" Cordie asked. "It's criminal."

"It's just a shirt," Jack commented.

It was the wrong thing to say.

"It was a beautiful blouse," Regan snapped.

"It was symbolic," Cordie added. "You wouldn't understand."

"A symbolic blouse with blood all over it."

Regan groaned. "We could have tried cleaning it. The bullet didn't tear it. That woman who cut it was barbaric."

"And that's why you threatened to kill her?" he asked, addressing Sophie as he walked into the room. "What's the big deal about a cabana anyway?"

"Gabbana," Cordie corrected.

"He knows what it is," Sophie said. "He's making fun of me."

He shrugged. He watched for her reaction as he asked her friends, "You tell her about the skirt yet?"

"No . . . not the skirt," Sophie whimpered. "I loved that skirt. It was—" His smile stopped her. "You're such a jerk."

His smile widened. "Bite me."

I finally had the opportunity to talk to Eric in private. I insisted that he accompany me to set up a temporary shelter to observe the pack.

I didn't beat around the bush. I told him I had a sample of Ricky's blood, that it was one of the first vials taken, and that there was no unknown hormone evident, not a trace, even though the samples he took showed high levels of the mysterious stuff.

Eric bluntly admitted he had been experimenting on Ricky, but he swore he hadn't injected any of the other wolves. He knew what he was doing would get him in trouble, so he begged me to keep silent until I had read the data he'd collected.

We spent hours and hours going back and forth, but in the end Eric convinced me to go along with the experiment. If his incredible claims prove to be accurate, he's stumbled upon a wonder drug.

THIRTEEN

SOPHIE WAS RELEASED FROM THE HOSPITAL THE FOLLOWING evening. Regan pleaded with her to come and stay at The Hamilton, and Cordie lobbied for her to move in with her in her not quite yet renovated brownstone. Sophie refused their kind offers, insisting that she would be just fine at home. She wanted to sleep in her own bed. There would be round-the-clock protection until the shooter was in custody.

Alec insisted on driving her home, which meant she also had a second escort, Jack MacAlister.

Once she was in her own place and had changed into sweatpants and an old flannel shirt, she could finally relax. She sat on the sofa, swung her feet up on the ottoman, and let out a sigh of relief.

"Have you talked to Detective Morris?" she asked Alec. "I don't remember his last name."

Alec smiled. "You mean Detective Morris Steinbeck?"

"Steinbeck, like the author?"

"Like the detective in charge of your case, and no I haven't talked to him yet. I'll call him in the morning."

"I'm curious," she said. "How come John Wincott didn't take the case? He's a detective and he's your friend, too."

"It wasn't assigned to John," Alec explained.

"So the locals are handling it?" Jack asked. "You're not going to take over?"

"I wanted to, but John told me that Steinbeck's a good detective and I should butt out and let him do his job."

"If you want the case, you should take it," Jack said.

"No, I'm too close to it," he said. "Sophie's a good friend. If Steinbeck doesn't keep me informed, then I might cause some trouble."

Such arrogance. Had Sophie's incision not been throbbing, she might have laughed. Were all men as arrogant and cocky as these two? *If Steinbeck doesn't keep me informed, I'll cause trouble?* Oh, brother. Power. Is that what it was about? FBI trumps police? Alec sounded egotistical, but at least he meant well.

While Alec and Jack continued to discuss territorial issues, she grabbed her sack of supplies. She'd left the hospital with an antibiotic, extra bandages, and pain medication. It was definitely time to take a pill.

Alec turned to Sophie. "Tell me about Steinbeck. What did you think of him?" Alec wanted to know.

"He seemed to know what he was doing. He was thorough. He certainly asked a lot of questions."

"There wasn't much to tell, was there?" Jack asked before disappearing into the kitchen. Sophie heard him rummaging through the cabinets.

"What's he looking for?" she asked Alec.

"Food. We're starving."

"There are some carrots in the fridge," she called out.

She heard Jack laugh. He came back into the living room with bags of potato chips and pretzels, two bottled waters, and a Diet Coke. He tossed the pretzels and one of the bottles to Alec.

"You couldn't have seen the shooter," he said as he sat down next to her on the sofa. "He was too far away." He kicked off his shoes and put his feet up next to hers on the ottoman.

"Comfy?" Sophie asked.

"I'm getting there."

The man obviously didn't understand sarcasm.

"You're right," she said. "I didn't see the shooter. I had to tell Steinbeck about the threats, and he asked me to give him names of people who would want to kill me."

"Bet that's a long list," Jack commented nonchalantly as he ripped open the bag of chips.

"Not funny," she retorted. "I told the detective that everyone loves me, that I'm kind and sweet, and no one would ever want to harm me." Except maybe Trainee Louanne, she thought, and the emergency room doctor. She'd made him shake in his boots. And, oh yes, the creepy guy who hit on her on the El, the one who wouldn't take no for an answer. There was also the woman at that boutique. . . .

"All right, maybe there is a long list," she admitted. "I told the detective that when Kelly's closed and it came to light that the pension was gone, there were a lot of very angry employees. Can you blame them? They were counting on that money for their retirement. My father happened to be a big shareholder in one of the companies in the hedge fund where the money was invested. As soon as the fund went belly up, the finger-pointing started. I'm sure you saw the press conference where the lying CEO came right out and said my father took the money before the stock crashed."

"The CEO didn't come right out and say it, Sophie. He was smart enough not to get charged with slander," Alec said.

"He implied it, and that's just as damaging," she countered. "Don't you think a few people believed him? And those same people might want to get even. Everyone wants a scapegoat. No one wants to be responsible for anything bad that happens. When Congress screws up, they find one or two scapegoats to feed to the public even though they were responsible. My father, in this instance, is the scapegoat just because he's had some questionable dealings in the past."

"Then those vengeful people should go after your father, not you," Jack said.

"Leave my father out of this."

Jack noticed she was having trouble getting the bottle open and took it from her. "Can't leave your father out," he said. "He's smack in the middle of it."

"I'm not going to discuss my father with you or anyone else."

Jack let it go for the moment. She wasn't in any shape to argue right now. She looked pale and her hands shook when he gave her the opened bottle. She would have spilled the pills all over the sofa if he hadn't taken the bottle from her again.

"Listen, since you haven't spoken to Detective Steinbeck," Sophie said, "I probably should tell you something . . ." She didn't get any further. This was going to be difficult to explain and she thought maybe she should let Steinbeck tell them instead.

Alec and Jack both waited for her to continue.

"How many?" Jack asked, holding up the pill bottle. "And who do you need to tell? Alec or me?"

She held out her palm, surprised to see how she trembled. "One, please, and I guess I'll have to tell both of you since you're sitting right here. I don't want to be rude."

"That ship sailed a long time ago." Jack looked at the label on the medication. "These aren't very strong. Sure you don't want to take two?"

"*One* pill is enough to swallow." She smiled. "Get it? You're the other pill."

"Did they X-ray your head at the hospital?" Jack countered.

The doorbell rang and Alec jumped up to answer it. "It's about time," he said.

"Is the security detail already here?" Sophie asked.

"No, Gil isn't coming until nine. Hopefully, Regan and Cordie are here with groceries and carry-out. I'm starving."

Jack got up to help. Cordie handed him a bag of groceries and Regan handed her husband the barbecue.

Sophie called from the sofa, "Did you get my batteries?"

"Triple A, like you asked," Regan replied as she stocked the refrigerator. "I'll put them here on the counter."

Sophie wasn't hungry, but Cordie coaxed her into drinking some of the hot soup she'd stopped to get at the Chinese restaurant down the street. The tasty soup picked her up.

Sophie's friends hovered over her. Cordie put the back of her hand on Sophie's forehead to make sure she wasn't feverish, and Regan shoved pillows behind Sophie's back and wrapped a blanket around her shoulders.

"It was *minor* surgery," Sophie protested. "Minor," she repeated. "Stitches come out in a week, and then I'm back to normal. I could even get back to the weights."

"When have you ever done weights?" Cordie asked.

"I'm just saying I could."

"Isn't there anything we can do for you?" Regan asked.

Sophie looked around the room. The drapes were closed for the first time in probably a year, and it reminded her of how the glass had been shattered by the bullet.

Alec followed her gaze. He and Jack had finished eating and were sprawled in easy chairs flanking her fireplace. "Gil took care of the window for you. He had people here early this morning."

"I just may have to marry that man," Sophie said. "He's so efficient."

"What else can I do?" Regan asked.

"You could put the groceries away and then go home. You're making me nuts hovering. I'm fine."

Cordie followed Sophie into her bedroom and would have gone into the bathroom with her if Sophie hadn't quickly shut the door. She changed the bandage and was surprised that the incision didn't look all that bad. After washing her hands and face, she grabbed a tube of moisturizing cream and opened the door. She burst into laughter. Cordie had made the bed and fluffed the pillows.

"Do you want to get into bed now?"

"Good God. No, I don't want to get into bed. I had minor surgery," she repeated. "It's not even seven o'clock, and I've got a lot of work to do."

Cordie followed her back to the sofa. "I have to call Mr. Bitterman," Sophie said. "Where's the cordless phone? I know he must be worried."

"I already talked to him," Alec said. "He called me on my cell phone when he heard you'd been shot, and I assured him you were fine."

She nodded. "Cordie, did you e-mail everyone to let them know I'm okay?"

"I did."

"Who did you notify?" Alec asked. He sounded mildly curious.

"Family and friends," Cordie said.

"What about her father? Did you notify him?"

Regan gave her husband "the look," which he completely ignored.

"We'd really like to talk to him," Jack said. "You know, take him out for a beer . . ."

"He's a hard man to pin down," Alec added.

"He moves around a lot," Sophie said. "My father is a busy man. At the moment, he's out of the country."

Cordie and Regan knew how uncomfortable Sophie was talking about her father, and they quickly changed the subject.

"One of my kids tried to blow up my lab," Cordie said.

"Cordie teaches chemistry at one of the high schools," Sophie explained to Jack. "Didn't one of your kids blow up the lab last year?"

"Sort of," she answered.

Jack smiled. "How does someone *sort of* blow up a lab?"

"It's complicated."

Cordie looked at Regan and tilted her head toward Sophie, a hint that it was her turn to keep the conversation away from Bobby Rose.

"I'm never going to forget that noise," Regan blurted.

"What noise?" Sophie asked. She remembered she hadn't taken her antibiotic and was now tackling the childproof bottle.

"Over the phone, I heard a booming sound and glass shattering and then a crash."

Sophie didn't have the patience for the bottle, and without thinking what she was doing, she tossed the bottle to Jack. He'd opened one bottle; he could open another.

"I thought you were dead, Sophie," Regan said and immediately became teary-eyed. "I really did. I called nine-one-one on one house phone and called Alec on another. But I kept the cell phone line open, hoping you'd answer me. Did you hear me shouting to you?"

"No, I didn't."

"How'd you manage three phones at once?" Cordie asked.

"I don't know how I did it, but I did. Alec and Jack were in a meeting, and usually the secretary won't interrupt, but I didn't have to do much explaining. I think I freaked her out, shouting about you getting shot."

Alec reached for Regan and pulled her into his lap. "We made it to the hospital before you did, Sophie," he said.

Regan dabbed her eyes. "I'm going to go home and have a good cry."

Alec patted her arm. "Why don't you go ahead and cry now? You'll never make it all the way back to the hotel dry-eyed."

Sophie laughed. Regan could cry at the drop of a hat. It was really kind of impressive. When the three of them were in elementary school, Cordie and Sophie would see who could make Regan cry first. Sophie always told a sad story she'd made up, and Cordie always sang a sad song. Now that she thought about it, what they did wasn't very nice. Fun, but still not nice. This was an odd time for these memories to surface. Maybe the pain pills had something to do with it.

"I'm sorry I made you cry when we were little," Sophie said, suddenly feeling guilty.

"When did you make her cry?" Alec asked.

"All the time," Cordie admitted.

"Until I caught on." Regan shrugged. She went into the foyer to get her sweater and purse. She turned around to Cordie and said, "I'll drive you home if you're ready to leave."

"If Sophie doesn't need me . . ."

"Please go," Sophie said. "I'm begging you, and take these two with you."

It took five more minutes before her friends made it to the door. Regan turned back one last time and asked, "I was wondering. Who was on the cell phone when you got shot? Whoever it was must have been freaked out, too."

"Oh, yeah, about that . . . we'll talk tomorrow."

Alec and Jack hadn't picked up on her evasive answer. They seemed rooted to their chairs.

Once Regan and Cordie were gone, she turned to the men. "You should go home, too," she suggested.

"We're going to wait until Gil gets here," Alec said.

"*Both* of you have to wait with me?"

"I'm Jack's ride home, so yeah, we both have to wait."

"Who was on the cell phone?" Jack asked. Now he was curious.

"I already explained it all to Detective Steinbeck."

"Explained what? Who was it?" Alec asked.

Up to now, she had avoided telling them, but she guessed this moment was inevitable. There was no getting out of it.

"The man who shot me."

JOURNAL ENTRY 290
ARCTIC CAMP

Something dreadful has befallen the pack. Allie, one of the females, died yesterday. We noticed she had been unusually quiet the last couple of days, but we didn't pay close attention.

Eric took me aside to assure me he had nothing to do with Allie's death. I believe him, but I'll be relieved when I find no unusual hormone in Allie's blood.

Two more wolves are showing symptoms. We're guessing the cause is a virus, but we've been unable to identify it. We all feel so helpless and pray the others remain healthy.

FOURTEEN

"**B**UT *YOU* WOULD HAVE LOOKED," SOPHIE PROTESTED.
"Are you nuts?" said Alec. "No, I would not have looked. Would you have looked out that window, Jack?"

"Of course not."

Sophie glanced from one to the other. "Oh, come on. If someone called you, and that someone's voice sounded familiar, and he told you that he didn't want to ruin the surprise . . ."

The two men appeared so incredulous that she stopped trying to justify her actions.

"You're pretty much reacting the same way Detective Steinbeck reacted," she said.

"Did you ask him if *he* would have looked out the window?" Jack wanted to know.

"As a matter of fact, I did."

"And?" Jack prodded when she didn't continue.

"And he said he wouldn't have looked," she admitted reluctantly. "He's a homicide detective. What else could he say?"

"Don't you remember why your boss wanted you to work from home?" Alec asked. "Did you forget about the threats?"

"No, I didn't forget," she said quietly. "I just didn't take them seriously."

"Why not?"

"I get threats all the time—at least every time my father is in the news being unfairly accused of some crime or other. He's never been convicted, I might add."

"In the past, what kind of threats have you gotten?" Jack asked.

She gave a nonchalant shrug. "The usual stuff. You know: 'I hate you,' 'I'm gonna make you sorry,' 'I'm gonna rip your head off . . . blah, blah, blah . . .' "

"I've told her to report these the minute they happen," Alec told Jack.

"Tell the police?" Sophie scoffed. "And have them hovering around me even more than they already do? For what? The threats always stop within a week or two. Alec, I am not going to live my life in fear."

"What else did the shooter say to you before you looked out the window?" Jack asked.

" 'Be a sport.' I asked him to tell me his name, and he said, 'Be a sport.' He also said he didn't want to ruin the surprise."

"So you looked," Jack said, shaking his head.

"Obviously."

"Hmm . . . Yeah, I guess getting shot might be considered a *surprise*," Jack said.

"It's not helpful to be sarcastic."

Jack, sitting in the other chair across from her, leaned forward with his elbows on his knees. "So if I ask you to be a sport, you'll pretty much do whatever I want you to do?"

Sophie didn't appreciate his attitude. *If it involves shooting you, I probably would*, she thought.

Alec wanted her to continue. "You said the voice sounded familiar."

"Sort of familiar," she replied. "He was very cheerful, and he reminded me of a salesman. At the time I thought his voice sounded like I'd heard it before, but now I'm not so sure."

"The next time you get a threat, you call me immediately. Understand?" Alec said, his tone hard.

"I can take care of myself."

Wrong thing to say, she realized, especially since she had just been released from the hospital and was nursing a gunshot wound. Alec looked as though he wanted to shake some sense into her. Jack's expression was even worse.

"Stop looking at me like that."

"How am I looking at you?" Jack asked.

"Like you think I'm an idiot."

"Then I nailed it. Good."

What did they want from her? The truth? Not going to get that, she decided. Of course she was scared, and so tired, tired of pretending that none of the threats bothered her. They were both waiting for some contrition. "Okay, I'll admit it. I wasn't being cautious."

Jack nodded agreement and turned to Alec. While he recited a litany of all the horrible things that could happen to her if she were not more careful, she sat in silence and observed. He really was a jerk, she thought. Too bad he was so damned sexy. She couldn't believe she was actually attracted to him. But why not? He was one fine specimen of masculinity—tall, broad-shouldered, muscular. He had thick, dark hair, a chiseled face, and piercing eyes, and his bad boy smile made her stomach shiver when he looked at her a certain way.

She knew he was attracted to her, too. The way he watched her was awfully personal for an FBI agent. He looked at her the way a man looks at a woman he's interested in. She also knew he didn't want to want her. Considering that he thought she was an imbecile with a smart mouth, and considering who she was related to, who could blame him?

She studied Jack MacAlister closely as his conversation with Alec proceeded without her. Did he know she was attracted to him? She hoped not. Oh, God. FBI. What was wrong with her? What had happened to her standards?

She could go to bed with him, she supposed. It would just be sex, a lot of wild, amazing, passionate sex. No love involved, though. She couldn't allow herself to fall in love. She had to protect her heart. She wasn't like other women. She could never get married and have children . . . not with her family history.

Animalistic, crazed sex . . . no strings . . . nothing wrong with that, was there?

Hello. . . . FBI. *Stop it, Sophie,* she scolded. She had to be crazy thinking such thoughts. FBI. Why couldn't she seem to remember that when she looked at him?

She needed to occupy her mind with something else so she wouldn't have time to think about her warped choices of men. It was like dieting. Whenever she was on a diet, she had to keep busy so she wouldn't think about the quart of Häagen-Dazs chocolate chunk ice cream in the bottom of her freezer. Granted, she usually caved and ate the ice cream anyway, but she was determined not to cave with Jack. That was one craving she could resist.

William Harrington. With all the turmoil of the last twenty-four hours, she'd practically forgotten about him. Now there was a mystery she could concentrate on. What had happened to him? And why had he gone to Prudhoe Bay? Did he go there after leaving the race? Why, then, had she been told he'd gone to Europe? Something was wrong here, but what?

Sophie wasn't sure how to proceed. She thought about running her thoughts past Alec. She could tell him how she had met Harrington and explain the bizarre circumstances surrounding his death, but what could Alec suggest? That it was an accidental death? A horrible way to die, but still accidental?

She needed to talk to Mr. Bitterman. He was an expert on checking sources, and he would certainly know how she should investigate this. After all, he'd played in the big leagues, working at one of the most prestigious newspapers in the world for over twenty years. She should call him.

Alec and Jack had ended their discussion of her, and Alec was texting on his iPhone.

"Alec, do you think someone could be listening in on my phone conversations?" she asked.

He didn't look up as he answered, "Gil checked. He's positive no one is tapping the line. Why do you ask?"

"I was curious, that's all. Agent MacAlister, do you have someplace you need to be? You keep checking your watch."

"Don't you think it's about time you started calling me Jack? And no, I don't have any plans that can't be changed. I'll just make a quick call."

"Alec, for goodness's sake, drive Jack to his car. Let him keep his date. It's rude for him to cancel so late in the day." She couldn't leave it at that. "Besides, I've heard that some of the high-priced escort services charge for last-minute cancellations."

Jack flashed a smile and said, "Can't leave until Gil gets here."

The doorbell rang just then. Jack burst into laughter. "I swear I didn't plan that."

Gil was two hours early. He rushed inside carrying three large pizza boxes with two six-packs of bottled Kelly's Root Beer balanced precariously on top.

"Out of my way, Alec. We've got to eat these pizzas while they're nice and hot, and drink these sodas while they're nice and cold. Hey, Sophie, darling, how are you doing? Feel like eating a slice or two?"

"Maybe later. Where'd you get the Kelly's?"

"Black market," he answered with a grin.

"You went to a lot of trouble bringing hot food in," she said. She was about to add that it was a shame Jack and Alec had already eaten and Regan and Cordie had already left, but Jack followed Gil to the table while Alec went into the kitchen to get some napkins.

"What kind did you get?" Alec asked.

"What do you mean, what kind? The works, of course. If it's edible, it's on there."

Sophie crossed the room and nudged Jack out of the way to examine the huge pizza Gil had just opened. "You're really going to eat again?" she asked, looking up at Jack.

Jack glanced down and suddenly felt tongue-tied. Damn, she was pretty. Face scrubbed, not an ounce of makeup, and she still looked gorgeous. Seductive as hell, too. Another time, another place, he'd make a move.

"What?" he said, trying to remember what she'd asked him.

"I asked you if you were going to eat again."

"Yeah, of course I'm gonna eat. It's pizza. We've gotta eat while it's hot."

"That's a no-brainer, Sophie," Alec said.

It's more like gluttony, she thought. She left them to their Roman feast, which seemed to be close to an orgasmic event, and went into the kitchen to make a cup of hot tea. She spotted the package of triple A batteries on the counter and was reminded of the digital recorder she'd used to interview Harrington. Tonight, no matter what, she was going to listen to every single word Harrington had said. It was a fitting penance for calling him a narcissist. He *was* a narcissist, but she felt bad saying so.

This time she would pay attention. He might have said something relevant about Prudhoe Bay while she had zoned out, and maybe that something would explain the where, when, and why. The poor man was dead, and so she made a promise to herself not to complain while she listened to him drone on and on and on about each of his twenty-four races. And, oh yes, also the saga of his blisters. She would not fast forward through any of it no matter how strong the urge. She sighed. That poor dead man. That poor, god-awful boring, dead man.

She sipped her tea and went into the bedroom to get the digital recorder. She thought she'd left it on her desk, but it wasn't there. As she was checking the drawers, she remembered she'd put it in her purse just before Regan called. Uh-oh. It was all coming back to her now. She remembered holding the purse, the call interrupt, and now the infamous "Be a sport" spoken to her in such a cheerful voice.

The memory caused her to shudder. The purse had to be in the living room.

It wasn't, though.

"Alec, did you see my purse? Red leather . . ." She glanced around the room again. "I was holding it when I got shot. It has to be here."

"I saw it," Gil said around a mouthful of pizza. "It was on the floor, right over there by the window," he added, waving a half-eaten slice in that direction. "It was covered in blood."

"Covered in blood? No, not my Prada!"

Jack looked at Alec and tilted his head toward Sophie. "Is this gonna be like the cabana shirt?"

She heard him. "It was a Dolce & Gabbana, and the Prada red leather tote is a one-of-a-kind."

"*Was* a one-of-a-kind," Jack corrected.

She felt like cursing. She slumped into the chair next to Jack. "Was? Care to explain what you mean by that?"

"I guess you could say the Prada helped save your life," Jack said. "The bullet went through the latch before it got to you."

She sat back. "Okay, I can have that fixed. If the leather isn't stained . . . if I can get the blood out . . . where is it?"

"It isn't here," Alec told her.

"It was part of the crime scene," Gil explained, "so it was taken to the lab."

"I want it back. My recorder is inside, and my wallet with all my identification, and oh, my God, my credit cards."

"I'll call Steinbeck in the morning," Alec promised as he finished the last of the pizza and began to clear off the table.

Sophie yawned. The pain medication was making her sleepy

and she was worn out. "Don't you two have someplace better to be?" she asked Alec and Jack. "Maybe some bad guys to catch?"

"Not me," Jack answered. "I might be taking a leave of absence. If I do, I'm going to find a secluded beach where it's hot all year long and set up a hammock. I hate the cold, and Chicago's already getting there."

"Well, I'm sure you'll have a lovely time," Sophie said. "Now, if you will please excuse me, I'd like to go to bed."

"Jack and I'll head out," Alec said, "but Gil's staying here tonight."

"But—" Sophie began.

"Don't argue with me on this one, Sophie," Alec warned.

Gil winked at her. "That sofa looks mighty comfortable to me. I promise to be quiet as a mouse. You won't even know I'm here."

Reluctantly, Sophie gave in. She no longer had the energy to argue.

After locking the door behind Alec and Jack, she went to her linen closet to get a blanket and pillow for Gil. She straightened up the kitchen and turned out the lights, then headed for her bedroom. The living room was illuminated by the glow of the TV. Gil was watching a basketball game with the volume turned down.

"Good night, Gil," she said. "And thank you."

"Good night, Sophie, darling," he answered through a yawn.

Sophie dressed in her nightgown and sat on the edge of her bed. She was so weary she could hardly keep her eyes open. The clock on her nightstand said 11:30. She couldn't go to sleep yet. She had to stay awake another half hour, so she picked up a magazine and read. Finally, at 11:55, she slipped quietly out of bed. She tiptoed to her bedroom door and cracked it open a sliver. Gil was snoring loudly. Gently closing the door again, she crossed the room to her closet and pushed aside a stack of shoe boxes on the floor to reveal a small wooden panel. With a couple of taps the panel came loose. Behind it was a cavity the size of a paperback novel. She reached inside and pulled out a thin cell phone. Glancing across the room at the night-stand, she squinted to see the clock. It now said 11:59. She waited.

At precisely midnight, the phone vibrated in her hand.

Sophie quickly flipped it open and put it to her ear.

"Hi, Daddy."

I cannot describe how distraught all of us are. Lucy, the other adults, the pups, all gone. The only survivor is Ricky.

Ricky was at death's door, too. Eric convinced Brandon and Kirk to return to the base facility. As soon as they left, Eric sedated Ricky and then, with my help, gave the wolf another injection of K-74. I urged him to increase the dosage.

Within hours of injecting him, Ricky was up and as strong as ever. His remarkable recovery in such a short time stunned Brandon and Kirk.

For the first time, I saw emotion in our alpha male. Ricky went into deep mourning over the loss of his family. He couldn't seem to find his bearings and wailed long into the night; in the daytime, he paced.

FIFTEEN

EVERYTHING WAS GOING TO BE ALL RIGHT, ACCORDING TO her father anyway, and ninety-nine percent of the time he was right. Things did have a way of working out for the better, and, as he constantly reminded her, there would be a light at the end of the tunnel. It was just that crawling through that tunnel to get to the light was always such a pain.

Getting shot was a perfect example. What possible good could come from that? Too soon to know, she supposed, but she chose to believe her father and to embrace his optimistic outlook on life. She also thought she'd start embracing another of his philosophies: get even. Sophie would welcome the opportunity to shoot the man who had shot her. See how much *he* liked it.

Over the phone her father promised her that Kelly's employees would get justice, and she trusted him. She hoped they would get their money back, too, which she mentioned several times. Her father's response was a simple, "We'll see."

After they finished discussing the current sorry state of affairs with Kelly's Root Beer, she told him all about William Harrington, sparing no details of his gruesome death. He suggested that she pack her bag and take a trip to Prudhoe Bay. He reminded her that she was a reporter, and that there was obviously a story to be had there. Sophie recognized her father's real motive. He wanted her out of Chicago until all the hoopla over Kelly's closing calmed down. What he suggested made good sense, though. There *was* a story to be told in Alaska.

The next couple of days went by surprisingly fast, yet Sophie didn't get much of anything accomplished. She slept a lot, ate a little, and felt dull as oatmeal. Gil spent only that first night in her apartment, but he was never far away. When he wasn't guarding her apartment, someone else was on duty. No one got past the lobby without identification and permission. The added security was Alec's doing, and Sophie didn't know how she was ever going to repay him for keeping her safe.

She had company, lots of company, and there were Get Well cards and fresh flowers. Mrs. Bitterman came by with a pot of homemade spaghetti sauce and meatballs. There was enough to feed a family of twelve. Even complete strangers sent good wishes for her speedy recovery. Most insisted they didn't believe Bobby Rose—Chicago's very own Robin Hood—had stolen money from Kelly's retirement fund. The vast majority blamed Kevin Devoe, Kelly's investment money manager, for being inept and making bad stock purchases.

Sophie couldn't escape from the scandal. Every night there was something in the local news about the company closing and also about the bitter divorce. Kelly's daughter, Meredith, and her soon-to-be-ex, Kevin Devoe, were involved in a nasty, hateful fight. Accusations were being flung by each side, and all of them were caught on film and shown like a sick soap opera on the six o'clock and ten o'clock local TV news. Their vile, angry sneers were right there in the middle of the screen for everyone to see.

How could a couple who obviously had loved each other when they married turn into such gargoyles? Love one day, hate the next? No wonder the thought of marriage made Sophie want to gag.

Mr. Bitterman called her every day, but he refused to come and see her until she had recovered from her injury, and he refused to let her say a word about work.

"I know if I do, you'll hound me to let you get back to the newspaper, and I'll feel sorry for you because you were shot, and I might give in," he told her.

When she opened her mouth to talk, he cut her off. At first she was infuriated by his obstinacy because she was dying to tell him about Harrington's fate, but she soon realized Bitterman's stubborn insistence could work to her advantage. She needed more time to gather information before approaching him with her plan.

Sophie couldn't get Harrington out of her mind. She wanted to call Paul Larson in Prudhoe Bay and ask him if he had found out anything more about the deceased. Paul had given her his cell phone number and had told her she could call him anytime night or day, but she didn't want to bother him. He had a full-time job working as a security officer for the oil companies, and he had promised that he would call her if and when he had further information about Harrington. Still, waiting to hear something was driving her to distraction.

She kept a notebook close, and every time she remembered something Harrington had said during that endless interview, she jotted it down. Guilt plagued her. She should have paid more attention to him.

Her attention now, however, was focussed on her missing purse. What she should do is find out where the crime lab was located, go there, and demand that they give her back her personal possessions. They still had her digital recorder with every word Harrington had said on it.

THE DAY HER STITCHES WERE REMOVED started out as a very good day indeed. Paul Larson, the security guy from Alaska, called with all sorts of interesting information.

"They found Harrington's wallet. It was thirty yards from the remnants of a tent that had been set up about twenty miles from nowhere. I mean it. It was smack dab in the middle of the most desolate land you could ever imagine. Nothing around for miles and miles. A small plane flew over looking for Barry, and they set down to put some new markers up."

"Who's Barry?"

"The male polar bear that ate . . . I mean that killed William Harrington. I've discovered that Barry is quite the celebrity up here."

She was horrified. "Because he killed a man?"

"Oh, no, no. He's a celebrity because he's been part of a scientific study on polar bears. There's always one scientific group or another up here collecting data about something. If it's not the polar bears, it's global warming."

"You said they were checking up on Barry?"

"That's right. The pilot spotted a long strip of red fabric flying in the wind. A big wad of it was part of a tent, but then there was another smaller strip frozen to the wallet. If the tent hadn't been such a bright color, he never would have seen it. Even so, when you think about how huge this place is, it's pretty amazing they found anything. They call it a frozen wasteland."

And William Harrington pitched a tent in the middle of it? What in God's name was he doing camping twenty miles from . . . frozen nothing? Sophie couldn't even begin to imagine what he had been up to. She wondered aloud: "You don't suppose Harrington was in Alaska because of one of these scientific studies, do you?"

"What kind of study?" Larson asked.

"This might be a stretch, but I keep thinking about the project Harrington mentioned. He called it the Alpha Project. It's probably nothing," Sophie said. "Harrington was pretty boastful, so he most likely was exaggerating about some superman club he was a part of, but it might be worth a little investigating."

"Alpha Project?" Larson laughed. "Sounds a little sci fi to me."

"I'm sure you're right, Paul," Sophie admitted, "yet I can't help but be intrigued. I still wonder why Harrington was in Alaska. What was inside the wallet?"

"His driver's license, a couple of hundred-dollar bills, and a twenty, and a Visa bank card. There wasn't a scratch on that skinny leather wallet. Not a scratch they said. Amazing, huh? Considering . . . you know . . ."

Considering that good old Barry had chewed up William Harrington?

"They sent the wallet down to the lab in Anchorage. The remains had already been taken there. I talked to a guy down there, told him I was real interested in the investigation, and that I would appreciate it if he would let me know what was going on.

"I guess they started with the bank that issued the credit card and from there they tracked down the name of a law firm handling Harrington's affairs. They even got the name of the one and only relative, who, I understand, is going to inherit a hell of a lot of money. Dwayne Wicker. A second cousin. Pretty sad he only had the one relative."

"I don't know who his friends were or if he even had friends," Sophie said. "We only discussed the twenty-four races he'd won. And blisters. We talked a long time about his blisters."

Paul laughed. "Blisters? You're making that up."

"No, I'm not. I'm ashamed to admit I sort of daydreamed while he talked. I feel bad about that. Those races meant so much to him."

"Then why did he blow off the twenty-fifth race?"

"If I had to guess, I'd say he knew he wouldn't win, but the fact that he was still wearing his racing socks in Alaska is making me wonder if there isn't much more to his disappearance."

"Listen, I've got an idea. Since you're not going to be writing about races, come up here and write about Alaska. We've got a five-star hotel just outside of Barrow. How about I make a reservation for you? I really want that candlelight dinner."

"Do they put chocolates on the pillows every night in this five-star hotel?"

He had a nice laugh. "Okay, I made up the hotel, but you still have to come up here. We have a no-frills hotel here with clean rooms and clean sheets, and you've really got to see the northern lights. The view here is spectacular."

"I thought you said it was a wasteland."

"A beautiful wasteland." He laughed again. "I guess that's a contradiction. You just have to see it to understand. Alaska will fascinate you."

"Let me think about it," she said.

"Think about me, too."

She didn't respond to his comment. "You'll call me if you get any more information on Harrington?"

"I'm going to call you anyway. Bye now."

SOPHIE WAS DESPERATE. "I need Kelly's Root Beer, and I need it bad."

"And you're calling me because . . . ?" Cordie asked.

"Because you know how to get things from the street . . . the 'hood."

"The what?"

"The 'hood, like in neighborhood. Can you get me some or not?"

"I've got a couple of bottles in my refrigerator. I could bring them over after my last chem lab."

"That's not enough. I need cases of the stuff."

"Okay. I'll ask the obvious. Why?"

"Because Mr. Bitterman is coming over tonight. There's a story I want to investigate and it might be necessary for me to take a trip. My hope is that he'll approve the story and cover my expenses. I'll tell you everything when we get together. But now I need root beer and lots of it. I lured Mr. Bitterman to my apartment with a promise, and I exaggerated just a bit."

"How much is a bit?"

"I suggested I had a closet full of the stuff."

"There's an easy solution. Call the grocery store and have them deliver a couple of cases of another brand of root beer."

"Mr. Bitterman would have heart failure. It has to be Kelly's Root Beer."

"What about Regan? Maybe she can help."

"I've already given her an assignment. She's supposed to work on Alec to help me get my things back from the crime lab. There's absolutely no reason for them to hold on to my personal possessions."

"Gil told me there was blood all over your purse and that the bullet went through the clasp. Poor you. They had to take it because it was part of the crime scene. Don't you ever watch any of those CSI shows on television? You're lucky they didn't cut your rug up and take that, too."

"But what about the things inside my purse? Why do they need to keep my wallet and digital recorder and my cell phone? I guess I can kiss that battery good-bye."

"Talk to Detective Steinbeck."

"I have talked to him. He keeps telling me he'll get my things back real soon, but I've stopped believing him. He's just humoring me."

"I don't know what you think Alec can do. This isn't a federal investigation."

"He has friends in the police department, and I'm hoping he can get one of them to help. I really need my recorder. There's an important interview I have to listen to," she explained.

"Ah, the runner interview."

"Yes," she said. "I'm desperate. I even left a message on Alec's cell phone telling him that if I don't get my recorder back by tomorrow, I'm going to break into the crime lab and get it myself. If I have to tear up the place, so be it."

Cordie laughed. "Oh, I bet he just loved listening to that message."

After she finished talking with her friend, Sophie tried several other possibilities, but none of them could hook her up with Kelly's Root Beer. The beverage was as scarce as mascara at an Amish convention.

Nothing was going her way, and Sophie had reached the end of her rope. She wasn't asking for much, just a little good news.

And then it came. But why is it that most good news is accompanied by bad news? Sophie wondered.

Good news: She got her digital recorder back.

Bad news: Jack MacAlister came with it.

JOURNAL ENTRY 304
ARCTIC CAMP

Brandon called a meeting and proposed we keep the deaths of the pack "our little secret." He fears that our funding will be taken away. It had only just been renewed, and none of us wants to leave until we see what happens to Ricky.

We've all agreed to Brandon's proposal.

Ricky has found a new pack for us. He wandered alone for almost two weeks before he found another family. It's typical for wolves to move around in the fall and winter. Ricky came across a pack in migration, and though it's highly unusual, he has managed to blend in. It remains to be seen if this alpha male will cause trouble in his new community.

SIXTEEN

AGENT MACALISTER WAS AS CHARMING AS EVER. AND SO was his greeting. He didn't waste time on "Hello" or "Hi there." She opened the door and heard, "It's a felony to break into a crime lab and steal evidence."

"But I didn't break into the lab, did I? I merely threatened to," she replied. "I suppose it would be impolite to ask you to give me my recorder and then go away, Agent MacAlister."

"Jack. Call me Jack." He smiled as he walked past her into the living room. "You're not getting your recorder back until you say my name."

He didn't look like he was going to be leaving anytime soon. He was making himself comfortable on her sofa.

"Why are you here?" she asked.

"It's a long story."

"Try me." She folded her arms across her chest and suddenly re-membered she wasn't wearing a bra under her T-shirt. The band rubbed against her incision. She grabbed her oversized cardigan. She had placed it on the back of a chair and planned to put it on before she opened the door to Mr. Bitterman, but she'd forgotten all about it.

Jack dropped her recorder on the table next to him, pushed the ottoman farther from the sofa to accommodate his long legs, then sat back and put his feet up. Sophie wouldn't have been surprised if he'd picked up her TV remote control and asked for a beer.

"I'm doing one last favor for Alec before I head to the ocean."

"How long is your vacation?"

"It's not a vacation. It's a leave of absence." His answer was abrupt, impatient.

"Is that good or bad?"

"Depends."

"What beach do you have in mind?"

"Don't know what beach yet. Someplace warm, though."

"What was the favor Alec wanted? He could have sent a messenger with the recorder."

"I have to listen to the interview."

He put his hand up when he saw she was going to object and said, "Detective Steinbeck told Alec he'd already listened to it, but when pressed, admitted he had trouble paying attention. Said that the guy you were interviewing . . . what's his name?"

"Harrington. William Harrington."

"Okay, so Steinbeck said it was a real dry interview . . ."

Her back stiffened. "I beg to differ. I don't do dry interviews."

Jack continued as though she hadn't interrupted. "Steinbeck said Harrington droned on and on in a monotone voice."

Sophie nodded. True. Harrington had droned on and on.

"The police are investigating anyone you may have come in contact with in the days before the shooting and Alec thought one of us should listen to it just in case there was some connection."

"He just talks about 5K races he's won."

"How many 5K races?"

She smiled. "Twenty-four. Are you sure you want to listen?"

"I'm here, aren't I?"

"I could tell you about it."

He shook his head. She tapped her foot impatiently while deciding what to do. Then she gave in. "Fine. You may listen to the interview."

"Sophie, I wasn't asking for permission. I'm gonna listen to it. I can do it here, or I'll take the recorder and listen to it at my place."

"Okay, listen to it here."

"You want to start now?"

"Not yet. We'll wait until Mr. Bitterman gets here. He probably won't want to listen to the interview, but I should give him the choice. And please, don't interfere when I'm talking to him about an article I want to write. You'll want to interfere, but try and restrain yourself."

"Why would I want to interfere?"

She sighed. "The polar bear."

"Polar bear? You want to write about a polar bear?"

"Not exactly about the bear. His name is Barry, by the way."

He flashed a smile. "Sounds like you're writing a kid's book."

"Only if my intention was to scar them for life," she said.

"Say my name, Sophie, or I worry I might just have to interfere."

"I don't want to call you by your first name because I don't want to get that friendly."

He laughed. "Yes, you do. It's okay. I want to get friendly, too."

She shook her head. "No, you don't. You don't like me."

"I don't have to like you to get friendly with you."

She had no idea what to say now, and so, feeling a bit like a coward, she retreated to the kitchen.

"Grab me a root beer," he called out.

"Absolutely not," she called back. "The root beer's for Mr. Bitterman."

He decided to join her in the galley kitchen.

"Word on the street is that you've got a whole closet full of Kelly's."

The pipeline from Cordie to Jack needed to be plugged.

"You may have a Coke, a Pepsi, diet sodas, or water."

He had to check out the refrigerator himself before making a decision. He finally settled on a can of Diet Coke, then went to the cabinets to find something to snack on.

She tried to push rice cakes on him. Regan had gotten them for her at the grocery store, but Sophie didn't like them. What she did like was kettle chips, and so, of course, that was the snack Jack wanted.

"Just because Alec can go through my cabinets doesn't mean you can."

He'd already opened the bag and was chewing on a chip. "You aren't being a very gracious hostess. What are we having for dinner?"

Her response wasn't clever. She sputtered.

"Use your words, Sophie. Use your words," he drawled as he strolled back to the sofa.

She wanted to use a meat cleaver. Good thing she didn't own one. While she enjoyed a few other murderous thoughts, she got a cold soda out of the refrigerator, took a couple of deep breaths, and then went to join him.

"I've been injured. I'm not cooking dinner tonight."

"From the looks of your kitchen, I'm guessing you don't cook at all."

"Of course I cook."

"Yeah? The price tags and stickers are still on your pots and pans, or rather, your pot and pan. Didn't see any lids."

She sat down next to him, reached across his lap, and grabbed a handful of chips. "I microwave."

He abruptly changed the subject. "When's your boss getting here?"

She checked the time on his watch and said, "He should be here now."

"How long is the recording?"

"A couple of hours, maybe a little more. Why?"

"I want to be in bed by ten."

"Ten, huh? You don't look ninety. Must be all that sleep you're getting?"

Mr. Bitterman didn't show up until almost an hour later. It was odd, but sitting with Jack while they waited wasn't at all uncomfortable. He wasn't hesitant to answer questions about his background, where he grew up, where he went to college, and how, after graduating from law school, he had decided to become an FBI agent instead of joining a law firm.

"Tell me why you're taking a leave of absence. Burn out?" she asked.

"No."

"Shoot someone you shouldn't have?"

"No."

"Mental problems? That's a yes, isn't it?"

He smiled. "No."

"Then what?" She nudged him in his side. She was as tenacious as he was.

"It's a forced leave of absence."

"Now that's interesting."

She waited for him to explain, and when he kept silent, she pressed again. "You know I'm going to ask. What did you do?"

He reluctantly told her about the YouTube video. Once he'd finished explaining, he added, "You're probably the only person in Chicago who hasn't watched the damned thing."

"The video. That's right. Regan and Cordie told me to watch it, but I forgot."

"Until something more interesting gets filmed, I'm being hounded by the press. At first the higher-ups wanted me to lay low in Chicago, but this isn't going away. Now they want me out of town, so I'm heading to an ocean until this blows over." He shook his head as he added, "I guess I know what it must be like for you every time your father's in the news."

Sophie didn't want the conversation to get anywhere near her father, and so she steered him away with a couple of other personal questions. The only topic he was reluctant to discuss was his love life. He admitted he'd never been married, but when she asked him if he'd ever come close, he changed the subject.

"Now it's my turn," he said. "Let's talk about your father."

"Let's not."

He didn't push. "I'd ask about your background, but I don't need to. I know all about you." He then proceeded to prove it.

When she thought he had finished, she said, "You read my file."

"I know a whole lot more that isn't in your file."

"Like what?" she asked suspiciously.

"Like you work hard to make people think you're superficial."

"I *am* superficial." She protested even as she realized how ridiculous she sounded.

He laughed. "It's your protection, isn't it? The only people who know the real you are Regan and Cordie, and maybe Regan's brothers."

"I don't hide who I am."

"Yes, you do." His voice softened as he added, "I've done a little checking, and I've got you all figured out, Sophie Rose."

She shook her head.

He nodded. "You're always saving for a new purse, aren't you?"

"I like purses." Jeez, she sounded defensive.

"You don't actually buy the purses, though, do you? You pick out the one you want, save enough to buy it—and I've heard some of them are way up there in price—and then you give the money to a two-hundred-forty-pound muscle man named Muffin, who runs a soup kitchen. It's become a game you and Muffin play. You send a photo of the purse in an envelope along with the cash."

"You don't know what you're talking about. I'm going to buy a Birkin."

"That's several thousand, isn't it?"

"I *am* going to buy the Birkin," she insisted. "Would I go to visit it every Wednesday at five p.m. if I weren't? It's a gorgeous buttery tan with gold markings."

He looked exasperated. "No, you're not going to buy it. What you're going to do is save the money and then give the money away. You do a lot of nice things you don't want anyone to know about, don't you?"

She started to protest again, but he stopped her. "Give it up, Sophie. You're not an artificial, money-hungry, label-loving dimwit. Sorry, sweetheart. It just doesn't fly with me."

Sophie was squirming in the hot seat, but Mr. Bitterman saved the day when he knocked on the door. She had never felt such relief. She hated that Jack knew so much about her. Why had he gone to the trouble to find out her secrets? Why was he interested? What was he up to? *Her father.* That was it. He wouldn't be looking into her history and her behavior if he weren't hunting for something about her father.

Bitterman handed her his coat. Tugging off his tie on his way into the living room, he sat down hard in an easy chair. While he and Jack discussed the attempted murder investigation—*her attempted murder investigation*—she hung his coat in the closet and went into the kitchen to get him a cold root beer.

Bitterman was rolling up his sleeves as he asked Jack, "So no progress on the case at all? No leads?"

"That's what Detective Steinbeck is telling me," Jack said.

Bitterman pointed a finger at Sophie. He took the root beer she offered but held on to his frown. "Then you're sitting tight, young lady. I don't want you running in the streets while there's some trigger-happy nutcase on the loose."

"Sir, I don't run in the streets, and as far as sitting tight . . . I asked you to come over to talk about something important." Without thinking, Sophie crossed to the sofa and sat down next to Jack. Bitterman noticed.

"Before this conversation turns to business matters, I have to ask you how you were able to get so much root beer," her boss asked. "I thought I'd nabbed the last case in Chicago."

She glanced at Jack. He was trying not to laugh. "Yeah, Sophie, how'd you do it?"

Her thoughts flashed back to the meat cleaver.

"Actually, sir, I was desperate to get you to come over so I could talk to you, and I might have exaggerated the exact amount of root beer on hand."

Bitterman leaned forward. "You might have exaggerated?" he asked warily.

She looked him in the eyes. "I did exaggerate. I don't have a closet full of root beer. Just a couple of bottles. That's all."

"In other words, she lied," Jack was happy to interject.

Sophie gave him a look that should have withered him but didn't. She didn't want Mr. Bitterman to dwell on his disappointment so she quickly tried to turn his attention to a more important matter.

"Sir, do you remember William Harrington and the 5K race?"

"Sure, I remember. He changed his mind at the last minute and didn't run the race, right? You told me it was because he knew he couldn't win."

"That's what I thought, but it turned out I was wrong. That wasn't the reason he didn't run."

Bitterman looked around the room. "Seriously, there isn't more root beer?"

"Sir, what I'm trying to tell you is important."

He nodded. "All right. So what was the guy's reason for not running?"

"He died."

Bitterman took a few seconds to absorb the information, then said, "What a shame. He was a young man, wasn't he? He had to be young to run all those races. I suppose dying is just about the best reason there is not to run a race. Where'd it happen?"

"In Alaska," she answered. "He died in Alaska."

From her tone, Bitterman knew something more was coming. He set his root beer on the coffee table and sat back. "He did, did he?"

"A polar bear ate him."

"What's this?" he asked, confused. "What did you say?"

She repeated the terrible news, and Jack chimed in at the end. "Barry ate him."

"My God, they named the polar bear that ate a man? That's awful callous."

"No, sir. He already had a name."

Now to the tricky part. Sophie had to convince Mr. Bitterman to let her investigate the story, and if necessary, send her to Alaska without making him think she might be in danger. Her boss was overly cautious about her. She hadn't quite rehearsed what she was going to say, but she thought she did a great job of piquing his interest and not hinting at anything other than a human interest story idea.

Then Jack started asking hard questions about living conditions, the wild animals, and the harsh climate—all questions she didn't want to answer in front of her boss. Sophie poked him in his side with her elbow. "We can talk about this later, Jack. Remember, you weren't going to interfere."

"The danger of—"

She interrupted. "I know, it's terribly cold up there, but I'll wear the appropriate clothing."

"That's not what—"

She poked him again. "Instead of this story, I could write about your leave of absence and remind Chicago of the video."

Jack leaned in close. "If you want to go to Alaska and freeze to death, I won't stop you."

"You say the sweetest things."

It turned out that Bitterman liked the idea of Sophie getting out of Chicago for a while. He also thought his subscribers would enjoy reading some human interest stories about the rugged people who lived in Alaska. If she made the trip, he might as well get his money's worth.

"I read somewhere that the high school in Barrow has started a football team. It was a clever way to keep the kids in school and off drugs and alcohol. It's working, too. You might want to go there. You've sold me, Sophie. You can do the story. I'll fund the trip."

He started to stand, then changed his mind. "Just wondering . . . how did you find out about Harrington?"

"He had my business card with him. The police up there found it and called me to tell me he had died."

Before he asked another question, she rushed on, "Jack and I are going to listen to the interview I did with Harrington. I'm hoping he said something I missed that would explain why he went there. It's a bit of a puzzle I'd like to solve. Would you like to listen to the interview with us?"

Bitterman declined. "It's been a long day. I want to get home and relax."

The second the door closed behind him, Jack started toward her. She backed up.

"A bit of a puzzle?" he asked. "Care to explain what you're really doing?"

She shrugged. "I'm giving William Harrington the last word."

Eric and I have become brothers of a sort. Since we're both still in our twenties, the bond comes naturally. We keep no secrets from each other. I confessed to him that I was doing research on my own, that I had thought to study the effects of the bitter cold and the isolation on Brandon, Kirk, and Eric, too. I admitted I wanted to increase the stress with various experiments but had decided to forget that plan and concentrate on Eric's amazing discovery.

I wanted to be bolder. I urged Eric to inject more of the new pack. I have certainly changed, for now I believe that scientific discoveries that can benefit others justifies whatever means necessary.

SEVENTEEN

THE MORE JACK HEARD ABOUT SOPHIE'S PLANS, THE CRA-
zier he thought she was, and he made the mistake of saying so.

Her response was sharp. "You don't have the authority to stop
me from going there or anywhere else, for that matter. I have to do
this."

"Why?"

"Because no one else will." She brushed past him as she added,
"I don't think William Harrington's death was an accident. He was
excited about being asked to join some secret group or project because he was so physically fit."

She suddenly remembered something else Harrington had told
her and whirled around to face Jack. "Tests. Harrington told me that
they did a CT scan and an MRI, and they took gallons of his blood
to test. They were looking for flaws. Admit it, Jack. That's weird."

She stood with both hands on her hips. Her face was flushed
with excitement. Jack had trouble concentrating on her words.

"Did he happen to mention who *they* were?"

"No, of course not. He wasn't supposed to talk about any of it, but wouldn't it be easy to find out? The list of places where one can get an MRI can't be all that long. I could start there."

He followed her into the living room. She bumped into him when she abruptly turned around again.

He shook his head. "You can't get medical records. You know that."

"Hmm. You're right," she admitted. She folded her arms and stared into space, thinking. "There's got to be some way for me to check."

"Could we listen to the interview now? I want to get this over with."

"Yes, I know," she said, "so you can leave and go look at an ocean somewhere." She couldn't keep the censure out of her voice.

"What's with the attitude?"

"You should care and you don't."

"When a crime is committed, I damned well do care. Harrington's death was an accident."

Hands were back on her hips. "I think it was murder."

Jack didn't laugh, but he wanted to. "A polar bear murdered him. Was it a premeditated act? Barry could end up on death row if . . ."

He sat down before she could push him.

"Do you think that's funny?" she said with a scowl.

"Yeah, I do. Kind of."

Sophie rolled her eyes, "You are such an idiot. No wonder you work for the FBI."

He patted the cushion next to him. "Sit down and convince me Harrington's death wasn't an accident."

"Okay, then," she said, pleased he had decided to be open-minded.

"William Harrington was all set to run what was for him a big race, and then *boom!*" She snapped her fingers for emphasis. "He dies alone in Alaska in the middle of nowhere with a tent nearby. In the meantime, his home phone and his cell phone were disconnected, and his website was shut down. I went to his apartment building and was told he'd packed a bag and left for Europe, but he was actually in Alaska. Now I ask you, does that make any sense to you?"

She didn't give him a chance to answer. "Oh, I know what you're going to say. Harrington had his phones disconnected because he didn't know how long he would be in Europe—which is a stupid reason, but logical—and he simply changed his mind about Europe and chose instead to go camping miles from nowhere alone in the Arctic.

"Then you would say, all that talk about being so super-fit and being invited to join some kind of Superman project was a lie he made up to impress me. I don't think it was a lie, though."

He smiled. "Do I need to be here for my part in this conversation?"

Embarrassed, she said, "I'll admit I can get a little eager."

"Because you're searching for a story?"

"No, because I'm searching for the truth. It's the right thing to do."

"I'm not waiting any longer. I'm listening to the interview."

With that, he pushed the button on the recorder. Harrington's voice filled the room.

Sophie ran into her bedroom to get her notebook and pen. Very professional now, she returned to sit on the edge of the sofa, pen in hand and notebook balanced on her knees, poised to take copious notes.

An hour later she was sprawled out next to Jack sound asleep. Her feet were in his lap; the notebook was on the floor, and her pen had disappeared between the cushions.

Jack lasted another half hour before giving in. At that point, he either had to take a break or throw the frickin' recorder out the window. When he stopped the recording and moved her feet off his lap, she woke up.

Sophie opened her eyes and saw him. The hubba-hubba hunk,

she'd decided to call him. One of her socks was hanging off her foot, and he was pulling it up for her. When he caught her staring at him and smiled, her heart missed a beat. She was sure of it.

Bizarre, she thought. Absolutely bizarre. She'd never had such an instant love/hate reaction to a man before. Jack was different, and that made her worry. This man could hurt her. The big jerk.

She slowly sat up and brushed the hair out of her face, clearing her mind of hubba-hubba thoughts.

"What did I miss?" she asked.

"If you're lucky, races one through twelve."

"You only got that far?" she asked, frowning.

"At least I listened. I didn't fall asleep five seconds after Harrington's voice came on."

"You're right," she said. "I shouldn't have criticized you."

"Refresh my memory. How many more races do I have to listen to?"

"Twelve."

"Ah, come on," he groaned. "This is brutal." Standing to stretch his legs, he said, "The CIA could use this stuff in interrogations. Stick a pair of headphones on the suspect, and in three hours tops, he'd crack like a piñata."

"You don't have to stay." She picked up the notebook and put it on the table next to the recorder then started searching for her pen. "You could come back tomorrow and listen to the rest."

"If I leave, I'm taking the recorder with me."

She knew it wouldn't matter if she pointed out it wasn't his to take. He would still be difficult. Did she expect less? Of course not. He worked for an agency that had no misgivings about such things.

"Then you have to stay."

"Yeah, okay."

"Meet you back at the sofa in five minutes."

Sophie went into the bathroom off her bedroom to wash her face and brush her teeth. The cold water revived her. Now all she needed was a little more caffeine, and she could get through the rest of the races without falling asleep. After glancing in the mirror, she decided to comb her hair and put on a little makeup. She had a bottle of perfume in her hand and was about to dab some on her wrist and her neck when she suddenly realized what she was doing and, worse, why she was doing it. She wanted to look pretty . . . for him.

"Have you lost your mind?" she whispered. She stared at her reflection a full ten seconds waiting for an answer. "Apparently so," she said then. "FBI. Remember what that stands for?"

The reminder helped. And so did Jack. If he noticed she'd fluffed up, he didn't comment. The fact was, he barely glanced at her. As soon as he heard her coming, he turned the recorder on.

William Harrington had just begun his riveting chat about blisters. To his credit, Jack managed to get through all the races without cursing.

"Nothing Harrington said would be helpful to Steinbeck in his investigation," he concluded as he flipped the Off switch.

"Did you think there would be something? Whoever tried to kill me had to be someone who lost his pension when Kelly's closed, or maybe was a relative or friend of someone who lost his pension. Harrington didn't have a thing to do with it."

"Maybe" was his noncommittal response.

"I don't understand why Detective Steinbeck didn't bring my recorder and listen to the interview himself."

"Steinbeck is following up on leads and questioning people, and this interview is low on his priority list. Alec knew you wanted to get your recorder back. Like I said, I was doing him a favor."

"Now you can tell Detective Steinbeck and Alec that there wasn't anything relevant to the investigation."

Jack headed to the door. "I *could* tell Alec, but *will* I? Doubtful," he said. "Real doubtful."

She could hear the mischievous smile in his voice. "What are you saying?"

"I'm saying my partner would have to listen to the entire interview if I were to suggest that there were some suspicious comments made."

"You'd lie to your partner?" she asked, pretending shock but inwardly thinking it was a great idea.

"I'm seriously considering it."

"What about Detective Steinbeck?"

"I'd tell him the truth."

He unlocked the deadbolt, then turned around. Sophie took a step back, but she was still entirely too close to him. The foyer was cast in shadows.

"Sorry your evening was ruined," she said. "It's just a little after nine now, and didn't you say you wanted to be in bed by ten? You can still make it."

"I did say that, but I think I'll go home instead."

It took a second for her to understand what he was telling her. He had planned to be in some woman's bed by ten, not his own.

"There's always tomorrow." She tried to sound cheerful.

"Or the day after. You can wait that long, can't you?"

"Me?" she asked indignantly. "Are you suggesting that you'll be in my bed? A bit presumptuous, wouldn't you say?"

"You haven't thought about it?" he asked.

"I . . . um . . . I might have . . . but it's too complicated . . . it's all . . ."

He smiled and said, "Trust me. It will be worth the wait."

He pulled her into his arms and slowly lowered his head, his lips lightly brushing hers in a sweet, no-nonsense, see-you-around kind of kiss. When he raised up, their eyes met. She could have pulled away, but instead she put her arms around his neck, and this time there was nothing sweet or hurried about their kiss. His mouth was hot, wonderfully hot. He didn't have to force her lips apart; she willingly gave him what he wanted. His tongue slowly penetrated and rubbed against hers, igniting such heat inside her. He stroked and explored her mouth, learning the taste of her.

A kiss shouldn't be lazy and erotic at the same time, but this one was unbelievably arousing. He acted as though he had the rest of the night to seduce her, and when he ended the kiss, he could have taken anything he wanted.

He knew it, and so did she.

He didn't say good-bye. He simply turned her into Jell-O and left. She didn't know how long she stood there leaning against the wall, but she finally got it together and turned the deadbolt. She switched off the lights in the kitchen and the living room, then went into her bedroom.

She held her hands up in front of her face. They were trembling. But that was all right—she had simply been surprised by his kiss. Her curiosity was appeased, and she could move on. She'd just forget about it.

Sophie fell back onto her bed and stared at the ceiling, trying to convince herself that it hadn't been any big deal. All the while, a little voice in the back of her mind whispered, *Holy Crap!*

JOURNAL ENTRY 400
CHICAGO

Our work in the lab has given us incredible results. K-74 doesn't stop the aging process completely, but it slows it measurably. By what percent, we still don't know.

More amazing to us is the correlation between stress factors and physiological reactions. No matter how horrible the conditions, the animal demonstrates no fear and the heart rate never fluctuates. Is this drug a way to control or completely eliminate the ravages of prolonged stress on the body?

The rat placed in the tank with the python showed no fear, even while he fought to his death. Did K-74 make him feel invincible?

How will the wolves react to an increase of the drug? We'll soon find out.

EIGHTEEN

THERE WAS AN "INCIDENT" AT WILLIAM HARRINGTON'S apartment.

Gil had made a phone call to a Mr. Cross, the manager of the building, and with a little charm and a bit of bullying was able to get Sophie inside Harrington's home.

Mr. Cross was waiting for them in the lobby. Fortunately, the thug masquerading as a security guard/receptionist wasn't on duty. She didn't think she would be able to get past him even with Mr. Cross attached to her elbow.

"We'll miss Mr. Harrington," Cross said as he followed them into the elevator. "He was the ideal tenant. Paid his dues on time, kept to himself, didn't cause any problems, and he rarely had late-night visitors.

"I'm afraid you're going to run into Mr. Harrington's second cousin in the apartment. He's been coming and going all week. He isn't anything like Mr. Harrington. Quite the opposite," he whispered. "A tad uncouth, if you ask me."

Uncouth? Mr. Cross was being kind. Dwayne Wicker was stunningly crude. Sophie wasn't one to make rash judgments about anyone, for first impressions were often deceiving, but she made an exception with Dwayne. While Mr. Cross was making the introductions, Dwayne felt the need to adjust the crotch of his pants. Couldn't get much more uncouth than that.

A toothpick dangled from the corner of Dwayne's mouth. "What do you want? What are you doing here?" The toothpick bobbed with each word he spoke.

"I need to go through Mr. Harrington's papers," Sophie told him.

He squinted at her. "Why? Were you like his secretary or something?"

"You could say so."

"Oh, then that's okay. I don't care about his papers. I already know where his cash and investments are," he said.

"You hit the lottery, didn't you?" Gil asked.

"Sure did."

"How well did you know William?"

"Didn't know him well at all. He didn't have much use for me. He loaned me money a few times, but then he stopped. Bet he's burning you-know-where for that. He had more money than he knew what to do with, and I was just scraping by. It wasn't my fault I couldn't hold down a job. I've got back problems. Being blood relation, he should have shared. Right?"

Neither Sophie nor Gil said a word. Dwayne took their silence to mean they fully agreed.

"He was stingy is what he was, but he couldn't take it with him, could he? Now I get it all."

Dwayne was making Sophie sick to her stomach. "Where are William's papers?"

"They're all in a pile on the floor in the dining room. I already sold the table and chairs, so you'll have to sit on the floor while you sort through it."

"Isn't it premature to be selling his things so soon after his death?" Gil asked.

"Nope," Wicker answered. "I figure the minute the police confirmed that William was dead, all this was mine. I'm the closest relative he had. I could have gotten to this sooner if the police hadn't insisted on absolute proof. They sent hair out of a brush up to Anchorage so they could run DNA tests. I'm sure it's William." He pointed to the dining room. "You'd better hurry up. I got movers coming any minute now, and a Realtor to tell me how much I can get for the place."

Harrington's apartment had been quite elegant at one time: high ceilings with beautiful, deep crown moldings, spacious rooms with lots of light. It now looked like Dwayne was getting it ready for a garage sale.

The pile of papers turned out to be a gold mine. Sophie found phone bills, letters from Harrington's physicians, medical test results, his address book, and credit card bills, all filed in manila folders. She collected a huge stack and stuffed it into her oversized tote. She would have taken more if Dwayne hadn't strolled in to see what she was up to.

"How come you're so interested in his papers?"

"I just am," she answered.

Dwayne was suddenly suspicious of her motives. "Are you looking for something in particular? Hey, wait a minute. What's going on here?" Before she could answer, he asked, "Were you and William together? You know what I mean. Were you giving it to him?"

"Giving what, Mr. Wicker?"

The disgust in her voice set him off. "Screwing him," he snapped. "You were, weren't you?"

He squatted next to her, saw the letter from a law firm in her hand, and tried to snatch it. "I know what you're up to. You think my cousin left you some money, and that's why you're going through his papers. I've got news for you, sweetheart. You're not getting a dime."

Gil sat on the window seat watching. He spoke before he

thought about the consequences and inadvertently threw gasoline on the budding fire. "Unless he wrote a new will and left his sweetheart every dime."

The possibility sent Dwayne into a tailspin. He nearly swallowed his toothpick. "The hell he did. Give me those papers and get out of here."

Sophie paused only long enough to stand and glare at Gil. "Seriously . . . ?"

A tug-of-war immediately ensued. Dwayne was no longer calling her "sweetheart." "Bitch" was her new name as he tried to pull the tote out of her hands. Each time he tugged at her bag, she pulled it away. He had a few other crude names for her, but Sophie wasn't bothered until he stepped over the line and slapped her.

She was so shocked by the attack, she froze. So did Dwayne, and then a smug smile began to spread across his face. Before Gil could bound across the room, Sophie curled her hand into a fist and, quick as a snake, struck, splitting Dwayne's lip and snapping his toothpick. She might have broken his nose, too, but she couldn't be sure.

After firmly locking the straps of her tote in her hands, she shook her head at Dwayne and said, "Shame on you, hitting a girl."

Retreat seemed the logical move before Dwayne regained his senses and his temper.

"Lovely to meet you," she said as she walked ahead of Gil out the door. "You have yourself a nice day now."

The foundation has given us the green light to finish our original study with the wolves. The old gang is back together again. We've made a few updates to the facility here in the frozen north, but for the most part things have remained the same. While we were back in Chicago, Eric and I set up our own lab. We begged and borrowed and managed without assistance. I am now an equal partner, and we aren't owned or controlled by any pharmaceutical company or government agency. Our testing will remain secret while we gather data.

Amazing. The tracking device is still working. We couldn't believe our eyes when we found Ricky. He's at least nine years old now but looks as vigorous and young as the day we first spotted him. In fact, he is once again the leader of his own pack. He hasn't lost one iota of his virility. This warrants a study of its own.

While Brandon and Kirk identified and tagged each of the members of the new pack, Eric and I took blood and tissue samples from Ricky. It was not an easy task to sedate him, but we managed. Up close his coat doesn't have the same luster, but the blood work tells a different story. Ricky has a hormonal balance unlike anything we've seen before, plus we still see traces of K-74.

Ricky will get another dose of the drug soon. Once we see how he reacts, we plan to inject the others.

We won't be putting our findings in any official report. What we're attempting isn't within the parameters of our mission here and could get us thrown out of the program, but we're banking on the reward being worth the risks.

NINETEEN

SOPHIE SAT ON THE FLOOR OF HER APARTMENT WITH MANILA folders spread out in front of her. She had spent the afternoon combing through William Harrington's files looking for something that would explain his sudden disappearance and his untimely death. So far, all she could be certain of was that Harrington was obsessed with his health. The thickest folder was stuffed with medical reports and test results, and from what she could decipher from them, he was as fit as he claimed to be.

The latest examination report was on the top. Knowing that she would probably be rejected, she decided to try her luck anyway. She found the number of the clinic on the first page and dialed it. Sophie cheerfully introduced herself to the receptionist who answered the phone, and then she laid out her case. She told the woman that she was a reporter and that she wanted to write an article about one of the clinic's clients who had recently met an untimely death. She did her best to convince the woman that the article was to be a tribute and not an exposé, but the receptionist cut her off in midsentence, explaining rather forcefully that neither she nor anyone else at the clinic could divulge information about their patients. The answer was exactly what Sophie had expected, but she felt it was worth a try. She hung up the phone discouraged but not deterred. She'd have to keep looking.

Next she picked up Harrington's address book. There were very few entries, and most of them were professional contacts: the law firm, a couple of doctors, a hair salon, several restaurants. None of them appeared to be friends, making Sophie wonder if Harrington had any. If he did, he probably kept their contact information on his cell phone or PDA, and since she didn't have either, there was no way she could check. However, there was another solution: the cell phone bill. Sometimes the bills listed the numbers of incoming calls. She shuffled through the folders but couldn't find the one she wanted. It was probably still in Harrington's apartment. She had stuffed only half the files in her tote bag when Dwayne Wicker had intervened, and considering her last encounter with him, she doubted he'd welcome her with open arms if she visited the apartment again.

Sophie was contemplating her next step when the phone rang. Paul Larson was calling from Alaska.

"I was just wondering if you'd reconsidered my invitation."

Sophie laughed. She couldn't fault the man for his persistence.

"Actually, I'm thinking about it," she said.

"Great!" he said enthusiastically. "I'm excited to meet you." He hastened to add, "And it's not because I'm starved for female company."

"If I come, it will be for business only. I've been doing some research on William Harrington, and there are a few things here that I want to check out first."

"That's the other reason I'm calling," he said. "I've got news. I heard about two guys who talked to Harrington."

"When did they talk to him? What did Harrington say?"

"Slow down," Paul said with a chuckle, "and let me explain. You might not know this, but we've got trucks coming up and down the Dalton Highway pretty much all year long. The rigs come from Fairbanks with equipment and supplies.

"One of the drivers is a real nice guy named Sam Jackson. He told me he was giving two brothers a ride back up to Deadhorse. Their last name's Coben, and they're trappers," he explained. "According to Sam, they're kind of strange, but not scary. I think he means the brothers don't know how to be social. They're maybe awkward but still friendly and don't mean any harm.

"Anyway, to pass the time, Sam told them about Barry killing a man, and when he mentioned where it happened, one of the brothers asked him if the man's name was William. They had met a William who was all alone out on the flats. Neither brother could remember the man's last name, but they both recalled that William told them not to call him Bill. Odd thing to remember, don't you think?"

"Yes," she agreed. "What else did the brothers say?" she asked, trying to hurry him along.

"At the time, Sam didn't know William Harrington's name, but he was sure the brothers were talking about the same guy, though one of them told him that this William was setting up camp in a remote area, and he looked like he was going to be settling in for a long spell. They also told Sam that they talked to him for quite a while and offered to help him put some of his equipment together, but William wouldn't let them help."

"Did Harrington tell them what he was doing there?"

"Sam didn't say, but he did tell me the brothers spent several hours with him."

"I'd love to talk to them."

"Sam's already on his way back to Fairbanks," Paul said. "But I could dig up his phone number for you or have him call you."

"No, I mean the brothers. I want to talk to them."

"That's going to be a problem. Sam said they were picking up supplies and then heading toward Umiat. "

"Could I get their cell phone number?"

Her question gave him a good laugh. "Sophie, they're trappers. They don't carry cell phones. They've probably never used one. They live in the wilderness and don't have any need for cell phones."

"What happens if they get into trouble?"

"They have rifles and guns and hatchets and—"

"Got it. Wilderness men," she said. "Live in log cabins in the mountains."

"More like prefabricated trailers," he said. "And cell phones couldn't get signals where they are anyway. If you get up here fast, you can probably catch them before they head back to their camp."

She tallied up the work she needed to do for the newspaper. "It might take a couple of days."

"The sooner you get here, the more likely you are to find the Coben brothers," he cautioned.

"I'll make my reservations today."

"Let me know your arrival time, and I'll make sure I'm there to greet you."

"Yes, I will."

"How about I go ahead and reserve some rooms for you at the hotel. How many do you think you'll need?"

"Just one."

"You're traveling alone?"

"Yes, I am. Is that going to be a problem?"

"No, of course not. You'll be perfectly safe here. Probably safer than in Chicago."

Based on the fact that she'd recently been shot, she had to agree with Paul. Prudhoe Bay had to be safer.

"I'm not worried," she said.

"The accommodations in Deadhorse are a bit unusual. You can either get a room but share a bathroom, or share a dorm room with a bunch of guys. I'm guessing you'll want a private room."

"You guessed right."

"Oh, and I'll go ahead and tell the police in Deadhorse that you're coming. I want to tell them about the Coben brothers meeting Harrington, anyway. His death was ruled accidental, but they still might want to talk to the brothers. How long are you planning to stay? If you don't mind, I'll take some time off and show you around."

"That would be great—"

"You'll want to see where Harrington was camped, won't you?"

"Yes," she said. "And while I'm up there, I'll need to go to Barrow. My boss wants me to write a couple of articles about the high school football team he heard about."

"Barrow isn't a hop and a skip away. You'll have to fly there, but I can arrange that for you. You'll fly right over the accident site," he added. "You know, where Barry . . ."

Snacked on William Harrington? "Yes, I know," she said instead.

He mentioned several other places he thought she should see while she was in the bay, as he called the massive northern area of the state. Umiat, the Topagoruk River, and Alaktak were just a few. She couldn't spell the names let alone pronounce them, but Paul was familiar with all of them.

"You're going to see the Arctic Ocean. That alone is worth the trip."

Paul made it sound like such an adventure. Time to get educated, she decided. She still didn't know much about Alaska. She went to her computer and started reading. The north shore fascinated her. Nights that lasted over fifty days, winter winds that could pick up a man and toss him around like tissue paper, and temperatures that could drop as low as 60 degrees below zero. Who in his right mind would live there?

She called a travel agency to find the best way to get to Prudhoe Bay. After making her reservation, she called Paul Larson's phone. It went right to voice mail.

"Paul, this is Sophie Summerfield," she said. "I'll be on flight 459, Wednesday, five p.m. See you then."

She had much to do before leaving Chicago. Gathering all the folders into a pile, she stacked them on her dining room table and went to work on one of her assigned newspaper articles. When she finally turned off her computer, it was past midnight.

Her mind was filled with images of Alaska, but when she finally curled up in bed and closed her eyes, her thoughts turned to Jack MacAlister and the kiss. That frickin' kiss. Big, big mistake. Definitely. So how come she wanted to make the same mistake again?

THE SECOND MISTAKE SHE MADE was forgetting about the gossip grapevine. Gil picked her up the next morning. He was her designated driver to the doctor to have her stitches removed, and on the way home she casually mentioned her travel plans. He seemed genuinely interested and asked a lot of questions about the places she hoped to visit.

By the end of the day, Gil had a new name: Big Mouth.

She hadn't been home more than an hour when the phone calls started. She heard from Regan; Regan's brother Aiden, who was calling from the airport while he waited for his flight home, which meant that Regan had already squealed to him; and she heard from Cordie, who had to limit her tirades to coincide with the five-minute breaks between classes. It took her three phone calls to finish.

Sophie took the are-you-crazy calls in stride until she heard from Alec. Regan had obviously convinced her husband that it was his duty to keep Sophie from doing anything rash. He told her flat out that she couldn't go. She didn't get angry. She laughed and then reminded him that she would do whatever she wanted as long as it was legal. Then she lied. She told him she hadn't made up her mind to go to Alaska and promised that he would be the first to hear, once she made the decision.

Alec wasn't buying the lie. He'd known Sophie a long time now and understood how her mind worked. He'd bet a month's

salary she already had her airline reservations, and just for the hell of
it, he checked. He was right.

He knew he couldn't stop her, but he hated the idea of her going
alone. Harrington had ended up stranded in the middle of nowhere,
and he didn't want that to happen to Sophie, too. It didn't matter
that Harrington's death was ruled an accident. There was still something sinister in play, and knowing Sophie, she would want to find
out what it was.

Alec knew he could request assistance from the FBI office in Anchorage, but they couldn't give Sophie twenty-four-hour protection, and she wouldn't allow it anyway. Since he had married Regan,
both Sophie and Cordie had become like sisters to him. Cordie was
the more reasonable and practical of the three friends; Sophie,
though sweet and charming, was the daredevil. She always ended up
fighting for the wronged and the forgotten, and, despite the risk,
usually she got them the justice they deserved. Sophie, he'd learned,
was all about fairness.

Alec didn't care how Sophie felt about it. Someone had to go
with her, and there was only one person he could think of who had
the time and the mettle. He also had a gun and a badge, and both
would certainly come in handy.

Jack was the man for the job. Convincing him was going to re-
quire a little finesse and a whole lot of manipulation.

Only one way to make it work. Emergency poker night.

JOURNAL ENTRY 493
ARCTIC CAMP

Brandon and Kirk have returned home, and they believe Eric and I will be leaving the facility in the next few days.

They are pleased with their work with the pack, and Brandon has become quite attached to this family. He is sorry to leave them, but he fully expects to see them again next year.

Eric and I had our work cut out for us after they left. It took some time to locate all the wolves that were injected with K-74. They all seem to be as lively as when we last saw them. None has aged much at all.

Too bad we had to end their lives while they were still in their prime, but a more thorough analysis is called for to determine the effect of K-74 on a cellular level.

The most remarkable discovery we've made thus far is that the more stress an organism undergoes, the stronger and more youthful he becomes. How is this possible?

TWENTY

THEY WERE ALL IN ON IT.

Gil couldn't wait to brag. "I'm telling you, you should have seen Sophie. She split Wicker's lip wide open, and I think she might have broken his nose. I sure hope she did. The scumbag howled like the mangy dog he is."

Gil sounded like a proud uncle boasting about a goal one of his nieces had made at a soccer game. He had just taken his seat at the poker table and was recounting the incident at Harrington's apartment to the poker regulars: John, Alec, Jack, and Zahner.

"Don't mess with our Sophie," John said. "She'll take you down every time. Aiden made sure she and Regan and Cordie all knew how to take care of themselves."

Everyone at the table smiled and nodded, everyone but Jack. "That son of a bitch hit Sophie? Where were you, Gil? Why didn't you stop him?"

"Sophie didn't need my help. By the time I was halfway across the room, she had already let him have it. It was funny how she did it, too. She put her hand right up in front of his face, then slowly made a fist, staring him in the eyes the whole time—"

"She have rings on the hand she fisted?" John asked.

"Sure did."

"Good for her. Do more damage when you're wearing rings."

"Yeah," Zahner agreed. "Have enough rings on, and it's like you're wearing brass knuckles."

"Okay, so Sophie made a fist . . ." John prodded Gil to continue.

"She's about two, maybe two and a half, feet away from him, and he's wearing a real smart-ass expression, and then—*bam!*" Gil paused to smack his right fist into the palm of his left hand. "She goes straight at him. No swinging her arm up in an arch giving him time to duck. Nope, just straight on . . . hard . . . as quick as a cobra."

"She should have gotten him in the crotch," Zahner said. "I always tell my girls, kick them in the crotch."

"What girls would those be?" John asked.

"The working girls I'm trying to get off the street."

"You sound like a damned pimp," Alec remarked.

Zahner wasn't offended. In fact, he had a good laugh. "I'd make a whole lot more money if I were."

"What the hell, Zahner?" Jack asked. "When did you get the gold tooth?"

"It's a snap-on," he said. "My girls love it."

"Enough with the girls," John said, chuckling.

Alec's brother-in-law, Aiden Hamilton, walked into the room just as Jack asked, "Is Sophie okay? Did that bastard hurt her?"

"Someone hurt Sophie?" Aiden asked as he removed his suit jacket and casually draped it over a chair.

"She's fine," Gil said, and then proceeded to tell the incident once again.

When he was finished, Aiden asked, "Are the police going to be knocking on her door?"

"No worries about that," Gil told him.

"Possibility of a lawsuit?" he asked.

"Don't think so," Gil said.

"What are you, her surrogate father?" Zahner asked Aiden.

Alec answered. "Aiden was Sophie's unofficial guardian for a
while. He wasn't quite twenty-two when he petitioned the court.
Did you ever make that legal?" he asked.

"What does it matter now? She's over twenty-one," Aiden
pointed out.

"I don't get it," Zahner said. "She has a father."

"Yeah, but he was a wanted man back then. Sophie could have
gone into the foster care system if Aiden hadn't stepped in," Gil
said.

"Are you playing poker with us tonight, or are you just stopping
by to say hello?" John asked.

Aiden rolled up his shirtsleeves and smiled. "I'm playing."

A collective groan went around the table. A card shark, Aiden
rarely lost.

He pulled out a chair and sat. "You boys ready to lose your
money?" He looked at Jack, then glanced over at Alec and gave a
barely noticeable nod.

The con was on.

JOURNAL ENTRY 498
CHICAGO

We haven't quite defined the correlation between stress and the effectiveness of our serum, but it appears that the adrenaline produced in a stressful situation can exponentially increase the potency of the drug.

It is time to move to primates. Keeping our work a secret is the real challenge.

TWENTY-ONE

MARGARET PITTMAN CALLED JACK TO HER OFFICE FOR A sit-down. He passed Alec on his way, and from the sympathetic expression his partner gave him, Jack knew he was going to be hearing some unpleasant news.

Nothing could be more unpleasant than where he was being forced to go, thanks to the poker bet he'd lost. Alaska may be a beautiful wilderness, but he couldn't even say the name of the state without mentally shivering. He hated the cold. Always had, always would.

As it turned out, Pittman also wanted to talk about his leave of absence. Wanting to get him away from the media, she had approved his vacation plans, but now he was asking for something different.

By the time he finished explaining where he wanted to go and why, including everything he had learned about William Harrington, Pittman appeared interested. A little *too* interested, he thought, which put him on guard.

"Uh-hum, uh-hum, I see, I see," Maggie said briskly. "You want to start your leave today, and you're going to northern Alaska?"

"That's right."

"You're traveling with Miss Sophie Rose?"

"Yes," he answered. Sophie just didn't know it yet.

"Agent Buchanan was just in here giving me an update. He mentioned that Miss Rose has been doing a little investigative work. She's determined to find out why William Harrington went to Alaska." Pittman shook her head. "Death by polar bear. That's a new one for me. I think Miss Rose could write several interesting stories about the Arctic. Don't you agree?"

The ten-second rule had passed and Pittman was still looking at him expectantly. She actually wanted him to answer the question.

"Yes, I'm sure she could."

"You know, Miss Rose needs continued protection. Don't you agree, Agent MacAlister? Of course you do. Now, it's my understanding that Agent Buchanan and Aiden Hamilton have been paying for security; well, now it's time for us to take over. The woman's taken one bullet, and who's to say she won't be taking another if she stays in Chicago. I've spoken to Detective Steinbeck," she added, "and he admits they don't have any significant leads. The shooter's still out there."

She put her hand up to block any interruptions Jack might have wanted to make and continued, "We're not interfering in the investigation. We're just . . . observing. Detective Steinbeck knows he can call on us to assist . . ." she paused to smile and said, "to take over the investigation if need be. We're not good at assisting, are we? We like to take charge because we know what we're doing, and we get the job done. Isn't that right?"

Jack didn't bother to nod. He simply waited for her to tell him his answer.

"Yes, it is right," she said before abruptly changing the subject. "By the way, do you have any idea how many hits there have been on that video you starred in? We're over two million now and still climbing. I've had three major networks hounding me for interviews with you." She held up three fingers and wiggled them. "You're the new American Idol."

He groaned, and Pittman reacted with a glare. "One of my assistants asked me why we didn't just shut down the video. I told her, why bother? By the time we found out about the thing, it had been downloaded to about eight hundred sights," she exaggerated. "It's all over the Web now. And as you probably know, we did try the it's-all-a-hoax ploy, but that didn't fly."

Pittman wasn't one for idle chitchat. She'd brought up the video for a specific reason. Jack waited for her to tell him her real agenda.

A knock sounded at the door, and Pittman's assistant peeked in.

"Is that the DVD?" Pittman asked. "Good . . . good. Thank you, Jennifer."

The woman handed Pittman a large manila envelope and left.

She removed the disc from the envelope. "I want you to watch this in a minute. You'll find it enlightening."

Jack hoped to God he wasn't one of the stars on the DVD. His mind raced. He hadn't shot anyone since the hamburger joint.

"The video is the reason I'd like to start my leave today," he reiterated.

She shook her head. "No, you aren't going to be taking a leave. You're going to be working. Your new assignment is Ms. Rose, and she will be your sole responsibility. I don't want anything to happen to that young woman. Now, I'll bet you're wondering why I'm so interested in keeping her alive, aren't you? For one, she's a U.S. of A. citizen, and we've taken an oath to protect our U. S. of A. citizens. For another, her father. That's right. She can give me Bobby Rose."

Maybe in your dreams, Jack thought. "Sophie's extremely loyal to her father," he said instead. "She's not about to hand him over to anyone."

Pittman tossed the DVD to Jack. "Put that in the player for me."

The television sat on the credenza behind her desk. Jack did as she requested while she pushed her chair back.

"I understand she's loyal. She's his daughter, and she loves him, right?"

She didn't even give him time to start the silent counting ritual.

"Of course she does. Bobby Rose isn't a wanted man, not at the moment anyway. I would just like to have a visit with him."

Yeah, right. A visit. Pittman was too smart to think Bobby Rose would say something incriminating. What else did she have in mind?

She was now searching through the desk drawers looking for the remote that controlled the DVD player.

"He's been a person of interest too many times to count, and he did spend some time in a holding cell years ago. Couldn't keep him there, though. Lack of evidence. Every time, it came down to lack of evidence. Of course, there's also the fact that Rose is probably the most brilliant lawyer I've ever run across."

She located the remote in the center drawer crammed behind a manual, picked it up, and waved Jack back to the chair facing her desk.

"We have had our differences with Mr. Rose."

Jack wanted to laugh. Differences? Various government agencies had been trying for years to put Bobby Rose behind bars.

"He's a bloodhound," she said, nodding. "That man can sniff out money these criminals think they can keep for themselves. It doesn't matter where they hide it; he finds it."

"Then he hides it and keeps it," he pointed out.

"Yes, he does, but we can't prove that, can we?" She almost sounded as though she admired him.

She rolled back in her chair and turned the player on. "Bobby sent this DVD for us. The DVD was delivered by messenger service, and when questioned the young man said he picked it up at the front desk of the Hamilton Hotel. No one behind the desk knows how the package got there. The beginning is from the local news-cast two nights ago."

She pushed Play and the overly cheerful voice of a perky news-caster came on.

"And now for an update on the closing of Chicago's beloved root beer company. The bitter accusations are mounting, aren't they, Tom?"

The screen flashed to Meredith Devoe and her attorney stand-ing in front of the courthouse.

"I'm thankful my father isn't alive to see this. My soon-to-be-ex-husband has destroyed his company. My father trusted him," she cried. She paused to dab at her eyes with a tissue before continuing. "He invested the employees' retirement money in a risky stock fund. The values were overinflated, and now all is lost. Kevin Devoe should be behind bars because of his stupidity."

The reporter asked Meredith when she had last spoken to her husband.

"I have not exchanged one word with him since I filed for di-vorce, and I hope I never have to speak to him again."

The attorney stepped forward to add his two cents. "My client is penniless, thanks to Kevin Devoe's irresponsible behavior. He gambled and lost everything they owned."

Jack frowned at the DVD player. "Then who's paying the attor-ney bills?" he asked.

"I'd like an answer to that question as well," Pittman agreed.

The screen went black, and a second later Kevin Devoe was being interviewed.

"I have done nothing wrong. Those stock numbers were in-flated, yes, but all the reports indicated they were sound invest-ments. It was Bobby Rose who drove the price up. He got his money out and let the house of cards fall. If anyone should be taken to task, it's him."

When asked how he felt about his wife's accusations, he responded, "She's a fool. Her father, Kelly, had faith in me. He was a good man, but his daughter . . . well, let's just say she's a hard, angry woman. I don't know what I ever saw in her."

Pittman hit Pause, capturing and freezing Kevin Devoe's sneer.

"Note the date and time at the bottom of the next frame."

She pushed the Play button again. The next scene was a dark building that looked like a warehouse. A light hung above the single side door. A beat-up old Ford pickup entered the frame and pulled across the gravel parking lot to stop at the door. The date was yesterday; the time, 3:10 a.m. A man wearing a hoodie got out of the truck. He kept his head down until he heard a faint whistle. When he turned toward the light, his face was visible. Kevin Devoe. No doubt it was him. The door flung open as he rushed to it, and there, waiting with open arms in an open trench coat and little else, was Meredith Devoe. The greeting was hot and heavy.

"Guess this can't be shown on the six o'clock news," Pittman remarked.

"Maybe the porno channel," Jack replied.

The screen went dark and Pittman spun her chair around, emptying the rest of the envelope's contents onto the desk. "Bobby Rose also sent us statement copies of three accounts, all with rather large sums of money. The accounts were under fake names, but our people checked. The money belonged to the Devoes . . . and you'll notice I said *belonged*. The money was in the accounts, but it's gone now. We tracked it as far as we could, and the only thing we're sure of is that the Devoes didn't withdraw it. However, I rather doubt either one of them will report it stolen.

"I think the Devoes have been squirreling away Kelly's money for years, enough to tide them over until they can get to the big money: the retirement savings. If they play the victim and cry that they're penniless, people are less likely to accuse them of having anything to do with the lost retirement money. Those investment funds were stripped, all right, and I don't think Bobby Rose had anything to do with it. Maybe I'm being naïve, but my guess is that Bobby Rose emptied these accounts and knows exactly where the retirement money is."

Jack thumbed through the stack of account statements. "You're sure all of this came from Bobby Rose?" he asked.

"Positive," Pittman said. She picked up a folded card and handed it to him. "This came with the video and the records."

The card read: *More to come. Bobby Rose.*

Pittman continued. "If history has shown us anything, it's that Bobby Rose doesn't let innocent people suffer. He's got something up his sleeve, and we're going to let this play out. And we're also going to do right by his daughter, like we should have from the beginning. Plus, Rose will be grateful that we're watching out for her."

Jack nodded. "I'll protect her."

"See that you do," Pittman ordered. "Jennifer has your schedule. Oh, and Agent MacAlister, one last thing . . ."

Jack stopped at the door. "Yes?"

"Watch out for polar bears."

We have become masters of deception. Eric has a few friends from his old neighborhood who are willing to do anything for the right price. One of them has secured three healthy monkeys for us.

We had come up with an elaborate lie to tell Eric's friend, but he was only interested in the money and didn't care what we did with the animals.

He might come in handy in the future.

TWENTY-TWO

S OPHIE FOUND OUT JACK WAS GOING TO ALASKA WITH HER when he showed up at her door and told her so.

When the doorbell rang, she had assumed it was Gil. He had said he would be checking on her before she left for Alaska. He was such a nice man, he even offered to drive her to the airport to-morrow afternoon. She appreciated the kind gesture, but she sus-pected that at least part of his motivation was penance for squealing on her. Who *hadn't* he told that she was heading to Alaska?

Gil and his posse, as he liked to call his team, were still taking turns watching out for her. As long as the shooter was on the loose, Gil and his friends would be bodyguards. Alec and Aiden insisted on it. It was pointless to argue because they were going to do what they were going to do whether Sophie approved or not. Thankfully, once she was on the plane and away from Chicago, Gil's services wouldn't be needed.

She should have looked through the peephole before she opened the door.

"You're early— You're not Gil."

Jack looked exasperated. "No, I'm not. Move out of my way, Sophie."

She automatically stepped back, allowing him entrance—another dumb move. It would be easier to tell him to go away if he were in the hall.

"I'm going to Alaska with you," he matter-of-factly informed her.

It took a couple of seconds for the announcement to settle. Reeling from the surprise, she protested, "What? No! You're not going."

"Sorry, sweetheart," he replied. "I am, and that's final."

Dropping his duffel bag in the foyer, he walked past her. She caught the scent of his aftershave. Very appealing . . . musky and masculine.

Not relevant! her mind screamed. "You hate cold weather," she said aloud.

"Sure do."

"Then why—"

"I'm going, Sophie. Deal with it."

Deal with it? I don't think so. "I'm perfectly capable of traveling by myself," she argued. "I don't want anyone to go with me."

He tossed his heavy sheepskin coat on the back of her sofa. He was wearing a T-shirt that showed off his muscular arms and chest, and a pair of jeans that looked as though they'd been purchased at the fifth-hand store. Did the jerk have to be so . . . built?

"*Want* and *need* are two completely different things," he answered as he settled into an easy chair, kicked off his shoes, and reached for the television remote. "I sure don't want to go with you, but here I am."

She took a tentative step forward. "You'll just get in my way."

"I probably will, but I'm still going. What channel is the Food Network on?"

"What . . . the food . . . ?"

"Never mind, I'll find it. You look a little confused. Have you packed yet?"

Sophie continued standing in the foyer, stunned. "No . . . I'll pack tomorrow. I don't leave until late afternoon. Why is your duffle here?"

"Our plans have changed, Sophie."

She ran her fingers through her hair. "*Our* plans? *We* don't have any plans."

"Sure we do," he said cheerfully. "We're leaving on a seven a.m. flight to Fairbanks, which is why I'm spending the night."

This announcement sent her rushing into the living room. "That can't be. I'm flying out tomorrow afternoon. I've already paid for my ticket."

She stopped in front of the television, blocking his view. He motioned for her to move to the left.

"Ah, here it is," he said. "Bobby Flay is doing paella. I've always wanted to know how to make it." He added, "The transaction was voided."

She tried to clear her head. "It's a nonrefundable ticket."

"I work for the FBI, Sophie. When I tell you the charge was erased, you can believe me."

Still incredulous, she asked, "Who changed my reservation?"

She shifted from one foot to the other with her hands on her hips; her elbow blocking his view. Once again he motioned for her to move. She complied without thinking.

"Jennifer," he answered. "She made the reservations. Ah, man, look at that food processor. I've got to get one of those."

"Jennifer who?" Sophie's frustration was brimming over.

"I don't know her last name."

"Of course you do."

"No, I really don't."

Sophie took a deep breath. This was maddening. None of it made any sense. She decided to approach the situation rationally. "Even if for some reason I have to take an earlier flight, there's absolutely no reason for you to come along, and there's certainly no reason for you to stay here tonight."

"Oh yes there is," he countered. "If we're going to make it to the airport on time, we'll need to be out of bed by four-thirty a.m."

"I'm not sleeping with you."

"Yeah, okay," he said, never taking his eyes off the television as he watched Bobby Flay toss clams and lobster claws into the pan.

"Just like that? Okay? No argument?" She was appalled by the disappointment she heard in her own voice.

"No argument," he said. "If you change your mind, let me know."

Without a word, Sophie went to her linen closet and pulled out a thick down comforter and pillow. After dumping them on the sofa, she said, "This discussion isn't over," then headed to her bedroom and shut the door.

She needed time to think. Why would Jack want to go to Alaska? He hated the cold. Alec had something to do with this; she was sure of it. She'd deal with him later. She had to think of a way to convince Jack to be reasonable and stay in Chicago, but for now she had a much bigger problem: Jack, just beyond the door, sleeping on her sofa.

It was one thing for Gil to camp out in her living room. He was old enough to be her grandfather. He was also sweet. Jack, on the other hand, wasn't at all sweet or considerate. He was rude, arrogant, and stubborn, but also sexy and gorgeous. Every time she looked at him, all sorts of crazy notions popped into her head . . . like jumping his bones.

It was that kiss, that stupid kiss that made her curious to know what it would be like to sleep with him. No, not curious. Hot. Hot for him. And what did that say about her morals? She did still have them, didn't she?

Sophie was determined to stay away from him until morning. No waffling on that. She'd let him drive her to the airport, and on the way she would surely come up with something to make him change his mind.

Okay, plan made. She showered, washed her hair, and took her time blowing it dry. She put on her sexiest nightgown, but only because she happened to like the pink lacy top. It was a short gown that didn't quite come to her knees. She probably should change into something more modest, but why? Jack wasn't about to see what she was wearing to bed.

She kept up the ridiculous pretense until she had applied lip gloss. Oh, yes, she always went to bed wearing lip gloss. Never know who might come knocking on the door in the middle of the night.

She stared at herself in the mirror, then reached for a tissue to remove the lip gloss. She sighed. She still wanted to rip Jack's clothes off and kiss every inch of his body. When it came to Jack, she didn't know right from wrong.

No matter what, she wasn't going to open that door. She circled her bed, pulled the covers back, and then set her alarm clock and her cell phone to wake her at the ungodly hour of four-thirty a.m.

Daddy! She suddenly remembered that her father would be calling her at midnight. She knew she couldn't stay up till then if she had to get up at four-thirty, and that meant she should call him now and leave a long message on his voice mail. She could hear Jack talking on the phone in the living room. This would be the perfect time for her to call, but as she was heading to her closet, Jack knocked on her door.

"Sophie, you got a minute?"

Say no. Just say no. "I'll be right there."

Okay, new plan, she decided. *At least take the time to put on a robe before opening the door. No reason to give him the idea that you might be even remotely interested in . . . what did he call it? . . . oh yes . . . getting friendly.*

She didn't reach for her robe. Yes, her nightgown was on the short side and a bit low-cut, but he couldn't see through it unless he had X-ray vision. The silk wasn't transparent. Besides, women wore much less clothing to a Chicago beach. What was the big worry?

The beach didn't have a bed, nor the privacy for a man and a woman to do whatever they wanted. That was one gigantic worry.

Do not open the door.

She opened the door. "Yes?" she said sweetly.

Jack stood with his phone in his hand for several seconds, never taking his eyes off hers.

"Jack? Did you want something?" she prodded.

"Alec called," he answered.

Sophie couldn't read his expression.

"What did he want?" She was becoming more embarrassed by the second as she waited for Jack to say something about her nightgown, but he didn't say a word about the way she was dressed . . . or undressed.

"To say good-bye, I guess. Your hall bath doesn't have a shower. Think I could use yours? Where are the towels?"

"Linen closet." She was surprised she managed to get the words out.

He shook his head. "I looked. None there."

"Look in the dryer. Laundry room is just off the kitchen."

"Okay, thanks," he said as he slowly pulled the door closed.

He was gone. Sophie's insecurities came roaring back. Had he even noticed? She glanced down at herself and shook her head. She certainly hadn't made much of an impact on him, had she? She had thought this nightgown was sexy, but if that were so, then apparently the woman wearing it wasn't. Maybe she was the problem, not the gown.

Sophie was used to men noticing her. She liked to flirt, but she didn't tease, and she knew the difference. She did not sleep around. Truth was, she was as much of a prude as Cordie—although her friend called it being old-fashioned. Unlike Sophie, Cordie allowed herself to have dreams. She wanted to get married and have children, but there was one little glitch in her happy-ever-after fantasy:

Cordie was madly in love with Aiden Hamilton, and he, stupid man that he was, didn't have a clue.

Sophie was thinking about Cordie's predicament when it suddenly dawned on her how foolish her own behavior was. She had never seduced a man, and why she thought it would be okay with Jack was beyond her. She didn't have an excuse except that she had let lust control her thoughts. Fortunately, she had come to her senses.

Jack knocked on her door again. This time Sophie didn't run for her lip gloss or play silly mental games about her appearance. She was through acting like an idiot.

"Come in," she said.

"Did you set your alarm clock?"

"Yes, four-thirty. Did you find the towels?" Dumb question since he had one draped over his shoulder.

As he disappeared into the bathroom, she wondered if he noticed that she was now wearing a robe. She heard water running in the shower, and that meant he was getting naked. She picked up a book from her nightstand thinking she'd get lost in a good novel, but several minutes passed and she hadn't read one word. Her imagination was in that shower.

Apple. She'd get an apple and stay in the kitchen until he was out of the bedroom, and she would quit acting like a budding nymphomaniac, but before she could leave, Jack stepped out of the bathroom wrapped in a towel. No shirt, no shoes . . . no service. Why that saying came to mind she couldn't imagine.

Jack barely glanced at her as he walked past, and that made her all the more bewildered. Damn it, he had kissed her. Didn't that mean he was attracted? Must have changed his mind.

She followed him into the next room. "Jack . . ."

"Yeah?" He turned to face her.

"I want the truth. Why are you really going with me?"

He didn't hesitate with his answer. "I lost a bet."

"Lost a bet? Very funny." He couldn't come up with a more believable lie?

"Really, Sophie, I lost a bet."

She shook her head. "I can take care of myself."

"Sure you can, except when someone calls and tells you to look out the window."

"You're never going to let that go, are you?"

"I'm going with you." Each word was carefully enunciated. He picked up the comforter and unfolded it. "And Sophie . . ."

"Yes?"

"I swear to God, if you open your door dressed like that again, I won't be sleeping on this sofa."

To keep things quiet, we have set up cages in the basement of Eric's house, which is out in the country and is the only house for miles. He inherited the home from his parents, and we are both thankful he didn't sell it.

It has been three months since we took tissue samples and blood from the monkeys and then injected them with K-74. They've reacted remarkably well, showing signs of increased energy and stamina. We will know more when we do the autopsies.

Killing has never been easy for either of us, but it's unavoidable if science is to advance.

TWENTY-THREE

"ALL RIGHT THEN." SOPHIE TURNED AROUND AND WALKED back into her bedroom, the sass back in her stride. She didn't smile until she'd closed the door. Her world made sense again. Her insecurities were gone, for the moment anyway, and she was feeling desirable once more.

Jack had noticed and had obviously been affected by the sight of her in her nightgown. Was she disappointed he hadn't taken her into his arms and kissed her? Of course not. But why hadn't he?

Oh, no, she wasn't going down that road again. She knew she could be neurotic and obsessive about certain things, but her feelings for Jack were making her all sorts of crazy. One minute she was convinced he was a jerk, and the next minute she thought he was the hottest man she'd ever met. If that wasn't crazy, what was?

Sleep would be impossible if she didn't stop thinking about him. She forced herself to be practical by going through her checklist of what she had packed and what she would need to buy in Fairbanks. If she needed an extra pair of wool socks or thicker long underwear, she was sure she could pick them up in one of the stores there. Should she take her laptop? What about her cell phone? She knew she could get a signal in Prudhoe Bay and probably in Barrow as well.

An hour later she hung up her robe and got into bed. Her head had barely touched the pillow when she remembered she needed to call her father and leave a message for him.

She crept to the door to see if Jack was asleep yet. She peeked out and saw the television was still on, but he wasn't sitting in the easy chair. She could only see the back of the sofa, but she assumed he'd fallen asleep.

The soft light from the bathroom spilled into her walk-in closet. Leaving the door open a crack, she got the cell phone from its hiding place and sat back against the wall with her legs stretched out and one ankle crossed over the other. Once she was comfortable, she called her father. She didn't have to leave a message. He answered on the second ring.

"It isn't midnight yet," he said. "Is everything okay?"

Sophie quickly explained that she was leaving for Alaska early in the morning, and she didn't want him to worry when he called at the scheduled time and she didn't answer. She didn't have any idea how long she would be away. One week, maybe two. Once she'd filled him in on her itinerary, she wanted to hear what he'd been up to. He told her that he was working on a resolution for Kelly's, but he wouldn't explain what that meant or even give her a hint of what his plans were. Her father liked to be cryptic, and she had learned not to ask questions.

Daddy was in a chatty mood and told her a couple of very funny stories that made her laugh, and by the time she ended the call and put the cell phone back in its cubbyhole, she was feeling relaxed and sleepy.

She was still sitting in her dark closet when Jack opened the door.

"Sophie? What are you doing?"

It should have been obvious, but apparently it wasn't. "I'm sitting on the floor."

"In your closet."

She looked around. "It would appear so."

With as much dignity as she could muster, she slowly stood and walked past him into the bedroom. She couldn't help but notice that he was wearing a pair of faded plaid boxer shorts and nothing else.

"I heard talking and then laughter," he said.

"Uh-huh," she agreed, nodding. "That was me . . . talking and laughing."

He had to think she was crazy. How could she have been so careless as to assume he was asleep and couldn't hear her? She had kept her voice to a whisper, but she shouldn't have laughed, no matter how funny the stories had been. If he had heard anything, it was inevitable he would figure she was talking to someone on the phone, and it wouldn't take a leap to guess who that someone was. She needed to distract him.

"How did you get that scar?" She took a step toward him and put her hand on his chest. His skin was warm, wonderfully warm. "This scar," she said as she traced a tiny circle above his heart.

"I don't have a scar there," he said.

"I know."

He grabbed her hand and held it against him. "Do you know what you're doing?"

She looked into his eyes. "Yes, I do. I'm distracting you. Is it working?"

He slowly nodded. "Pretty much."

She could feel his heart beating under her fingertips, and the way he was looking at her made her own heart race.

"You should get some sleep," he said.

He didn't move. Neither did she.

"You should kiss me," she said.

"Yeah?"

She nodded. "Yes."

He sighed. "Want me to tell you what will happen if I kiss you?" He started walking her backward to the bed.

"I'd rather you showed me."

His hand cupped the back of her neck, and he roughly pulled her toward him. "This is going to get complicated."

"I can do complicated," she whispered.

It was all the permission he needed. He tilted her head back and kissed her hungrily, letting her feel the passion inside him. His tongue delved into her mouth to mate with hers, and the sweet taste of her was so intoxicating he had to have more. He kissed her again and again until he was shaking with desire.

She threw her arms around his neck and melted into him. Her unrestrained enthusiasm overwhelmed him.

In the bedroom Jack was a master of pacing and control, always giving his partner the ultimate pleasure, usually multiple times, before he took his own. Slow and easy. Satisfaction guaranteed.

But Sophie changed all that. Kissing him with such abandon, her mouth so warm, her lips so wonderfully soft, she held nothing back, rubbing her tongue against his, her fingertips stroking his shoulders as she moved seductively against him. Her erotic sighs drove him wild, and within seconds she had turned him from a master to a novice with raging hormones. His breathing was harsh, ragged. He held her tight against him, burying his face in the side of her neck.

"Slow and easy, Sophie."

She gently tugged on his earlobe with her teeth. "Why?"

Before he could think of an answer, she pushed him back, keeping her eyes locked on his, as she seductively lowered the left strap of her nightgown and then the right, letting it slide down the length of her body.

Suddenly, slowing down didn't make any sense to him at all. She was beautiful. His gaze slowly moved over her golden skin, her full breasts, her tapered waist, and her long, perfect legs. Oh yes, she was magnificent. A tightness settled in his chest, and he was desperate to touch her. He stripped out of his shorts and wrapped his arms around her, groaning from the surge of arousal he felt when she moved against him.

Together they fell into bed. He wedged his knee between her silky thighs, then stretched out on top of her. His arms bore his weight so he wouldn't crush her. Her soft full breasts rubbed against his chest and sent tremors through him. He buried his face in her hair. Her feminine scent aroused him; her velvety skin felt so good against his. He wanted to touch her everywhere, to use his mouth, his tongue to excite her. Caressing her breasts, he kissed a path down her neck, her whispered sighs urging him on.

Sophie loved the way he stroked her, loved the feel of his hot mouth against her skin. When his hand slid down her stomach and moved between her thighs, the fire inside her intensified until it became unbearable. Her nails dug into his shoulder blades as she arched against him and cried out.

Their kisses became ravenous, their caresses more demanding, rougher. Sophie made him burn like no other woman had, and Jack could feel his control slipping away. When he knew he could wait no longer to make her his, he moved between her thighs and thrust inside, groaning from sheer ecstasy. Liquid heat surrounded him, and the jolt of pleasure was so intense, he thought her fire would consume him.

He stayed perfectly still for several seconds. "You feel so good," he whispered.

Her breathing was as ragged as his, her need as demanding. He kissed the base of her throat, felt the frantic pulse of her heartbeat.

Sophie wrapped her arms around his waist and raised her legs to take him deeper inside.

Jack moved slowly at first, but the urgency built inside him, and his control snapped. Their lovemaking was wild, passionate, and when at last they climaxed, she cried his name.

With a loud groan he collapsed on top of her, pinning her to the mattress. He stayed inside her for long minutes, savoring the intimacy. She'd taken his strength, but he was able to roll to his side, keeping her wrapped in his arms. He was reeling from the sensations coursing through him. What the hell had happened to him? Sex had never been like this before.

Long minutes passed before his breathing was once again steady. Sophie took a little longer to recover. She shifted onto her back and stared at the ceiling. Jack raised up on one elbow to look at her and was arrogantly pleased with what he saw. She looked dazed. Her eyes were misty; her face was flushed, and her lips were rosy from his kisses.

She was the most amazing creature. She was totally uninhibited with him, and in the aftermath of their lovemaking, she didn't hurry to cover up.

Jack couldn't stop touching her. His fingers slowly trailed down her neck to her navel. He gently touched the skin where the bullet had struck and was shocked by the surge of anger he felt that someone had tried to hurt her.

She looked into his eyes and asked, "Are you okay?" And before he could say a word, she asked, "I didn't hurt you, did I?"

His head dropped to her shoulder, and he began to laugh. "I think I'm supposed to ask you that question. Are you okay?"

"It was lovely," she whispered.

She turned toward him and began to stroke his chest. The mat of hair tickled her skin. She snuggled closer.

"Very lovely," she whispered.

"Yeah? Give me a minute. I'll show you spectacular."

Jack was a man of his word.

JOURNAL ENTRY 644
CHICAGO

We have tested and retested, and the results are conclusive. The adrenaline produced in stressful situations does increase the potency of our drug. No matter how terrified the monkeys become, their heart rates don't increase. The cellular degeneration seems to slow as well.

Is this serum the first step in discovering the fountain of youth?

TWENTY-FOUR

THEY MADE IT TO THE AIRPORT WITH TIME TO SPARE, quite an achievement considering Jack had to drag Sophie out of bed. She didn't wake up happy, but a quick shower revived her. Fortunately, she had laid out the clothes she would wear, and she was completely packed except for her makeup bag, which she dropped into her carry-on as she ran out the door.

Sophie didn't notice that Jack was carrying his gun until he showed his credentials at check-in. The airline had already been informed that an FBI agent named MacAlister would be on the flight, so it took no time at all to get through security.

With his gun holstered in plain sight on his hip, Jack naturally got some worried looks from passersby, but it was Sophie who attracted the most attention. Every man she passed stared at her. Although irritated, Jack couldn't blame them. Sophie was a beautiful woman. Gil had called her a bombshell, and he wasn't wrong. Dressed for the cold in a long-sleeved, fitted, black turtleneck sweater and a pair of snug jeans with boots, she held her coat and walked as though she were on a runway. She captured every eye, but Jack knew she was oblivious to the stares.

They were seated in first class. The attendant took their coats and offered them beverages while Jack stowed their carry-ons in the bin above. Sophie took the window; Jack, the aisle. The seats were wider in first class, but his legs were still too long to stretch out without tripping the people filing past.

Neither had mentioned what had happened last night. Their passion had reached a crescendo numerous times, so they didn't get much sleep. Sophie was exhausted. She clipped her seat belt into place, closed her eyes, and was sound asleep minutes later.

She didn't wake up until they were about to land in Fairbanks. When she opened her eyes, she saw Jack flipping through a magazine. He didn't notice she was watching him. The images of his hot, naked body rubbing against hers made her face warm, and she tried to block the memories. Only one way to get through this trip with Jack, she decided. She would take the stance that nothing out of the ordinary had happened. Like some of the corrupt men her father went after, she would deny, deny, deny.

Once on the ground and inside the airport, she went to the ladies' room to freshen up. After brushing her teeth and splashing water on her face, she felt good as new. She had assumed there would be a layover in Fairbanks, but she was wrong. The mysterious Jennifer without a last name had booked them on Chip's Charter Service, and the flight was scheduled to leave in less than an hour.

Jack leaned against a pillar, reading the sports section of a newspaper, waiting for her. Sophie's heart skipped a beat when she saw him through the crowd, and she was once again a little breathless. Was it any wonder? Jack was one fine-looking man. "Very fine," she whispered. Denying wasn't going to be easy.

"You ready?" he asked, folding the paper under his arm.

They stopped at a snack bar in the terminal, but Sophie was sorry she had eaten the muffin and juice when she reached the gate that would lead them outside to Chip's Charter Service. There were small jets and small planes, and then there was Chip's six-seater. Her stomach dropped to her feet when she saw it on the tarmac. She was certain jets flew to Prudhoe Bay. Why weren't they taking one of those?

She stepped closer to Jack. "You know what? I think we should drive."

He could see the worry in her eyes. "You do?"

"Yes. We definitely should drive. It's only five hundred miles, give or take, and we can't get lost." She hastily added when he shook his head, "Only one highway, the Dalton, goes up to Prudhoe Bay. We could do some sightseeing."

"Have you noticed it's snowing? Can't do much sightseeing—"

"Yes, I noticed, and I also noticed how windy it is, which is why we shouldn't fly in that paperweight plane."

He smiled. "It has two engines. We'll be fine."

"Big trucks go back and forth on the Dalton all the time. We could catch a ride with one of them."

She glanced out the window and saw a heavyset man, looking a little like Santa Claus with his white beard and mustache, circle the plane and head toward them. She kept her eye on him as she whispered to Jack, "This isn't a good idea. Have you ever flown in a little plane like that?"

"Yeah, I have. One of my brothers is a pilot. He's taken me up a couple of times. Relax, Sophie."

Jack went outside to talk to the pilot, and Sophie stepped close to the window to watch him. She was suddenly overwhelmed. In the last twenty-four hours Jack MacAlister had uprooted her plans and her life. What was she doing here in Alaska with him? She had taken him to her bed and done the most intimate things with him, but she barely knew him. He had told her a little about his background, but there was so much more she *didn't* know. *One* of his brothers? How many siblings did he have? Were his parents still alive? Weren't these things you should know before sharing the most private part of yourself with someone? The reality of what she had done sank in, and she was mortified. When it came to relationships, she had always played it safe. Cautious to a fault, according to her friends . . .

until Jack. He had made her forget everything she had ever promised herself, and it was time for her to regain control.

From this moment on, she was going to keep things polite and professional, and she would definitely *not* be sleeping with him again. No more foolishness, she told herself.

The door opened, and a blast of freezing air swept over her. The pilot was actually younger than he had appeared from a distance. He was probably still in his thirties; his dark brown beard was covered with a layer of ice and snow, which is why it had appeared white.

"Hello," he said as he pulled off his glove and extended his hand. "You must be Sophie Rose. My name's Chipper, but some like to call me Chip. Either's fine with me. As soon as your luggage is weighed and loaded, we'll be on our way."

"Can you fly in this wind?" she asked worriedly.

"I sure can. If you'll excuse me, I'll do my final check."

"Chipper . . . does the plane have heat?"

He turned back. "Yes, it does."

Jack started to laugh. "Of course it has heat."

She leaned close to whisper. "Chipper has ice chips in his beard."

"Bet you can't say that fast five times."

"Be serious," she said. "Chipper has either been walking around his plane for a long while or he's been flying without heat. *Ice* in his beard, Jack."

"We'll be just fine, Sophie."

His calm reassurance irritated her. Of course they'd be fine— unless Chipper accidentally tipped the plane into the side of a mountain, or misjudged the icy runway and dumped them into the ocean. Until today, Sophie hadn't considered herself a nervous flyer, but as she watched the small plane pitch back and forth from the force of the wind, she thought it was a perfectly sensible reaction to be a little freaked out.

A phone rang, and that reminded Sophie of Paul Larson. He was going to be at the airport to meet her plane, and she hadn't notified him that her flight had changed and she would be arriving in Prudhoe Bay ahead of schedule. She made a mental note to call him when she arrived.

Chipper opened the door and announced it was time to leave.

Sophie put on her gloves, picked up her bag, and took a deep breath.

Jack turned her toward him and pulled the collar up around her face, then took her shoulders in his hands and leaned close to say, "Everything's going to be okay. You trust me, don't you, Sophie?"

She looked into his eyes and was surprised to discover . . . she did.

We have had long discussions about the next step. We must test our serum on human beings. But how to go about it, that's the question. If we run our trials through a clinic, even if we were to patent our findings, our secret would be out, and we would be in danger of losing our edge.

People would kill for our formula. When the world discovers what we have, every pharmaceutical company in the world will want a piece of it, and we know there are many who would stop at nothing to nab the profits for themselves. We have to be cautious and do the tests ourselves. When we hit the market with our creation, all the money and recognition will be ours.

We've worked too hard not to enjoy the benefits.

TWENTY-FIVE

EADHORSE, ALASKA, SITS AT THE TOP OF THE WORLD. Some call it a town; others call it a camp.

From her research, Sophie had learned that Prudhoe Bay is a working community. At any given time there are approximately five thousand men on the drilling sites owned by the oil companies, but they don't mingle with travelers who come to Deadhorse. Each company has its own self-contained facility for its workers. The rigs and the housing for the employees are enclosed to protect the equipment from the climate, and the accommodations are comfortable despite the harsh environment. The men on the rigs work twelve-hour shifts for two weeks straight, then fly home for two weeks. The money is substantial, but the social life is nonexistent.

Tours to the oil fields and the Arctic Ocean are available during the summer months, but a week's notice is required so that background checks can be made. Security is tight. One hundred sixty men comprise the security force that protects the rigs. Two policemen are on duty in Deadhorse, and like the workers on the rigs, their shifts are two weeks on and two weeks off.

Planes fly in and out of Deadhorse all day, every day, weather conditions permitting, and there's even a helicopter pad by the airport.

Sophie was fascinated by what she had learned and, despite the bumpy plane ride to get there, couldn't wait to experience the area for herself. As the plane approached the airstrip, she could see massive rigs off in the distance, and below a white canvas spread out as far as her eye could see. The ice and snow created a solid surface now, but after the spring thaw, the land would look as though it were floating in puddles of water. Deadhorse was little more than a scattering of prefabricated buildings perched aboveground with steps leading up to the doors. They looked more like warehouses than homes or businesses.

Considering the wind and the snow blowing across the runway, the plane's landing was smooth. Chipper offered to fly Sophie and Jack back to Fairbanks or on to Barrow when their business in Deadhorse was finished, and then he took them to the Prudhoe Bay Hotel.

"Hotel" was not a term the Hiltons or Marriotts would have used to describe the structure, but it served the purpose. The prefabricated units, hooked together as one building, offered simple accommodations.

Sophie and Jack knocked the snow off their boots before they entered the small office. There wasn't a crush of people waiting for rooms. In fact, Sophie and Jack were the only customers. The manager, who stood behind a linoleum-topped counter sorting through paperwork, welcomed them warmly and told them to call him Zester. It was difficult to judge his age. His face was so weathered, he could have been fifty or thirty, but from his booming voice, Sophie pegged him at forty.

"I should have a reservation," Sophie told him. "Paul told me he'd make arrangements."

Zester didn't have to look in the register. "Not here you don't. Think you might have one at the Caribou Inn? I'll call for you and cancel. You'll like staying here much better." He didn't wait for permission but turned his back and dialed his competitor.

Jack nudged Sophie. "Who's Paul?"

Sophie pulled off her scarf and folded it. "Paul Larson. Didn't I tell you about him?"

He shook his head. "Tell me now."

Zester interrupted before she could explain. "Nope. You didn't have a reservation at the Caribou." He chuckled as he added, "When I told Charlie how darn pretty you are, he said maybe you did have a room reserved after all. I expect he'll be coming over to say hello."

Jack unbuttoned his coat, and Zester spotted the gun at his waist.

"Hold on now. We don't allow guns here. At least we don't allow our customers to carry them around." He leaned over the counter. "What kind is that? Doesn't matter," he continued before Jack could reply. "A thirty-eight or a forty-five or a Glock . . . none of those will take down a bear. A fox maybe, but not a bear. You'd end up in jail if you tried to shoot a bear," he warned.

"I'm with the FBI."

Zester looked shocked. He took a quick step back, then moved forward again. In a whisper he said, "FBI? Something bad happen? Someone break the law?" He shook his head and added, "No, I'd hear about it if someone broke the law. I can keep a secret, so you can tell me. Why are you here?"

Sophie answered. "He lost a bet."

Jack smiled at how disgruntled Sophie had sounded. "Yeah, I did."

Zester didn't ask for clarification. "How about I set you up with my deluxe two rooms with a bathroom in between? That's the best I can offer."

A few minutes later, after dropping their bags in their rooms, Jack and Sophie followed Zester into the small cafeteria. Sophie felt as though she were walking through an elongated mobile home. The lunchroom was small, sparse, and spotless.

"Meals are included in the price of your rooms," Zester explained. "You missed lunch, but I can offer you some cold sandwiches. There's always food, twenty-four/seven," he added. "As far as drink, we're dry here, so nothing stronger than coffee, tea, or soft drinks."

Sophie asked for hot tea, and Jack wanted a Coke. While they ate their sandwiches, Zester called the policeman on duty and asked him to come over to the hotel.

He handed the phone to Jack and said, "Tim wants to talk to you."

While Jack talked to the officer, Sophie used her cell to call Paul Larson. A recorded voice answered.

"Hi, Paul. It's Sophie. Call me when you get this."

Zester went back to the kitchen to get a cup of coffee for himself, and as soon as they were alone, Jack said, "Sophie, I'm still waiting to hear who Paul Larson is."

"He's with the security force here."

"Okay. How do you know him?"

In his FBI mode his tone was no-nonsense.

"I told you about the policeman who called me to tell me they had found my business card in William Harrington's sock."

"I remember."

"Not long after that call, Paul Larson contacted me."

"How did he get your phone number?"

"Obviously he got it from the policeman who found my card."

"Go on."

She tilted her head and frowned. "Are you interrogating me?"

"Yeah, I am. Keep going."

At least he was honest about it. "Paul's been very helpful."

"How helpful?"

"He called when they found Harrington's wallet, and he explained where Harrington's remains would go."

"Anchorage."

She nodded. "He didn't have any idea why Harrington had decided to camp out in the wilderness, but he said he'd ask around and find out if anyone had talked to him."

"He went to a lot of trouble for you, didn't he?"

Was Jack jealous? Sophie immediately discarded the notion. "Why so grumpy?" she asked. "There's probably not a lot to do up here when you're not working, and he thought it was a mystery, too."

"That Harrington would camp out—"

"Yes," she said.

Jack sighed. "Why didn't you mention Larson earlier?"

She shrugged. "I should have," she said, then added, "You'll like him. He's very pleasant over the phone."

"Yeah, right. Pleasant." He shook his head. "You know what your problem is? You're too damned trusting."

"I trust you."

"You should."

Sophie didn't know what to make of his attitude, but she decided to placate him. "I don't trust Paul the way I trust you. He works for the security force here, so you know the powers that be have done a thorough background check."

"You're getting riled, sweetheart."

The endearment flustered her. "I think I'll go back to my room and unpack. I've got to charge my phone," she said. "The battery's low. Are you going to stay here?"

He nodded. "Don't leave the hotel without me, all right?"

She glanced out the window. The snow was now coming down hard. Since she wouldn't be able to see two feet in front of her if she went outside, that was an easy request to agree to. With the lack of sunlight, she could easily get disoriented and end up wandering in a snowstorm. There was also the possibility of running into Barry or one of his furry relatives.

Polar bears, up close and personal. She shivered thinking about it.

Sophie stopped at the front desk to ask Zester if he had heard of William Harrington.

"Everyone's heard of him," he said. "He's the man Barry went after."

She nodded. "Did you happen to meet Mr. Harrington, or do you know anyone who might have spoken to him?"

"I never met him," he answered. "I didn't hear that anyone around here did. He might have flown into Barrow and taken a small plane to Alaktak and headed west, or maybe he went to Nuiqsut or Umiat and headed east. His camp wasn't too far from there. He was found close to the ocean, though, so I can't really say how he got there."

Sophie didn't have any idea where Alaktak or the other towns were located. She had a map in her bag and would have to look them up.

"What about the Coben brothers? Do you know them?"

"Who?"

She repeated the name. "They're trappers," she explained, "and I heard secondhand that they had talked to Mr. Harrington."

He nodded. "Could be. I'm only filling in here for a couple of days, but I know a lot of people come through here, and they don't all stay in the hotel, of course. The name's familiar, though."

Thank goodness for Paul, Sophie thought. If he hadn't taken an interest and helped her, she wouldn't have learned anything about the Cobens on her own. Paul had talked to a number of truckers who drove in and out of Deadhorse. He'd done the legwork for her.

Sophie thanked Zester and went to her room to unpack. She spread her map out on the bed and used a highlighter to mark the villages Zester had mentioned. The police could tell her where Harrington's campsite had been.

An hour passed as she was organizing, and when she was finally settled, she called Mr. Bitterman to check in. He was in a fine mood and asked a lot of questions about Prudhoe Bay.

"Have you seen the northern lights?"

"Not yet."

"What's the weather like?"

She answered that question and several others.

"Are you going to join the polar bear club?" he asked. "Be a heck of a story if you did."

"Sir, there are limits to what I will do for my job. I'm not jumping into the Arctic Ocean for a story."

"Give it some thought," he said. "Now tell me about Harrington, and then I've got a whopper of a surprise for you."

"We just got here so there's very little to tell."

"That's right. Jack's with you, isn't he? Alec called me this morning. It was a relief to hear that you've got an FBI agent with you. Can't be too cautious, you know."

"Okay, tell me the surprise," she prodded.

"Can you get to a computer and look at the newspaper?"

"Probably," she answered. "What paper do you want me to read?"

"Ours, Sophie," he said, exasperated. "I want you to read today's edition of our newspaper."

She laughed. "Of course. What am I looking for?"

"Oh, heck, I might as well tell you. Full-page, four-color ad, paid for with a cashier's check telling Chicago that Kelly's employees are going to get their pensions."

Tears came into Sophie's eyes. Daddy had kept his promise.

"Do you know who placed the ad? Was there a name?"

"Nope, but everyone in Chicago is celebrating. They're saying Bobby Rose is behind it. You should hear the call-ins on the radio. Lots of excitement, Sophie, and when times are hard with the layoffs and all, we need some good news, don't we?"

"Yes, sir, we do. You can stop hoarding root beer now."

"Oh, no. Not until the company's doors are open. Call me tomorrow to check in—and Sophie, you be careful."

She couldn't wait to tell Jack about the ad. If she couldn't find a computer to use in the hotel, she'd pull up the Internet article on her phone. She hurried back to the cafeteria and found two men sitting with Jack. He made the introductions. One of the men was a police officer in Deadhorse, and the other was an oil company security guard. Jack pulled out a chair at the table, and when she sat down, she noticed a stack of papers in his hand with a list of names that he handed to the security officer.

"Jack tells me one of our men has been helping you with your investigation. Is that right?" the security guard asked.

"Only on his time off," she explained, not wanting to get Paul into trouble.

The guard smiled. "I understand you've had several conversations with him?"

"Just a couple," she answered. "He said he was helping the police, and he provided some information about William Harrington's death."

When the two men glanced at each other, she became curious. "Why are you asking?"

"You're sure you talked to Paul Larson?" the policeman asked.

"I'm positive," she stated emphatically.

"Ma'am," the policeman said, "I don't know who you talked to, but it wasn't Paul Larson."

"But he—" Sophie began.

The security officer didn't let her finish. "We don't have a Paul Larson here."

JOURNAL ENTRY 680
CHICAGO

Eric and I are calling our study the Alpha Project.

We've had no trouble keeping our work secret in Chicago, but Inook was another matter altogether. Living in such close quarters with Brandon and Kirk made it difficult. Luckily, Brandon decided that he and Kirk should go off and observe another pack, and that gave us more freedom. Eric gets so nervous about being found out, I worry that he will let something slip.

I've been checking out pharmaceutical companies. What I've learned so far is that they're all mired down in bureaucracy. I don't think we can approach them about our findings. If we were to tip our hand now, we'd lose all control. I've also learned they pay a pittance for independent research because they have to factor in how long it will take to get government approval. That could be years, if not decades.

If Eric and I are going to get the money we deserve, we'll have to take matters into our own hands. There are plenty of other markets out there.

TWENTY-SIX

W HY WOULD HE LIE?
Sophie's initial reaction to the news was that there
had to be a mistake. Of course Paul Larson existed.
She'd spoken to him!

When Jack went to get her some hot tea from the cafeteria's
beverage service, she tried the phone number Paul had given her.
Once again, she left a message on his voice mail.

While she was waiting to hear back, Jack made a call to his
sources to run a check on the number. He received his answer minutes later, not surprised to learn that the number Sophie had been
calling was registered under yet another fictitious name at a fictitious address.

What kind of game was this man playing?

"They're getting a fix on the location of the phone, so we'll
know where this guy was calling you from," Jack told her.

"We've got employees flying in and out of here every day, but
they check in right away and get to work," the oil company security
guard said. "Truckers will spend the night in Deadhorse when they
need to, but they usually head back the next day."

"Even so," the Deadhorse cop added, "with so many people coming and going, we would notice a stranger hanging around." Looking across the table into Sophie's eyes, he said, "I checked with Joe Rooney, the officer who called you about Harrington, and he's never heard of Paul Larson. He certainly didn't give anyone your phone number. Joe's a reliable guy, so I don't have any reason to doubt him."

All three men took turns asking Sophie questions, but there was little she could tell them. The guard and the police officer assured her that they would ask around, but other than that, there was nothing they could do, concluding that she had been the victim of a twisted practical joke.

After they left, Jack continued grilling her about the details of her phone conversations with the man calling himself Paul Larson.

"He didn't tell me anything specific about himself. Why would he? Oh, wait. He did say he was single and asked to take me to dinner, but I don't think he was serious."

"How much did you tell him about yourself?" Jack asked.

Irritated, she responded, "Nothing personal. I wasn't talking to a dating service."

Jack stood and began to pace. Sophie drummed her fingertips on the tabletop while she thought about her conversations with the fictitious man.

"So this guy lures you up here—" Jack began.

"He did not lure me here," she interrupted. "I wanted to come up here to talk to people in hopes that someone had seen Harrington. He didn't just drop out of the sky and land in a tent next to Barry. I'm still determined to find out what happened to him." She shook her head. "I know what you're going to say: *Barry happened to him.*"

"I wasn't going to say that. Would you have started in Prudhoe Bay, or did you come here because Paul suggested it?" He rubbed the back of his neck while he waited for her answer.

"I don't know. He told me there were trappers near here that I could talk to," she said. "This is crazy. Was anything he told me true?"

"They did find Harrington's wallet, and his remains were taken to Anchorage, so yes, I guess some of what he said was true."

"When will you know where he was calling from?" she asked.

"That will take a little time," he said. "We're getting out of here first thing in the morning. I'll call Chipper and put him on standby."

"Is Chipper really Chipper?" she asked. She smiled at how silly that sounded. "Is he really who he says he is?"

"Yes, he is," Jack answered. He crossed the room and stood in front of her. "And do you know why I know?"

"I'm guessing you're going to tell me."

"I checked him out. I don't take anything on blind faith."

"You're an FBI agent. You're trained to be suspicious. I'm a reporter. I'm trained to be curious. My interest wasn't in Paul Larson, so why would I want or need to investigate him?"

Jack gave up trying to make his point. He could tell this was going the route of the "You would have looked, too" argument she'd used after she was shot.

Sophie now walked to the cafeteria window and stared outside. "Do you know it's against the law to lock your car doors here?" she asked.

"Yeah?"

"It's true. It's because of bears. I guess if you run into one, or one happens to be chasing you, you jump in a car." She sighed and turned around. Jack stood just a foot away. "I should have checked him out," she admitted.

He pulled her into his arms and rubbed his chin against the top of her head. "Yeah, you should have," he agreed. "Any other interesting facts you want to share?"

"Most foxes carry rabies."

"Good to know."

"The Barrow Whalers made the play-offs."

"The who?"

"The Whalers. They're the high school football team in Barrow. You'll probably get to meet some of them. They're a new team, and football has made a positive impact on the lives of these boys. I promised Mr. Bitterman I'd write their story."

"So we're going to Barrow, huh?"

"Yes."

JACK WAS PREOCCUPIED at dinner, but Sophie didn't mind. It had been a long day, and she was weary.

They returned to their rooms, and Sophie went into the bathroom to get ready for bed. After showering, she opened the bathroom door into Jack's room and overheard him talking on the phone. "It has to be connected" was all she managed to hear. Who was he talking to, and *what* had to be connected?

Jack looked up and smiled when he saw her. She wasn't wearing a skimpy nightgown, but she was just as sexy in her oversized, blue and white cotton pajamas. And fuzzy pink socks. After he finished his call, he took his turn in the shower.

The wind was picking up outside, and the window rattled. Sophie had read somewhere that the winds could get as strong as a hundred miles an hour. The thought made her shiver.

The bed wasn't a double or a twin, but something in between. She pulled back the covers and stretched out on top, leaning against the headboard. Her mind wouldn't quiet down, racing from one thought to another. If the man calling himself Paul Larson was playing a joke, what was the point? Why go to all that trouble? There must be a reason. Had any polar bears ever gotten inside the hotel? She should have asked Zester.

Sophie was rubbing on hand lotion that smelled of jasmine when Jack entered her room. He obviously didn't mind the chill in the air. He wore just shorts and a T-shirt.

"Aren't you cold?" she asked.

"I'll get warm in a minute. Did you set your alarm? We're getting up early."

Sophie noticed him staring at her socks. She felt a little silly, but what did she care? She had made up her mind to keep their relationship simple and professional.

No, not relationship. Association.

"The phone calls were made from Fairbanks," he told her before he reached down and pulled one pink sock off, then the other.

"So Larson had no intention of meeting my plane tonight?" she asked. "What was the point? Don't you think that was a rather strange prank?"

Jack went to the door to make sure it was locked. "I don't know what his motive was, but I'm going to find out."

Sophie got under the covers. The sheets were cold. Jack was walking toward his room when she remembered the ad Mr. Bitterman had mentioned.

She told Jack about Kelly's Root Beer, then asked, "What do you think?"

"I'd like to see the ad."

He disappeared into his bedroom, and Sophie felt a pang of disappointment. She wasn't going to let him sleep with her. Still, it would have been nice if he'd asked. A minute later, Jack came back carrying his gun and holster. He didn't ask permission to join her. He put his gun on the table next to her pillow, pulled the covers back, and told her to scoot over.

He slid in next to her and turned toward the wall with his back to her. The heat radiating from his body warmed her in no time at all. She slipped her hands under his T-shirt. "I didn't say you could sleep with me," she whispered against his neck as she cuddled up against him.

"Go to sleep." He reached over and turned out the light.

"Jack?" Sophie said in the darkness. "I'm a terrible reporter, aren't I?"

Eric and I are weary from our trip, but it's been worth it. We've found a buyer. Our contacts in Asia and Europe produced nothing. Don't know why we didn't think of the Middle East in the first place.

To the Dubai billionaire, fifty million means nothing, and he was willing to agree to it on the spot. All he requires is that we give him hard data on our human experiments.

I've been having dreams about how I'll spend my share. Always wanted to visit Fiji. If the sands are soft and the women softer, I may just stay there.

TWENTY-SEVEN

JACK DIDN'T EMBELLISH OR COMPLIMENT HER ON HER RE-porting skills. He simply answered her question. "You're not a terrible reporter."

A few minutes passed. Sophie asked, "How many brothers do you have?"

"Three."

"Any sisters?"

"No."

Jack slowly turned toward her. He was a big man, and the bed was small. He rolled Sophie toward him so that she rested on his side.

"Why all the questions?" he asked, his face close, their eyes meeting in the dark.

"You know everything there is to know about me, and I don't know much about you."

"Yeah, you do. You know where I grew up, where I went to school, and when I joined the FBI. You also know I like the way you kiss me."

She smiled. "Good night, Jack."

He laughed. "Good night, Sophie."

Jack made it until around two in the morning, and then Sophie began to move restlessly against him. He wasn't sure if she was awake or asleep, but after removing her clothes without any resistance, he didn't care. It was his turn to seduce her. And, ah man, it was better than the first time. She was so responsive to his touch, and he loved the sexy sounds she made when his fingers caressed her. This time he made sure she climaxed before he did, and when at last he found release, she squeezed him tight inside her. And that was better, too.

He was just drifting off to sleep when a thought popped into his head. Had he done the seducing, or had she?

DENY, DENY, DENY.

Again Sophie was furious at her lack of self-control. Why couldn't she keep her hands off Jack? If they were in Chicago, it would be so much easier to stay away from him, but here they were forced to be together. Fortunately, he respected her unspoken decision not to mention last night's activities.

Chipper was waiting for them by his plane. He stowed their luggage while Sophie climbed into the backseat. Jack took the seat by the pilot, and while they were waiting for Chipper to finish his checklist, Jack asked Sophie if she was feeling okay.

"I'm fine. Why would you think I wasn't? Do I look like I'm not fine?" She couldn't stop blathering. "Why do you ask?"

"You've been unusually quiet, that's all, and yeah, Sophie, you look fine, considering neither of us got much sleep with the—"

"Barrow is considered a desert, did you know that?"

Jack grinned. She was once again pretending that nothing had happened. "It is?" he asked.

"Yes. It gets very little rainfall, but lots of snow. Temperatures drop below zero in early October and stay down until the end of May or early June. It never gets warm."

Chipper climbed into the plane, heard Sophie's last comment, and added, "Barrow generally gets around seven inches of snow in October. It's not snowing today, though, not yet anyway."

"Jack wants to see the ocean," Sophie told Chipper. "His ideal vacation is to sit and watch it."

"You're in luck then," Chipper said. "The ocean's on three sides of Barrow. You'll get to look at it every which way you turn."

Because of crosswinds, the flight to Barrow ended up being even bumpier than the one to Deadhorse, and Sophie's stomach did a couple of flips. She was, however, willing to delay their landing when Chipper insisted on circling so that Jack could see the ocean up close.

Barrow wasn't a fancy place, but the people were the warmest she had ever met. Everyone was friendly and helpful. They were proud of their city, and they were especially proud of their football team. Sophie had called ahead, and the coach was waiting to greet them. She interviewed him about the boys on his team and their backgrounds, but it was Jack who knew what questions to ask about the games. While the men discussed the season, she took notes.

Coach Smith told them about the first game the Whalers had won. It was quite an event in the small community. The players and coaches had celebrated by jumping into the Arctic Ocean. A pizza party wouldn't have been enough? Sophie wondered.

The coach called a couple of his players over to talk to Jack and Sophie. While they were with the boys, Sophie noticed two teenage girls sitting on the sideline with their heads together, laughing. One girl stood up and the other pushed her friend toward the field, giving her the nudge to approach them. The girl slowly came closer and closer, until she was standing just a few feet behind Jack.

She gently tapped Jack on the shoulder. "Excuse me," she said shyly.

Jack turned around. "Yes?" he said.

"My friend and I were wondering . . ." she began. She looked back at her companion who was gesturing for her to continue. "We were wondering if you're that guy on YouTube."

Sophie burst out laughing.

Jack patiently talked to the girl for a few minutes, and after thanking Coach Smith for his time, he quickly ushered Sophie off the field.

"I really must see this video," she said.

Jack was not amused, but Sophie was still laughing as they walked into a nearby restaurant.

A couple who were having lunch at the next table struck up a conversation and were glad to talk about their community. They had lived in Barrow all their lives and were able to give Sophie some interesting background for her story. They suggested places to stay the night, and Jack chose the one closest to the restaurant.

By the time Jack and Sophie walked to the hotel, they were frozen to the bone.

Jack paced in the lobby trying to get warm. "Couldn't do it. Couldn't do it," he repeated.

"Couldn't do what?"

"Live here. The cold would kill me."

"It's not so bad. After all, Chicago's winters are no cakewalk."

"Your lips are blue," he countered.

"After we get our rooms, I'd like to walk around town and talk to some more people."

"We're getting one room, not two, and we're not walking anywhere, Sophie, we'll find a ride to the police station. The headquarters for Deadhorse and the other northern towns is here in Barrow. I want to talk to them about Harrington."

Unfortunately, the police couldn't tell them anything they didn't already know. Harrington's death, they had concluded, was unfortunate, but it had been an act of nature. The file was closed.

Sophie asked them how she could get in touch with Joe Rooney, the officer who had called her to identify Harrington.

"Joe lives just outside of Barrow," the officer told her. "He's off this week, but I'm sure if we gave him a call, he'd come in to talk to you."

When Jack asked how Harrington would have reached the remote spot where he was camped, one of the officers suggested the possibility that Harrington had flown on a commercial flight to Fairbanks and then chartered a small plane to Inook.

"That's the closest village to Harrington's campsite. Few people live in Inook. Someone there would certainly have seen him. Small planes fly in with supplies. I'll bet he was a passenger on one of them. That would be easy enough to check."

"How close to the ocean was he?" Sophie asked.

"Real close," the officer replied, turning and pointing to the map pinned to the wall.

Later that evening, Jack slid into bed beside Sophie and took her into his arms. This double bed wasn't as cramped as the night before, but he still wanted her close to him.

"Tomorrow we'll talk to Rooney, and afterward we'll fly to Inook, but then home, Sophie. Agreed?"

"Agreed," she said.

Sophie didn't fall asleep for a long while. Her thoughts were on Harrington. He hadn't gone camping voluntarily. She was sure of it. He was all about labels and country clubs and impressing people with his money. Camping on his own? No way. Something or someone had drawn him to that barren, frozen place.

Everyone she spoke to was quick to write him off, and she could understand their rationale. But a doubt gnawed at her. She couldn't tie up Harrington's death in a neat package and let it go. Sophie was determined to get to the truth.

JOURNAL ENTRY 748
ARCTIC CAMP

We've been back in camp for a week now.

K-74 has exceeded our wildest dreams. Ricky's stronger and more alert than ever. Fortunately, Brandon and Kirk are off with their little study and won't be nosing around. Eric wants to speed things up with the human data. I have to be the patient and thorough one. If I don't rein him in, I'm afraid he'll run off cockeyed and screw up this deal for both of us.

Nerves are on edge all the way around. I wish we could get rid of Brandon and Kirk. Their high-handed, self-righteous opinion of themselves is getting a little old. They think the world will bow to them when it reads their research. If they only knew how menial their work is compared to ours.

Brandon's been the worst. He whines constantly about the pressure he's getting from the foundation to get something published. His anxiety has been a real pain in the backside for the rest of us. He hasn't slept a wink while he's been here—working nonstop. Can't say that I sympathize. He acts as though he's so important and the rest of us are just riding his coattails.

TWENTY-EIGHT

JACK HAD A LOT ON HIS MIND. HE CHECKED IN WITH THE Chicago FBI office and spoke with one of the agents who was gathering information for him, then called Officer Joe Rooney at his home and set up a time to meet.

It was easier for Rooney to come to them as he lived several miles southwest of Barrow in an area that was difficult to navigate for anyone who didn't know his way around. Besides, he was a newlywed, and his wife wanted to do some shopping. They agreed to meet at Rooney's favorite restaurant, the Red Seal Café.

Rooney had arrived first and stood at a table near the back, waving to Sophie and Jack as they entered. After shaking hands and taking their seats, Rooney suggested they try the whale meat stew.

"It's kind of tangy, but I grew up eating it, and I love it. Unfortunately, my wife is from Anchorage, and she hasn't figured out how to cook yet, so the only time I can get it is when I come here."

Jack was more adventurous than Sophie. She ordered a sandwich, and he ordered the stew. He was able to get down only two bites before he decided he also wanted a sandwich.

Joe dug in with gusto. "Guess you have to be raised with this kind of food to love it."

Jack got down to business. "Start at the beginning and tell me who found Harrington's remains."

"A helicopter pilot found him. His name is Massack, and I've known him for years. Went to high school with him, as a matter of fact. Anyway, he and another pilot, Walters, were flying near the coast checking bear movement. He told me he set the chopper down near some markers and almost tripped over the foot. He was pretty shocked to look down and see that."

Jack nodded. "That would be a surprise."

"When he was wrapping up the leg, he saw the corner of the business card. He pulled it out and found your name, Sophie."

Joe pushed his empty bowl aside and leaned forward on his elbows. "The tracks leading away from the remains were fresh. He knew it was a polar bear that got him, and from the size of the prints, he was pretty sure it was Barry. There isn't any other bear up here that big."

"When was the wallet found?" Sophie asked.

"About a week later. We did a thorough search and found strips of a tent." He shook his head. "Strange place to put up a tent, but there it was."

Jack leaned back and rested his arm on Sophie's chair. "Find anything else?"

"Some plastic," he said. "Bits and pieces of what looked like part of a camera. Sent it to the lab with what was left of the tent."

Sophie turned to Jack. "How did Paul get my cell phone number? He called me right after Joe did."

"Paul Larson?" Rooney asked. "They called me from Deadhorse and asked if I knew a guy by that name."

"Yes, he said he was working with the police and doing some investigating on his own," Sophie said.

Rooney shook his head. "I can tell you right now, no one outside the department works with us. He called you just after I called?

That is strange. I wouldn't even have had time to put it in my report. What do you suppose he's up to?"

"I wish I knew," Jack said.

They talked about Harrington a few minutes more, then Sophie said, "I understand his remains were found near a village called Inook. I'm hoping someone there saw him. The man didn't just drop out of the sky into a tent." She suddenly thought of something else to ask. "Paul told me about two brothers named Coben who were trappers. He said the brothers talked to Harrington, but I'm assuming that was a lie, too. Have you ever heard of the Cobens?"

"No, I haven't," Joe said. "It's surely another lie, but I'll ask around."

"Tell me about Inook," Jack said.

"Not much to tell. Only a handful of people live there, but they aren't spread out, and that's good if you want to talk to all of them. Straight north is the ocean and straight east of Inook is research housing. There are some scientists studying the habits of wolves. They're biologists I think."

"How many are there?"

"Four, I think. They close down in the late fall and go back in the spring."

"The habits of wolves?" Sophie asked.

"You know, the way the pack interacts, who's in charge, that kind of stuff. People must want to know about them because the docs keep getting grants to continue their study. I have to admit, I think it would be real boring to watch a bunch of wolves for months on end."

He continued telling them about Inook. "Small planes bring in supplies, and the people stock up for the dark days of winter. There's a little cabin that was abandoned years ago, and if the weather should turn ugly, pilots hole up there. They make sure it's always stocked with supplies."

"What do the people who live there do?" Sophie wondered.

Joe smiled. "They fish. Their grocery store is the ocean."

"Would you mind setting up a meeting for me with the pilots who found Harrington?" Jack asked. "I'd like to hear their version. I'm not doubting you," he hastened to add, "but they may have forgotten to mention something."

"I understand. I'll set it up. Want me to sit in on the meeting with you?"

"That'd be good."

"I know they're both in town. Listen, do you think I ought to go to Inook with you two? I could leave midafternoon."

"No, thanks, Joe. It will be getting dark," Sophie said, thinking they'd have to wait until the next morning.

Jack grinned. "Look outside. It's always dark."

"No, it's just a little cloudy," Rooney said. "Sun won't go down for another hour. By mid-November, it will stay down."

"How long does it stay down?" Jack asked.

"About sixty-five days, but it won't get totally dark. My wife's not used to our days yet. She was raised in Iowa and only lived in Anchorage a couple of years before I met her. I'm trying to convince her it's romantic here."

That, Jack decided, would be one hard sell.

Later, Joe brought pilots Massack and Walters to the hotel to meet with Jack, while Sophie stayed in the room getting a head start on the articles she wanted to write about the people of Barrow. She needed to think about something other than William Harrington for a while. Her mind was cluttered with the lies Larson had spun.

It was late when Jack returned. Sophie was already asleep, but she'd left the desk light on. Her notebook was sitting beside it.

Jack dropped the room key on the desk. He read the first couple of sentences of the story she had written. They captured his interest, so he picked up the notebook and read the entire article.

It was about the older couple they had met in the restaurant. Their names were Samuel and Anna. Jack was impressed by how accurately Sophie recalled the details of the information they had given, but more important, he was struck by how beautifully she captured the essence of the pair, telling of their lives as though they were the hero and heroine of some epic tale. Samuel and Anna had known each other since first grade, and had laughed when they said, "It was love at first sight." They had watched their children grow and now, after forty years of marriage, were watching their children's children grow. When Sophie described the way Samuel looked at Anna, as though she were still the most beautiful girl he had ever seen, Jack could picture the old man's face. In Samuel's eyes, he saw an entire lifetime of loving one woman.

Jack sat on the edge of the bed thinking about the article. Thinking about Sophie, too. When he got under the covers, he gently wrapped her in his arms. He kissed her forehead and fell asleep.

THE FOLLOWING MORNING, while Sophie showered, Jack checked in with Alec. She was dressed when she stepped out of the bathroom, and while she packed, Jack paced the room. She closed her carry-on bag, put it by her coat, and sat down on the end of the bed, waiting. Jack finally noticed she was watching him.

He tilted his head. "What?"

"You tell me," she said. "You're worried. Did something happen while I was in the shower?"

"Just trying to work something out. Did you remember anything else Larson said to you?"

She nodded. "I did. He Googled me."

"What the . . ."

"He said he Googled me and was looking at my photo. That kind of gives me shivers now," she admitted.

"Where did he find your photo?"

"My newspaper sometimes runs my photo above my articles," she explained. "Come on, Jack. You know these days anyone can find out anything about a person using the Internet."

"This guy went to a lot of trouble to get you up here. We don't know who he is, and we don't know his motives. I'm leaning toward changing our plans."

Sophie put up her hand. "I know what you're going to say. Back to Chicago, right? And that's fine, after we go to Inook. I've come this far. I don't want to leave just yet. What's a couple of hours going to hurt? It's a tiny coastal village. I'll talk to whoever's there, and then I can put this to rest."

"No, I think it would be—"

She cut him off. "Jack, I'm going with or without you."

"Ah, Sophie," he said, a smile in his voice, "that's sweet."

Suspicious now, she asked, "What's sweet?"

"It's sweet that you think you have a say. You go where I go, not the other way around."

She folded her arms defiantly. "Wanna bet?"

Horrible day!

Brandon became so agitated this morning, I worried he would do something drastic. I made the offhanded remark to Eric that Brandon could use a dose of K-74—never imagining that he would actually give it to him.

Brandon went into cardiac arrest around 3:00 p.m. We called for the medical helicopter, but it was too late. By the time they arrived, he was dead.

I could tell Eric was scared. When I confronted him, he admitted he'd injected Brandon with the K-74, telling him that it was a mild sedative. Now we find out that Brandon had a heart condition he was keeping a secret. According to Kirk, there won't be an autopsy. Lucky for us.

TWENTY-NINE

J ACK AND SOPHIE LEFT FOR INOOK TWO HOURS LATER. ONE
of those hours was spent arguing. Sophie was pretty sure he
finally gave in just to shut her up.

Once they were in the air, Chipper asked Jack if he would mind
making a stop on the way back to Barrow.

"I've got supplies to drop off at another coastal village. It won't
take long, and it will save me a trip tomorrow."

"We're going to be in Inook most of the afternoon. Why don't
you make the trip and come back for us?" Jack suggested.

Chipper was grateful. "I won't keep you waiting."

"When we get close to Inook, circle so I can get the lay of the
land. I want to see where the cabins are."

The pilot was happy to oblige. He flew over the water, then
passed over a cluster of prefabricated buildings hooked together like
the hotel in Deadhorse.

"That's where the people watching the wolves stay. I hear it's a
slick setup. They've got satellite and DVD players. I know because
I've brought disks for them. They watch a lot of movies when they
can't get out."

It looked deserted, but with the fresh snow, any footprints would have been covered up. No lights shone from inside.

"Must be locked up for the winter," Sophie remarked.

The noise from the engine drowned out her voice, and neither Jack nor Chipper heard her comment.

They passed over Inook and landed. Jack unzipped his bag, took out extra gun clips, and put them in the pockets of his ski jacket. He handed another to Sophie and told her to put it in her coat.

"You expecting trouble?" Chipper asked.

"No, just like to be prepared."

"You're overreacting," she told him as she stepped out of the plane. "We're not going to war."

Jack didn't respond. Standing side by side, they watched the plane disappear. Suddenly, they were all alone in the middle of a white wilderness.

Sophie made a complete circle looking for signs of life. Not a sound could be heard. She shuddered. "Jack, could I have a gun?"

"Finally getting nervous?" he asked. He took hold of her hand and started walking. "Time to knock on some doors and hope to God no one answers with a rifle."

"You're too distrustful," she told him. She was already gasping for breath. The cold made her lungs feel as though they were freezing and would crack at any second.

"Out here in the wild, would you open the door without a little protection? Never mind, I know the answer. You'd open it."

"You're never going to let that go, are you?"

He was ahead of her, and she couldn't see him smiling. "Never let what go?"

"I looked out the window and got shot. That's what."

Jack thought of Samuel and Anna. Did they ever argue the way he and Sophie did? If so, did they have as much fun?

The terrain was flat, but to Sophie it felt like she was climbing a mountain, a big one. She couldn't help but notice that Jack wasn't at all winded. The man was definitely in shape. She ought to know, she thought, remembering the play of his muscles under her fingertips.

"Didn't Joe say the homes were close together?" she panted.

"Yes, he did. Must be by Alaska measurements."

They walked for what seemed a mile before reaching a house, but Jack assured her it wasn't even a fourth of that. The structure was another prefab building, with one window on the side of the door and two snowmobiles parked beside the steps.

The Native American woman who opened the door looked stunned to see them.

"I don't think they get a lot of salesmen here," Sophie whispered to Jack.

She motioned them inside. Sophie sighed with relief when she felt the heat.

Jack asked several questions, but the woman was hesitant with her answers.

"You have a lovely home," Sophie said.

She then told them where she was from and why she had ventured here. Within minutes, Sophie had the woman telling her her life story. Her name was Mary, and she had three strong children. Her husband was fishing with a neighbor. As Mary became more comfortable with them, she offered information about the village and about her neighbors.

"If one of us had met this man you speak of, all of us would have heard about it. By tonight everyone will know about the woman with the blue eyes and her handsome husband." She shook her head and with authority said, "No Harrington here. Did this man get lost?"

"No, he had an unfortunate accident. A polar bear killed him."

Mary nodded sagely. "Ah yes, Barry ate him. We never knew the man's name. Now we do. William Harrington."

"Have you ever met the scientists who study the wolves?" Sophie asked.

"No, they keep to themselves. They watch the wolves, and sometimes they watch us. I think maybe they study us, too."

Mary insisted on feeding them. Knowing it would insult her to refuse the kind offer, Sophie spoke up before Jack declined. "We just ate before we came here, but I would love something hot to drink, please."

While Mary brewed tea, she told them about the other villagers. Later, she pointed the way to the three neighbors she knew to be home.

They spent the next hour knocking on doors and asking questions.

As they left the last house, Sophie said, "We should have listened to Mary. She told us no one saw Harrington, and she was right. She's a sweet woman, isn't she?"

Jack nodded. "You put her at ease."

"Do you think we could stay inside the empty cabin Joe told us about? I'm freezing. The cold seems worse since I got warm at Mary's house."

He put his arm around her shoulders. "Sure. I think we're through here. Chipper should be back soon." He pointed to a small wooden building sitting fifty yards off in the distance. "That should be it over there," he said.

He pulled her close as they made their way to the cabin, and Sophie prayed that there was a heater inside ready to start.

"I guess I may never know why Harrington came here," Sophie admitted.

They walked up the two steps to the door. Jack reached for the handle just as a loud crack split the air and splintered the wood, the chips flying past Sophie's face. His reaction was instantaneous. He threw the door open and shoved Sophie inside, covering her with his body as she landed on the floor.

We can't afford another mistake like the one Eric made with Brandon. If the Alpha Project is to continue, we have to be prudent and cautious. We've refined the formula and believe we've found the right dosage.

We've set up a human trial and were amazed at the number of applicants. It's incredible how many people will sign up for something if we play to their ego. Even when we swear them to secrecy, they seem eager to prove themselves.

They believe they are testing dietary supplements. We have given them only enough information to gain their trust and their cooperation.

The results have been phenomenal, even better than we expected. The added variable of the adrenaline has been especially exciting. The next step is to increase the stress factor to see how it affects the results.

THIRTY

A NOTHER CRACKLING BOOM. IT SOUNDED AS THOUGH INOOK
had been snapped in half by a demonic force.

Jack kicked the cabin door shut and dragged Sophie out
of the line of fire.

Stunned, she whispered, "Was that—?"

"High-powered rifle. Stay down!" Jack's voice was hard, angry.

He didn't have to tell her again. Her mind took a few seconds to
grasp the horror of someone trying to kill them, but her body reacted instantly.

Jack ripped his glove off and, gun in hand, rolled next to the
window. He leaned against the wall, listening to the silence, waiting
for some sound that would tell him where the shot had been fired.
Ten seconds passed. Ten more. Nothing. He slowly edged up to
look out the corner of the window. Impossible to see much of anything. The wind was stirring up the snow on the ground, and more
was falling.

Sophie crawled on her stomach to the far wall, then quietly
turned and sat with her back against a cabinet. She looked around
the cabin, searching for anything that would help them defend

themselves. It was sparsely furnished with a table and chair, a cabinet, and a cot. A thick drape meant to keep out some of the cold was pulled back on a hook beside the small window, which was their only source of light.

Another round of bullets slammed into the wall outside. Some of them spit through, hitting the table and chair.

"Get behind the chest!" Jack shouted.

Sophie hurried to do what he ordered and crouched down just as a bullet hit a can on a shelf above her. Pork 'n Beans. The can spun around, flew into the wall, and crashed to the floor.

The shooter was getting bolder, coming closer. Jack heard the sound of a motor humming in the distance. He looked out again and through the snow saw a light bouncing across the flat area where Chipper had landed the plane. It had to be a snowmobile. The beam of light was widening, and the sound of the motor getting louder.

"No matter what, you stay down," Jack shouted to Sophie.

"Careful, Jack. Careful . . . please."

Sophie watched him turn and reach for the door handle. He cracked it open an inch, no more. Stretching out his arm, he aimed the gun and waited for the snowmobile to stop. It was still too far away. He needed it to come within range.

"A little closer. Just a little closer," he said, deadly calm.

He got his wish. The snowmobile moved toward the cabin. When it stopped, the shooter turned the motor off but left the spotlight on as he swung his leg over and stood next to it, raising his rifle again. As though realizing he could be seen in the light, he lowered his weapon and leaned across the shield to turn off the beam.

For an instant he was in the light. That was all the time Jack needed. Shoving the door open with one hand, he fired with the other. The first bullet wounded the man in his shoulder and spun him around. The second bullet went through his neck. He was dead before he hit the ground.

The wind blew the door toward Jack, and he held it back with his arm as he scanned the area, looking for another target. Motioning for Sophie to stay where she was, Jack disappeared into the snow.

Sophie lay trembling for what seemed an eternity. She felt helpless. There was no signal on her cell phone, and the people in the tiny village didn't have telephones, so there was no way to call for help. Every minute Jack was gone felt like an hour. What was happening? Was he all right? Why didn't he come back?

The cabin was as cold as a meat locker, and her teeth chattered violently. She couldn't wait any longer. She got up and ran to the door. Just as she reached for the handle, it opened. Jack was coming up the steps holding the shooter's rifle in his left hand.

He wrapped his right arm around her and pulled her back inside, bolting the door. After lighting a candle that sat on the table, he looked around for something that would warm the room.

Sophie cautiously edged her way to the window and glanced outside. She saw the dead body sprawled on the snow. "Where did he come from?" she asked. Before he could answer, she thought about the village. "What about Mary and the others?" she worried.

"If they're smart, they'll lock their doors and stay inside."

Sophie could barely make out the shapes of the houses in the distance. She couldn't see any signs of movement. Again she looked at the dead man.

"What are we going to do?" she asked.

"For now, we'll stay put," he answered. "If no one else shows up, we'll move the body. Someone might come after him."

Jack had found a kerosene heater and was lighting it. Sophie rubbed her arms and stomped her feet while he got the heater working. The rifle he'd taken from the dead man lay on the table. It had a scope on top.

"Who was he, Jack?" she asked.

"I've never seen him before. Do you recognize him? Maybe you saw him in Deadhorse or Barrow."

"I can't see his face from here," she answered. She dropped the curtain across the window.

Jack walked over to stand in front of her. Her face was pale, and she was trembling. He surrounded her with his arms and tilted her chin up. "I'm not going to let anything happen to you."

She grabbed hold of the collar of his jacket, drawing him to her. "I know. And I'm not going to let anything happen to you. You've got a gun. Can I have the rifle?"

"You think you can handle it?"

"If you show me how." She glanced at the door. "Why is this happening? Why would anyone want to shoot at us?"

"I don't know," he answered, "but I'm going to find out."

"Where did he come from?" she asked again. "Mary told us the men in the village wouldn't be back until late."

"His snowmobile came from the east," he said. "The only thing in that direction is the scientists' camp."

"I remember," Sophie said excitedly. "Chipper told us the people staying there have all the latest equipment. If they have a satellite phone, we could call the police in Barrow and get some help."

"We'll wait it out until Chipper gets here. We can't take any chances."

"How can you be so calm?"

"Practice," he said.

Jack managed a quick smile, but inside he was in a rage. He wanted to shoot the bastard a couple more times. He crossed the room to stand next to the window, moving the curtain aside just enough to watch the area in front of the cabin. Minutes passed and no one else appeared.

Finally, he said, "I'm going to move the snowmobile and the body behind the cabin. You barricade the door behind me."

"Oh no, you don't," Sophie cried. "I'm not waiting in here without you again."

"Then stay behind me," Jack cautioned. He went out first. It was deadly quiet now, the silence eerie.

Sophie followed Jack to the snowmobile. The halo of blood around the shooter's head was black against the white snow. Bracing herself, she looked at his face.

She gasped. "I know him."

JOURNAL ENTRY 874
CHICAGO

We've found the perfect subject. He's extremely fit, and he signed on to the project knowing that he could be tested at any time. His considerable ego makes him willing to prove himself. In addition, he has no family and very few ties. If he were to disappear for a few weeks, no one would miss him.

THIRTY-ONE

S OPHIE STEPPED AWAY FROM THE BODY. "CHICAGO," SHE SAID. "I talked to him in Chicago. He was rude, and I thought he looked like Bluto."

Jack knelt on one knee and methodically went through the man's pockets, searching for identification. He found a gun, engaged the safety, and handed it to her. In another pocket he found two clips and gave those to her as well.

"He was the security guard," she said. "No, I thought he was a security guard. I remember thinking he was filling in for someone else at the reception desk."

"Where, Sophie?" Jack asked patiently. "Where exactly did you see him?"

"In the lobby of William Harrington's apartment building."

If Jack was surprised by the news, he didn't show it. "Go back inside before you freeze to death."

His expression told her he didn't want an argument. She headed toward the cabin but dropped one of the clips in the snow. She scooped it up and held it against her so she wouldn't drop it again. Inside, she carefully placed the gun and clips on the table next to the rifle and felt a little calmer, knowing if anyone else were to start shooting at her she had weapons to defend herself. It wasn't relevant that she had never even held a gun until just a moment ago. Jack would show her how to unlock the safety and load the weapon. By God, she'd shoot to kill if she had to.

She remembered the bloodstains on the snow and went outside again. While Jack moved the snowmobile and the body behind the cabin, she scooped up handfuls of snow and covered the blood. Then she stomped it down so the wind wouldn't carry it away. It seemed to her that the temperature had dropped again. Did it ever get too cold to snow, or was that a myth? She didn't know. She should have paid attention in earth science class instead of flirting with Billy Gibson.

By the time she and Jack were back inside the cabin, they were feeling the early effects of hypothermia. Sophie's feet were numb, but after pacing in front of the heater, her toes began to sting, a good sign, she knew, though it was painful.

Jack was going through the drawers of the cabinet looking for anything they might need should they be stuck in the cabin all night. In the bottom drawer he found a stack of porn magazines, which explained how some of the stranded pilots passed the time, and a flashlight. The batteries were weak. He added the flashlight to the pile on the table and kept looking.

"This is the most ill-equipped cabin," he muttered.

"What should it be equipped for?" she asked. She pulled off her gloves and warmed her hands in front of the heater.

"Anything and everything. We'll need more kerosene, and I don't see any."

"Chipper will be here soon." She tried to sound optimistic.

Jack nodded. "There's a small utility shed close. I'll look there."

"It might be locked," she said as she put on her gloves again.

"If it is, I'll break the lock." He pulled the curtain away from the window and scanned the area in front of the cabin.

"Jack, what are you thinking?" she asked.

He didn't want to scare her, but he wanted her to be prepared. "If the man I killed had friends waiting for him, they might come looking. We need to be ready for anything . . . just in case."

He looked at her to see how she was handling the dark possibility.

She simply nodded and said, "Okay." She wrapped her scarf around her neck and tucked it inside her collar. "Show me how to use the gun."

He smiled.

"What?" she asked.

"You're a lot tougher than you look."

He gave her the man's gun and made her release and engage the safety several times before he was convinced she wouldn't forget it in a crisis. Then he showed her how to load the clips and fire the weapon.

Sophie put the extra clips in her left pocket, zipped it closed, and checked the safety one last time before slipping the gun into her right pocket.

"I'm going to the shed. I'll be right back," he told her. He looked outside before opening the door. Sophie was right behind him.

"I'm going with you. I can help carry if there are things we can use." She nudged his back. "Hurry. You're letting the cold in."

He pulled the door closed. She walked beside him, and he slowed his pace so that she could keep up. "You just had to come to Alaska," he grumbled. "I hate this cold."

She ignored his complaints. The snowfall had diminished, and Sophie looked off to the east. On the dark horizon, she could just make out the silhouette of a building. Joe had told them that the scientists closed down for the fall, but maybe Bluto had gotten inside and been waiting there for them to show up.

"How did Bluto . . . I mean, how did the man who shot at us know we would be here? He must have followed us," she said.

They had reached the shed, and as Jack tried to pry open the

door, Sophie pulled the wool scarf over her mouth and nose to warm
the air before she inhaled it. Hearing a sound in the distance, she
looked up at the heavy clouds hanging over them, expecting to see
Chipper's plane.

"Do you hear—?"

Jack grabbed her and pulled her to the side of the tiny building.
"Someone's coming. Stay here."

He slowly looked around the corner. Two . . . no, three lights
were coming toward the cabin from the east. Three men on snowmobiles were riding at full speed. It was too dangerous for Jack and
Sophie to try to make it back to the cabin, so they waited. The men
slowed and fanned out as they got closer. One headed toward the
front, halting before he reached the cabin so he couldn't be seen.
The other two circled to the back. When they passed the snowmobile Jack had parked there, they stopped abruptly.

"They found the body," Jack whispered.

One man motioned to the other, and they turned their machines
around and retreated a few hundred feet, pausing to confer. Jack saw
one of the men lift a fuel can from the back of his snowmobile. On
foot, they crept up to the cabin again. The third man moved closer,
drawing a gun and aiming at the front door while the other two bent
low and ran under the window. One took a rag from his pocket,
dipped it in the can, and set it afire. Giving the signal, he broke the
glass and tossed the rag inside just as the man with the fuel threw the
open can through the window. The light from the flame flashed
across the opening, and the cabin ignited. The men crouched in the
snow, waiting for Sophie and Jack to run out the door.

Sophie couldn't get the gun out of her pocket with her gloves
on, so she pulled one off. Flexing her hand for circulation, she
wrapped it around the handle with her finger on the trigger.

One of the men turned to the side and saw motion coming from
the shed. By the time he raised his gun in their direction, Jack had
aimed and fired. Solid hit. The man dropped on the snow facedown.

Jack swung to the left and fired again. He wounded the second man, got him in the shoulder, and fired again. The bullet hit him in the back of the knee as he tried to turn to shoot. Screaming, he went down hard.

The third man disappeared. A second later, they heard a snowmobile revving up. Jack ran toward the bastard writhing on the ground and kicked the gun away from him.

Sophie followed. "This one's not going anywhere," she shouted as she pointed the gun at his head. "Go after the other one."

"If he moves, shoot him," Jack ordered. Running to a snowmobile, he jumped on and took off. The man he followed headed east, then veered north at full speed. Jack thought he must be disoriented. There was nothing in that direction but the ocean.

The sky had turned dark, and the lights on the snowmobile made it easy to follow him. The light wavered, and Jack heard gunshots. The man was shooting at him. At this speed, it was only a matter of time before he lost control of the snowmobile and killed himself. Jack slowed down, widening the distance between them, and followed as the man zigzagged across the snow, the light on his vehicle bouncing at every bump.

How many miles had they gone? Jack's face stung from the cold; his eyes burned from the wind. Where did the bastard think he was headed? Had he lost his bearings? They had to be getting close to the ocean.

The guy would have to veer again or turn back in his direction. Keeping him within sight, Jack slowed down even more.

Suddenly, he heard a loud echoing crack. It was followed by a terrified scream, and then a splash. The lights on the snowmobile aimed toward the sky and disappeared. Another scream . . . then silence.

"Son of a birch," Jack whispered. "Son of a bitch."

Jack looked at the ice beneath him. Not a good way to go, he thought. He instantly turned his snowmobile around and sped away from there as fast as he could. As he headed south, he saw a light in the distance. The fire from the burning cabin was his beacon.

Sophie was getting frantic. Jack had been gone too long. When she heard the hum of a snowmobile, she let out a deep breath. It had to be him, she thought. Had to.

The man she was guarding glared at her. "FBI's on the way," she told him, as she shifted from one foot to the other. The heat from the fire warmed her face, but her feet were still freezing. Fire and ice, she thought. It seemed so bizarre to be standing there watching the fire burn and the snow melt, and then instantly refreeze. Crazy. Fire and ice.

Sophie had never been so happy to see anyone. When Jack walked toward her, she wanted to run to him and throw her arms around him, but she restrained herself. He was going to have to help her release her grip on the gun first. She thought her finger might be frozen to the trigger.

After Jack took the gun from her hand, he faced the man on the ground. "Who are you?"

"I need medical attention," the man yelled. He was actually outraged.

"Who are you?" Jack repeated.

"I need medical—"

Jack kicked his leg. "Who are you?"

The man screamed. "Carter. Dr. Eric Carter. Now get me help."

"You're a doctor? Fix yourself."

Eric sneered. "I'm not that kind of doctor. I'm a Ph.D. in biology."

"You study the wolves?" Sophie asked.

His gaze turned to Sophie. "All ruined. You've ruined everything. Why couldn't you let it go?"

They heard the drone of a plane's engine.

"Chipper's here," Jack said.

"Why wouldn't I let what go?" she asked Carter.

"Our test subject. Why wouldn't you leave it alone? You kept pecking away."

"You're talking about William Harrington?" she asked.

"Stupid female. You kept pecking away."

"What were you testing?" she asked. "What did you do to him?"

He didn't answer.

"Come on, Sophie," Jack said. "I'll put you in the plane and come back for him. You need to get warm."

Dr. Carter wasn't going anywhere. Jack got on the snowmobile with Sophie behind him. She rested her face against his back. Jack motioned for Chipper to stay where he was as they drove the snowmobile toward him. He opened the plane door for Sophie, and a burst of warm air poured across her face. Once she was seated in the back, Jack climbed in and shut the door. He didn't give a damn if Eric had to wait for him in the snow while he got warm. A few minutes wouldn't kill him.

"Radio the police in Barrow," he told Chipper and then quickly explained what had happened.

Chipper's brown eyes got so big that, by the time Jack finished explaining, he looked like a cocker spaniel. "What are you going to do with Carter?" he asked.

"Tie him up and put him with the cargo."

Once he could face the cold again, Jack headed back to where he'd left Eric Carter. Thinking he saw something moving up ahead, he slowed, and then stopped. The light from the snowmobile was being reflected by a pair of tiny circles. Eyes. Glowing red eyes, watching him. He turned the light and saw the others. Four of them. Wolves standing together about twenty feet from Eric.

Jack heard their hungry growls. He concentrated on the biggest one at the front of the pack. He was huge. His white coat was marked with a dark strip across the back. He stared at Jack, and their gazes locked. As Jack reached for his gun, the wolf turned toward Eric and pounced with lightning speed. His fangs punctured the doctor's throat before Jack could draw his weapon. The others leapt, and it was too late. Too late to save the man. The wolf he had been watching lifted his head and looked at him again, then continued to feed.

Jack got the hell out of there.

Once he was inside the plane, he could breathe again. "I've never seen anything like that," he said.

"Like what?" Sophie asked.

He shook his head.

"Where's the doctor?"

"He didn't make it."

"He must have bled to death," she guessed.

"Yeah, he definitely bled out."

The planes engines drowned out the wolves' howls.

Jack leaned back in the seat and closed his eyes. "Damn," he whispered. "Damn."

Sophie tapped his shoulder. "Jack?"

"Hmm?"

"What happened to the man you were chasing?"

He didn't open his eyes. "He went swimming."

William Harrington remained unconscious when we injected the K-74. After placing him in position, we observed off site.

    Though confused when he gained consciousness, he was reacting as we had expected: disoriented and frightened.

    Our mistake was in failing to factor in all the variables— especially indigenous species.

    We observed Harrington's stress level increase dramatically. He appeared to be terrified, but we could not discern the cause of this reaction because our remote cameras were not picking it up. Harrington's screams drowned out the sounds. Within minutes a polar bear, the size of which we had never seen, came into view. There was nowhere for him to run or hide. He was no match for the animal.

    Test invalidated.

THIRTY-TWO

S OPHIE INSISTED ON GOING BACK TO INOOK THE FOLLOWING morning with Jack. She was determined to look at the scientists' home away from home and, hopefully, find out what Dr. Eric Carter was doing.

FBI agents were on their way from Anchorage, and the police from Barrow had already made a complete sweep of the property.

The bodies in front of the burned cabin—or what was left of them once the wolves had finished—were on their way to the morgue.

Jack had watched them being put into body bags. Eric Carter was unrecognizable. Identification would be made from his fingerprints. Jack stood over the second body and examined his face. He had seen him before, but where? Replaying the events of the last few days in his memory, he came to it. He and Sophie had walked past him on their way to Chipper's Charter Service. The man had stood outside their hotel and had almost been hit by a truck as he rushed across the street toward his own vehicle. Okay, so the son of a bitch followed them.

Jack had made sure that Sophie stayed away from the gruesome scene at the cabin. He'd argued that she'd been through enough. She was with the police as they searched the four rooms of the scientists' quarters, and she walked through each one looking for some clue as to why Harrington had come to Alaska. She knew he had been connected with the Alpha Project. She still didn't know what that was, but she was positive it had something to do with the scientists who ran this facility. What had Eric Carter been afraid she would discover?

There were notebooks full of data, but they all were about the wolves. There were videos as well. The disks were labeled and numbered. The subject of disk one through disk twenty was the alpha male named Ricky. One of the officers put a disk in the player, and several others gathered around to watch Ricky and his pack attack a caribou.

"How were they able to film this without the wolves coming after them?" he asked.

"Look at the jaws on that beast," another officer said. "I think he could take down a polar bear all by himself."

Jack joined the group. He saw the wolf and recognized him immediately. As he watched the video, he felt a strange connection with the animal, probably because he had stared into his eyes and seen the power in him. He also felt a weird sort of fondness for the wolf because he hadn't attacked him. Scared the hell out of him, but had left him alone.

"He's magnificent," an officer remarked. "Think he was one of the wolves that killed the doctor last night?" he asked Jack.

"Yes," Jack answered but didn't elaborate. "He was there."

Sophie sat at the desk in the small room the doctors used as a study, looking through notebooks. Jack checked up on her every few minutes. He'd stop in the doorway and just watch her until she looked up. He'd ask her if she needed anything, and he'd also ask each time if she was ready to go back to Barrow.

She knew he was concerned about her, but couldn't understand why. She was surrounded by men with guns, and she had her own FBI agent bodyguard.

"Are you worried I'll read something that will freak me out?" she asked the fourth time he appeared.

"There is that possibility."

"Oh, please. After yesterday, nothing here will spook me . . . bore the wool socks off me, but not scare me."

He smiled. "You don't like wolves."

"Yes, I do," she replied. "But every little detail of their day? Eat, sleep, kill, eat, sleep, kill . . . repetitious."

"It's what they do."

She nodded. "They were interested in the behavior within the pack. The alpha interested them most, how he controlled the others . . . family dynamic stuff." She closed the notebook, put it back on the desk and stood. "I don't know how these scientists stood it. Day in and day out watching wolves . . . and in these conditions." She walked over to him as she asked, "Have they found anything that connects Harrington to the project?"

"Not yet," he answered. "But they've only just started."

When she looked up at him, he felt a tightness in his chest. She was beautiful, yes, but there was so much more to her. She was loving and trusting and fiercely loyal. He lifted her arms and put them around his neck.

"Guess what I'm gonna do," he drawled.

She moved into him and pulled his head down toward hers. Then she brushed her lips across his mouth, teasing, tempting. "This?" she asked. She deepened the kiss, rubbing her tongue over his lips. She pulled back and whispered, "Or this?"

Hungry for her now, Jack slanted his mouth over hers and his tongue moved inside. He loved the way she felt pressed against him, and from the way she eagerly responded, he knew she loved it, too. He would have liked nothing better than to rip her clothes off and make love to her now, in this room, but he lifted his head. His breath was shaky.

"This isn't the time or the place, sweetheart . . . unless you want to make the six o'clock news."

One of the officers interrupted. "Your pilot wants to know when—"

Jack didn't let him finish. "Tell him to start the engines. We're leaving now."

A few minutes later, Sophie was all bundled up and heading toward the plane with Jack. The wind had kicked up again, and the short walk was miserable.

"I hate . . ." Jack began.

She patted his arm. "I know. You hate the cold."

THE FLIGHT BACK to Barrow was turbulent, but Sophie's stomach barely complained. After her experiences of the last twenty-four hours, a bumpy ride in a tiny plane was child's play.

Once back in Barrow, she spent several hours in the police station. She tried to be helpful and apologized over and over again because so many of their questions were left unanswered. Was she ever going to discover what happened to William Harrington?

"I know that Harrington was involved in something he called the Alpha Project. I just don't know what his role was."

"How was Harrington connected to the scientists?" one officer asked.

"Bluto."

"Excuse me?"

She looked at Jack. "You explain."

"One of the men who attacked us . . . Sophie met him in Chicago. He was at William Harrington's apartment, and he told her Harrington had gone to Europe," he said.

The interrogation continued, and when they'd finally concluded that she had told them everything she knew, she was given the chance to ask them some questions.

"The men who came after Jack and me . . . who were they?"

"You've already named Dr. Eric Carter for us, but we haven't identified the others yet," the lead officer answered. "We're looking for IDs. The FBI will run prints."

Joe Rooney had been standing by Jack listening intently. He joined the conversation. "As far as we know, there were never more than four scientists at the facility. Besides Carter, there were Dr. Brandon Finch, Dr. Marcus Lemming, and Dr. Kirk Halpern. We've spoken to Dr. Lemming and Dr. Halpern. They're in Chicago, and they swear they didn't know what Eric Carter was up to. Lemming said Carter often stayed behind after the others had gone home, and he didn't tell them what he was doing on his own time."

"Did you speak with the fourth doctor, Brandon Finch? Where is he?" Sophie asked.

"In an urn on his wife's mantle, I imagine," Joe said. "He died of a massive heart attack a couple of months ago. Evidently he had a heart condition and didn't let the others know about it because he was concerned they wouldn't let him continue his work. Agents will go through Eric Carter's house and his lab in Chicago. They'll check out the other doctors, too."

"What about the man Jack chased on the snowmobile?"

"We haven't had time yet to get a search team together," Joe said. "They're going to have a tough time with the ice shifting."

"One of those men who died was pretending to be Paul Larson. That's what I think," she said. "I wish I had heard their voices."

"We'll get some help up here from Anchorage," Joe assured her. "We should know more in the next few days."

It had been a very long day by the time the police had finished their questioning. Jack invited the officers to join them for dinner, and most of them took him up on his offer.

The Red Seal Café was packed with customers. When Jack, Sophie, and the policemen walked in, a hush fell over the crowd. The whole town had heard the news of what had happened at Inook, and Sophie felt as though she were a guppy in a fishbowl. There was little doubt that she and Jack were the subject of every conversation at every table.

There was another whale meat special, and Jack decided he would try it again. He shuddered at the first bite.

"You've got to keep eating. By the third swallow, you'll like it," Joe told him.

Jack could only get two bites down before he gave up. "It must be an acquired taste," he told the others.

Sophie took the opportunity at dinner to get more information about Barrow. She got up and went to the table next to theirs and asked a father and son if they would mind answering a few questions. By the time Jack was ready to leave, the entire restaurant was crowded around Sophie, helping her with her notes.

"Don't forget to mention the lack of crime," one man suggested.

"Until yesterday," another said.

"Oh, right," the first man admitted.

Later at the hotel, she sat down at the desk and started writing while Jack made several phone calls. When she had completed her article, she looked at the clock. Two hours had passed. She turned around. Jack, wearing only a pair of shorts, was sitting in bed reading.

She slipped into the bathroom and showered. Wrapped in a towel, she came back to the bedroom and stood beside the bed, waiting. When Jack looked up and smiled, she let the towel drop to the floor. He pulled the covers back so she could slip in next to him. He warmed her body with his and began to kiss her neck.

"Jack . . ."

"You like this?" he asked as his fingers slid down her chest to her stomach.

She inhaled sharply. "Yes, I do, but tonight is the last . . ."

"Do you like this?"

His hand moved slower, and his fingers were doing magical things to her, robbing her of her thoughts. She knew she wanted to tell him something, but his touch was such a distraction. She gasped, then moaned. Jack leaned up on an elbow to watch her as he stroked her. The warm glint of his eyes made her heart race even more. She couldn't stand the torment any longer. She pushed him onto his back, straddled him, and then proceeded to drive him out of his mind.

When they both had reached the peak of ecstasy, she collapsed on top of him. She lay there for a long time, content to listen to his heartbeat.

It took Jack a while to control his breath. "Where did you learn . . . ?" he began.

"I didn't learn," she whispered. "It just felt . . . right."

Her mind cleared and she remembered what she wanted to tell him. She rolled away, pulled the covers up, and said, "That was the last time we'll do this."

"Yeah?" He reached for her. "How come?"

"I'll be back in Chicago, and I can't get involved with an FBI agent. I just can't."

She thought he would be more understanding, but he wasn't. He laughed.

"You *are* involved," he said.

She'd have to give him that. "Okay, yes, but once we're home, no more. Jack, you aren't falling in love with me, are you?"

"Hell no. Absolutely not."

"Good. I wouldn't want to hurt you. Good night."

She had trouble falling asleep. Why hadn't he asked her if she was falling in love with him?

Maybe because he already knew the answer.

This may be my last entry for a while.

When I began this journal years ago, I had intended to create a personal record of my experiences should I one day want to write a memoir. I never could have imagined the journey it would chronicle.

The Dubai contact is willing to pay the fifty million next month and not wait for further experiments. I wish we could have expanded the testing. I'd especially have liked to try it on female subjects. We might have been able to negotiate another ten million.

I'm packing up and heading home. Eric will follow later. Our primary objective now is to make sure all of our data on K-74 is secure.

We regret that William Harrington's death was in vain, but then, fairness has never been an attribute of science.

We can't reveal any knowledge of him or his death, of course. Our voice monitors picked up on some pilots finding evidence of him. They found a business card. They'll take it to the police, I suppose, and eventually he'll be identified. We've been very careful to prevent any trail leading back to us, but it would probably behoove us to keep an eye on how this plays out.

THIRTY-THREE

DADDY WAS IN THE NEWS AGAIN.

Sophie came home to a celebration. She had just unpacked and was about to listen to the messages on her recorder when Mr. Bitterman called.

"Turn on your television. Hurry. It's in the news. The FBI is going to owe your father big for this one."

He hung up before she could ask him any questions. She dutifully turned on the local news, hit the Record button, and sat down on the bed to watch.

Natalie Miller was reporting live from the courthouse.

"Kevin Devoe and his wife, Meredith, have been arrested and taken into custody by the FBI. From what we've learned, the FBI was sent proof that the Devoes had stolen the money from the Kelly's Root Beer employees' retirement fund and had hidden it in several secret accounts using dummy corporations."

The scene flashed to another reporter standing with an older man who was waving a cashier's check.

"It's all here," he said, beaming at the camera. "It's the exact amount I should have gotten when Kelly's closed. To the penny. All of us got the checks at the same time. I know. I've talked to my friends. Bobby Rose did this. He found that money, and he got it back for us. He knew what those crooks were up to."

"How do you know it was Bobby Rose?" the toothy reporter asked.

The man chuckled. "Who besides Bobby has the brains to figure it out and find our money? I'll tell you this," he added, waving his finger in front of the reporter's face. "Bobby takes care of his own. Chicago," he explained. "Oh, it was Bobby Rose, all right. Our Robin Hood. You can't convince me it was anyone else."

The reporter looked directly into the camera. "Natalie, the FBI will neither confirm nor deny that they know who was behind this. There will be a press conference tomorrow. Stay tuned for the latest developments."

No mention was made of reopening Kelly's. Mr. Bitterman would be disappointed if that didn't happen. Sophie called him, and after discussing the good news, she gave him a few details about her trip. They talked about Harrington and what she had learned about the scientists, but she couldn't bring herself to tell him about the killings just yet. She would wait until they were sitting face-to-face. Besides, she needed time to process it all.

She discussed a few articles she wanted to write about the people of Barrow, and he suggested she could work from home where there wouldn't be any interruptions. She was happy to comply and, after hanging up, immediately went to work. She wrote the story of the football team first. After that, she put some finishing touches on her story about Samuel and Anna. She even wrote about the hotel in Deadhorse, but she wasn't ready to write about Harrington. There were still too many holes in that story.

On her second day home, she received another piece of good news. Detective Steinbeck called to tell her the police had identified the man who had shot her in her apartment. Working with the FBI, they had checked the fingerprints from one of the bodies in Alaska and discovered they belonged to an ex-convict who lived in

Chicago. His name was Ivan Brosky, and he had a record a mile long. When they searched Brosky's apartment, they found a cache of weapons, and ballistics was able to match one of the guns with the bullet. They had their man. Any further investigation would be handled by the FBI.

Steinbeck's call was followed immediately by one from Gil.

"Great news, huh, Sophie?" he said. "They got the guy."

"How did you—" she began. She didn't finish because she wasn't really all that surprised. Gil had his ways of knowing everything.

"I've got Tony downstairs today, and Alec said it's okay to send him home. I just wanted to let you know. I'll check back with you in a few days to make sure you're okay."

Sophie thanked him and hung up. Maybe her life could get back to a modicum of normalcy once again.

Cordie called her at five o'clock. "Get dressed up. Regan and I are taking you to Fortune's."

"I'm not in the mood," she said. "Maybe tomorrow."

Cordie would not take no for an answer. "You love Fortune's. We'll pick you up at seven. Be ready."

Maybe it would be good for her to be with friends, after all. Sophie needed something besides work to take her mind off Jack. Hopefully, one of them would have a horrible problem, and she could concentrate on that.

She quickly finished her work and changed into her favorite black silk dress. She added a bloodred scarf over her wool coat. If the restaurant got chilly, she could use it as a wrap.

The three women caused quite a stir when they followed the waiter to their table in a cozy alcove with drapes on either side.

"Where's Alec tonight?" Cordie asked when they were seated at the round table.

"He and Jack were working on something, but he wouldn't tell me what it was," Regan answered.

Cordie talked about school, and Regan caught them up on her

search for an apartment. "I don't want a big house to take care of. Not yet. Besides, Alec might be reassigned. Okay, enough chitchat. Talk to us, Sophie. Tell us what you found out about Harrington."

"I want to hear about Alaska, too," Cordie chimed in.

Sophie didn't know where to start. She talked about the trip all through dinner. Her friends sat wide-eyed, barely touching their food as she narrated the story of the last few days.

"Oh my God, Soph . . ." Regan gasped, the tears welling up in her eyes. "You could have been killed."

"So the man who shot you . . ."

"Bluto," Regan said. "She called him Bluto."

"He followed you to Alaska. It wasn't all about Kelly's like everyone thought."

"Speaking of Kelly's . . ." Regan said. "Your dad is now a hero."

Hero today, criminal tomorrow, Sophie thought. "How much do you want to bet the FBI will be looking even harder for my father now?"

Her friends nodded. They had known her father for years and were well aware how elusive he could be.

"Have you talked to Jack since you got home?" Cordie asked.

"Do you think Kelly's will reopen? Mr. Bitterman thinks it will," Sophie said.

Regan and Cordie exchanged a look. Cordie said, "Don't change the channel. You were with a gorgeous man for days—and nights—and you haven't mentioned him once. Why do you think that is . . . oh my God, I know why. You slept with him."

Deny, deny, deny . . . except with her friends. Sophie couldn't lie.

"Yes, I did," she admitted. "I don't know what came over me. I do have principles . . . especially when it comes to the FBI . . . but. . . ."

Regan opened her mouth to protest, but Cordie cut her off. "We know, you're married to an agent, Regan, but your father isn't a career criminal."

Sophie looked miserable. "Maybe he'll go away."

"Jack?" Regan asked.

"Of course, Jack," Cordie said, clearly exasperated. "And if he doesn't go away, Sophie?"

"I can't let this happen. I'm in way over my head."

"You fell in love." Regan nodded.

"You know she did," Cordie said. "Sophie doesn't sleep around. If she didn't have feelings for him, she wouldn't have slept with him." Turning to Sophie, she said, "So you don't want to sleep with him again?"

"Of course I want to sleep with him again. That's the problem!"

Cordie looked sympathetic. "Maybe you're worrying for nothing. Maybe he doesn't plan to see you again. He might have moved on now that you're back in Chicago and safe."

The possibility made Sophie's heart ache.

IN BED THAT NIGHT, the images of Harrington and Inook and the scientists' camp came flooding back to Sophie. She had gone to Alaska to write William Harrington's story, but since returning home, she had done everything she could to avoid the task. A pang of conscience stung her. She had vowed that she would give him a voice, and she owed William at least that much.

She threw off her covers and went to her computer. For the next hour she wrote of what she knew about the man and his ambitions and his ultimate demise.

She thought long and hard about the ending to the story. After all, she didn't really have all the pieces to the puzzle. And so she wrote:

William Harrington loved challenges. He thrived on them. What took him to Alaska remains shrouded in mystery for now, but someday that shroud will be lifted, and we will know the truth. His story is not finished.

THIRTY-FOUR

HIS STORY IS NOT FINISHED.

Marcus Lemming read the words in the newspaper and was enraged.

He was close to his goal, and nothing was going to get in his way now. Eric had almost destroyed the dream with his stupidity, and he had paid the price. Marcus, on the other hand, was too careful, too intelligent, to let it slip through his fingers. Every last piece of research was compiled, recorded, and filed away in a secure place. No one would find it before it was time to hand it over to the buyer. And no one would ever know about the deal he'd made, the fifty million dollars for his research and Eric's formula. What the buyer did with it was of no concern to him. It was all part of the confidentiality agreement. The buyer wanted his scientists to take the credit for the discovery, and that was fine with Marcus. If they revealed the truth, they'd look like fools.

There was just one little problem Marcus had to handle before he was home free: Sophie Summerfield Rose. Eric had said she wouldn't stop. The article she had written for the newspaper said as much: *His story is not finished.*

Marcus had to silence her. He supposed he could find another one of Eric's friends to eliminate her, but the last one had bungled the job, so why would he go to that well again? He'd see to the job himself, and since there is a purpose behind everything a scientist does, he would gain some benefit from the undertaking. Sophie would become his first female subject. After the experiment, he would give her a lethal dose and cremate the body. No body, no crime. But he would have the data for the sake of science . . . or at least for his own gratification.

How to grab her without being seen was the problem he still needed to work out. Preparation and patience—that's what the situation called for. If she didn't make any hasty moves and gave him time, he could work out a plan down to the most critical detail. He hoped to have the opportunity to talk to her before she died. He would ask her why she had gone to such lengths to find out the truth. Why did she care? William Harrington was a nobody. He didn't have any friends or lovers or hovering relatives. He was a loner, and she had done only one interview with him. Just one. She had barely even known him.

When Eric heard that Harrington had mentioned the name Alpha Project to her, he feared she would dig for the truth and get too close, so he had hired one of his unsavory friends to get rid of her. But Marcus had thought Eric had acted rashly. No one, not even Harrington, knew what the Alpha Project really was. Now things had gotten so screwed up, there was no telling to what extremes she would go to unravel their secret.

If luck was on his side, he'd have a month before he had to deal with her—a month before he received his fifty million.

THIRTY-FIVE

M R. BITTERMAN LOVED THE ARTICLES. HE WAS ESPE-
cially fond of the story Sophie had written about the
football team, and was moved by her story about Harrington. It was good to be back to work, back to her routine.

She hadn't seen Jack since he'd left her apartment after bringing
her home from the airport. He had checked every room to make
sure no one was waiting to pounce, kissed her on the forehead, and
walked out the door.

Sophie struggled to keep him out of her thoughts, but late one
evening she decided to watch the video on YouTube. She replayed it
several times, and each time she saw something new, the way he
calmly handled a horrible situation, the way he coolly kept everyone
else from panicking. She wasn't surprised by his courage. She'd already seen him in action and knew how he handled himself in a crisis, how he protected others. He had certainly protected her.

The alpha male. Jack was that, all right.

At five minutes to twelve, Sophie went to her closet, got the cell
phone out of its hiding place, and waited for her father to call.

He was always on time.

"Hi, Daddy."

"Tell me about your trip," he said in greeting.

She wanted him to tell her about Kelly's first.

"Now your turn, Princess," he said after giving his account.

Sophie glossed over the shootings and the fire and told him about the weather and the people and the food, but her father had a way of finding out information, and he already knew down to the last detail what had happened. He sounded like a scolding parent when he said that he would never have encouraged her to go had he known the dangerous trouble she would get into, and he promised to send a team of bodyguards the next time she wanted to travel. She assured him that wouldn't be necessary. She didn't plan on going on any more adventures.

Wanting to move on to more pleasant topics, he said, "I enjoyed the story you wrote about Mr. Harrington. You did an excellent job."

After a few more minutes of conversation, her father paused. "Something's bothering you. I hear it in your voice. What is it?"

"You won't like it."

"I'm your father. You can tell me anything."

She took a breath. "I did such a stupid thing. I fell in love."

"That's wonderful."

"With . . . him."

"Him?"

"The FBI agent." She thought she heard a gulp. She took another breath. "There's more."

"You're pregnant?"

"No. He went to law school."

She knew how her father felt about attorneys. He was one of the best, but he understood what the unscrupulous ones were capable of; he'd witnessed it firsthand. Many years ago, as an enthusiastic young lawyer, he had unwittingly gone to work for the most corrupt law firm in Chicago: Ellis, Ellis, and Cooper. They had turned Bobby Rose into the man he was today.

The Bridget O'Reilly case had been the turning point. An automobile explosion took her husband, her three children, and her mother. Bridget was left with severe burns over half her body. Had the auto company heeded the warnings from the dealers and mechanics about the faulty connection, the explosion never would have happened.

The court awarded Bridget thirty-two million dollars, but by the time the appeals were disposed of, and Ellis and Ellis took their cut and reimbursed themselves for expenses, Bridget was left with two hundred thousand dollars. The amount didn't even begin to cover her medical bills. Bedridden and settlement gone, Bridget couldn't get the health care she needed. Before she could get state aid, she died of an infection.

Meanwhile, Ellis, Ellis, and Cooper celebrated their windfall.

Bobby Rose had been a young, idealistic attorney at the time. His research had helped win the case for Bridget, and in spending a great deal of time together, they had become good friends. He naively believed that she would receive the justice she deserved, but watching Bridget die penniless as the law partners went on lavish vacations and built colossal homes to match their colossal egos, Bobby changed. He resigned his position with the firm. He didn't have to tell them why. They knew, and they had a good laugh over his moral indignation.

Six months later, some of the investments the firm was using as tax write-offs suffered unforeseen and severe losses, and that was followed by unexplainable withdrawals from several accounts. Their assets were dwindling before their very eyes. Since many of their transactions were of a dubious nature to begin with, the lawyers tried to keep the losses quiet. Not only were they afraid of the scrutiny of the authorities, but they also feared for their reputation. They were high-priced attorneys. Who could trust a firm that couldn't even protect its own accounts?

From that time on, Bobby vowed that the fat cats who came to their wealth by underhanded and ruthless means would not enjoy

their riches. Over the years, he gained a reputation for being involved in the downfall of several notorious businessmen. Of course,
to do this, he had to resort to some questionable methods himself,
which was why the law was constantly looking for him. Bobby was
not only shrewd, he was street smart, and when necessary could disappear. He was never sought for criminal charges, but, rather, for
questioning.

His one regret was that he had not been present for most of Sophie's growing up. Her mother died when she was a baby, and circumstances kept him from being the kind of father he wanted to be.
Still, Sophie had never once doubted that her father loved her.

"Say something, Daddy," Sophie prompted when her father
didn't speak. "I said he's a lawyer."

"It's a shock, Princess, I don't deny it, but we'll get through
this."

"I don't want you to be concerned. I just felt I should tell you,
but it isn't going anywhere. He's moved on, and I will, too."

Sophie realized she'd never really been in love before, and if this
was how it felt, it sucked.

"Do you think you can get away for a while . . . just to clear your
head? Why not join me in Monte Carlo?"

"That sounds nice," she said, her voice lacking enthusiasm. "I'd
have to wait until after Thanksgiving. There are too many people
depending on me."

"I understand. I know what you have to do. After Thanksgiving
then. You go to sleep now, and don't worry so much. Things have a
way of working out."

She pretended to believe him.

WORK BECAME HER SALVATION. She buried herself in it, writing for
hours on end. She managed to block out all thoughts of Jack . . .
until she got into bed. She'd close her eyes, and he was right there.

"Get out of my dreams," she whispered.

What was he doing? Where was he now? Had he taken time off and found the warm beach he wanted? Or was he back at work?

Had he handed off the Inook investigation, or was he still involved? She hadn't heard anything for days. Surely they were still looking for answers. Had they found a motive behind the men who tried to kill Jack and her? Alpha Project . . . four scientists . . . William Harrington. She fell asleep trying to connect the dots.

THIRTY-SIX

NOW THAT THE FUROR OVER THE YOUTUBE INCIDENT HAD died down, Jack was able to get back to work. His star had faded because there were two new online superstars for the world to watch. Both were gorgeous Hollywood A-list movie icons, and they were caught duking it out at a high-powered producer's swank wedding reception, the guy having had the bad taste to dump one sexpot to marry the other. What made the video so popular was the X-rated language and the footage of the scantily clad actress punching her way through the crowd to get to the blushing bride. The acid-tongued starlet throwing the first punch ended up sprawled across the ten-thousand-dollar wedding cake. This disaster movie was a huge hit.

In the meantime, Jack found himself reassigned to a fraud case, but since the investigation labeled "Inook" was ongoing, he went to Pittman and argued that he would be far more effective working on the information coming in from Alaska. His argument was valid, and Pittman was swayed.

"I know you, Agent MacAlister. You're going to work this case with or without my permission. Isn't that right? Never mind, don't answer. Okay, you're back in. I'll make the call and let everyone know you're the agent in charge. Finish this soon. I don't like my agents getting shot at."

All the boxes of information that had been gathered from the scientists' facility in Alaska had been shipped to Chicago. Anchorage didn't have the manpower, and since the first crime had been committed in Chicago, the case was theirs. Agents had already pored over every scrap of paper in every box and had viewed the disks. Wolves. Hours and days and months of video about wolves. There was only one thing unusual about the recordings: they stopped before the final year. Had those last months been recorded? If so, where were the disks?

Jack watched the footage, fast-forwarding through scenes with no activity. Sophie had been right. They did eat, sleep, kill, eat, sleep, kill.

He was going through a spiral notebook when two assistants came in, rolling a cart with more boxes.

"Where are those from?" Jack asked.

"The TNI Foundation archives. The research from past years that the doctors had compiled."

So far everything the FBI had examined had proven to be mundane scientific research, but they were leaving no stone unturned. Jack kept going back to what Carter had said to Sophie before Ricky got to him: *You kept pecking away.* What was he afraid she would find? What the hell was he hiding?

Agents had talked to the two remaining scientists several times, but they were unable to shed any light on Carter's motives. Jack familiarized himself with the files on each of the four doctors and wasn't satisfied with what he found. Somebody at TNI had to know something about Carter's secret.

Jack decided that it was time he talked to them face-to-face. He would start with Dr. Marcus Lemming in Chicago. He stopped by the doctor's office unannounced and was told by the secretary that Dr. Lemming had gone to North Dakota for a seminar. The other scientist, Dr. Kirk Halpern, lived just outside of Minneapolis. Jack grabbed a morning flight and was knocking on Halpern's door early that afternoon.

The scientist showed him into his cluttered living room. A slight man with hunched shoulders and an old man's demeanor, his file indicated he was forty-five years old. His obvious fatigue made him look older.

"Could I get you something to drink, Agent?" Dr. Halpern offered. He moved some newspapers off a chair and motioned for Jack to sit. "My wife used to keep me organized. She died six years ago." He glanced around the room. "I'm afraid I've let things go."

"How did your wife handle your long trips to Alaska?" Jack asked.

His face lit up. "She went with me. She loved my work and helped. It was after she passed that I joined Eric and Marcus and Brandon at Inook."

"Tell me about them, Doctor." Jack stood and removed his top-coat. Noticing Halpern staring at his gun, Jack draped the coat on the back of the chair and took his seat again.

"Please call me Kirk. I can't tell you anything I haven't already told the other agents."

"I would appreciate it if you would go over it again," Jack urged.

"There isn't much to tell." He moved a needlepoint pillow from the chair and sat down. "I'll begin with our team leader, Brandon . . . Dr. Brandon Finch. He was very organized. He even made charts so that we wouldn't waste time. Brandon got on our nerves after awhile. Things had to be just so. He was obsessive about everything from how we prepared our food to when we went to bed. It was irritating. I got along with him all right, but occasionally we bickered. After a while, the isolation and the weather gets to you.

"I felt just terrible when he died. None of us knew about his heart condition. He was overweight, but not too out of shape. He kept up with us in the field."

"How did the other doctors get along with him?"

"They put up with him, just like I did. Every now and then they'd get into it with him, but there weren't any hard feelings after they let off steam."

"What about Eric Carter?"

"Young, eager, intense. He and Marcus became close friends right away since they were the same age. They worked together well and shared similar interests—at the beginning anyway. Eric began to stay by himself more. The longer we were there, the more their friendship was strained. One afternoon while Eric was examining some blood samples he'd taken, Marcus took Brandon and me aside and told us he was worried about Eric. He asked us if we'd noticed any changes. Indeed, we had. Eric had become so withdrawn, he wouldn't let any of us look at his notes until he had them organized. Most of it was gibberish to us anyway. Marcus said he couldn't read his scribbles."

"You didn't have any idea what he was hiding?"

"No, I didn't. The agents told me that before he died, he said something to Miss Rose about a test subject. He was concerned about something she was looking for. I have no idea what he meant."

Jack was about to move on to Marcus Lemming when he thought of another question to ask. "Which of you did the recording?"

"At first we all took our turns with the camera, but the last couple of years, Eric insisted on taking it over."

"So there were videos from the last year?"

"Of course. Eric watched them over and over and over. It drove the rest of us crazy. We finally moved the player into the small room so we could shut the door. Hour after hour he'd watch. He loved Ricky. But then, all of us did. He was a splendid alpha male. I only wish I could have observed him to the end. Don't imagine he'll be around long. Arctic wolves don't have long life spans, you know. I had to leave that phase of the study because the last couple of years Brandon wanted me to go with him to track the pups from Ricky's second pack. I guess you could say we were creating a family tree of sorts. I will admit we learned a great deal, but we didn't get to film the new packs as much as we would have liked. Eric hogged the good audio and video equipment. He had thirty disk files marked. At night, he'd watch with the sound muted. He didn't want to hear, just to watch. One through thirty—when he finished the last one, he'd start all over again. Marcus thought Eric was having a breakdown of some sort. He wanted him to go home for a while, see a medical doctor. We would have sent him home, but we were going to close up soon anyway, so we put up with his odd behavior awhile longer. I believed that, once Eric got back to the city, he'd snap out of it."

Jack wanted to go back to the videos. "You said one through thirty disks. Are you sure of that number?"

"Oh, yes, I'm sure."

"I've found only twenty-three disks."

Kirk sat back. "What happened to the other seven?"

"You tell me."

He scratched his chin. "I don't know. Eric must have done something with them. Maybe he shipped them home. Did you check?" He smiled as he continued. "Of course you did."

Jack moved to the last scientist: Marcus Lemming.

"Like I told you, he was close to Eric until Eric started acting strange. Marcus was dedicated to the study and the pack, and by the time we finished, he was closer to me than Eric. In the evening, while Eric watched his videos, Marcus and I played Scrabble and cards.

"We've talked a few times since we left Inook. Marcus is thinking about moving back to North Dakota to be near family. This study burned him out."

Jack spent another hour talking to Kirk. He was putting on his coat and heading toward the door when he stopped to ask, "You never called your study the Alpha Project?"

"I've been asked that question about a hundred times now. I told the agents no, and I told Miss Rose no. We didn't call it the Alpha."

"You spoke to Sophie?"

"Yes, she called yesterday. She said she'd like to come see me. We spent a long time on the phone. She asked about the Alpha Project, but then somehow we started talking about my wife. It felt good to reminisce. I'm afraid I got carried away, but Miss Rose seemed genuinely interested."

That was his Sophie. She could get anyone to tell her his life story. But then, she wasn't really his Sophie, was she? Jack thought about her a lot. He missed her.

She was on his mind as he flew back to Chicago. She was still "pecking away," as Eric had accused. She wasn't going to let it go, which gave him an uneasy feeling. Jack needed to call her and tell her to stop. He needed to talk to her, convince her to back off. He needed to see her again.

THIRTY-SEVEN

"**G**OBBLE, GOBBLE, GOBBLE."

Sophie watched the protesters picketing in front of the grocery story with a mixture of disbelief and shock. Mr. Bitterman had given her the assignment, and this one was going in her I-hate-this-job notebook. It might even make the top five.

Seven protesters holding placards marched back and forth at the store entrance. Three were dressed up as turkeys.

Sophie crossed the parking lot. Bracing herself, she tapped on the shoulder of the woman at the end of the line. "Excuse me. Could you tell me who the head turkey is? I'd like to find out what you're protesting."

A gentleman with a round face framed in feathers and an orange wattle hanging from his chin stepped forward.

"That's me. I put this together," he announced with great seriousness.

"I'm writing an article for the *Illinois Chronicle*, sir. May I ask you some questions about your protest?"

"Of course. We want to draw attention to this horror."

"What horror would that be?" Sophie asked.

"The heartless cruelty to turkeys."

"It's barbaric is what it is," a woman shouted over her placard. "The assassins raise them just to kill and eat them. It's murder!"

"You don't want grocery stores to sell Thanksgiving turkeys?" Sophie asked calmly.

A thin older woman with thick glasses stepped forward. "That's right, and we're going to stay here until the killing stops."

Each of the protesters had something to add, and they made extra sure that Sophie spelled their names correctly. When she couldn't think of another absurd question to ask, she thanked them for the interview and turned to walk away. Behind her, the small but vocal group chanted, "Save the turkeys! Save the turkeys!"

Holding up her phone, Sophie took some pictures. Cordie and Regan would never believe her unless she showed them the proof.

She took her time walking back to the office. Pedestrians were rushing about all bundled up in their heavy coats with their collars over their ears and their wool hats pulled down. Sophie hadn't noticed the cold and was surprised when she looked up at the First Commerce Bank building and saw the temperature in big red letters below the time: twenty-eight degrees. Considering where she'd been, this was balmy weather.

What was she going to write about the turkey people? She couldn't call them crazy, and the article needed to be upbeat and cheerful because that's what people wanted to read. Okay, she'd make them cheerful turkey people.

Oh God, how had she come to this? Turkey protesters and the heartbreak of static cling—that's what she was writing about these days.

Enough with the whining, she told herself. She would write the story without balking because that was her job, but as soon as it was finished she thought she just might run out into traffic and hope she got run over by a very large bus.

Gary was in her cubicle again. He was getting so bold, he didn't even pretend to be looking for something.

Sophie didn't pretend to be gracious. "Get out." She wanted to push him, but knowing Gary, he'd probably sue her for assault. "This is my space, not yours."

"Just looking around," he said sullenly.

She didn't ask what he was looking for. He'd told her once that she always got the good stories—he obviously hadn't heard about the turkey people—and he wanted to see if he could snatch one for himself. After she looked around to make sure he hadn't stolen anything, she sat down at her computer, typed in her password, and started writing her article. It took her twenty minutes from start to finish. She attached a note asking Mr. Bitterman not to run her photo with the story.

She looked at the stack of assignments she needed to catch up on. What next? she thought. Sitting back in her chair, she took a deep breath. Her old notepad was sitting on top of her desk. She picked it up and thumbed through the pages, thinking yet again about her interview with Harrington. She knew she was missing something, and it was driving her crazy. Having read her notes at least twenty times already, she went over them again.

Selected to join an exclusive club. Was that the Alpha Project? He'd called it a club and had compared it to an Olympic trial. He'd bragged to her that he had taken a battery of tests to qualify.

"Just look at me." That's what he'd said. *A superman club?* She'd made that note a question. "Just look at me."

She needed to talk to Kirk Halpern again, so she made the call.

Kirk was happy to hear from her.

"I really hate to bother you," she began, "but I was wondering about the wolves you studied."

"I'd be happy to tell you anything you want to know," he offered.

"Were these particular animals unusually vigorous or strong?" she asked.

"I wouldn't say they were unusual," he answered. "They were what we expected for that particular subspecies."

"Did you notice any tremendous improvement in their condition while you observed them?"

"Actually, I didn't get to observe the same animals throughout the study. Dr. Finch and I branched off to another group the last couple of years. Eric and Marcus continued with the initial alpha male. He, of course, was the strongest of the pack. As you might know, we called him Ricky. He was mature when we first began our observations, so the likelihood of his growing stronger was remote. We couldn't tell the exact age, but we estimated him to be older based on the wear and tear on the teeth. The life span of the arctic wolf is only about seven years. It was amazing, actually, that Ricky was still alive at the end of the study."

"How much of your observation was recorded on video?"

"Dr. Carter was diligent with his recordings, though I've just learned that the later ones are missing. An FBI agent, Jack MacAlister, was just here asking about that very thing."

"When did he leave?" she asked.

"About fifteen minutes ago."

"Thank you so much, Kirk," she said. "You've been very helpful."

"Call me anytime."

Sophie put the phone down and tapped her pencil on her chin as she thought. How was she going to get to those videos? Everything that had been in the Inook facility was evidence in an ongoing investigation, and it would be heavily guarded.

She was going to have to get tricky. Kirk unknowingly had helped her by mentioning that Agent MacAlister had just left. Assuming Jack would get on the first available flight back to Chicago, she had to hurry. Timing was important.

She called Alec, and without explaining why, asked him if he would meet her in the lobby of the FBI building. Since he was already at the office, he agreed.

She smiled sweetly and kissed his cheek when she saw him.

"Jack told me I should watch some of the videos of the wolves," she said. She shrugged and sighed. "I know it will be boring, but he did ask, and I promised I would. Could you get them for me?"

Alec smiled back. He had known Sophie long enough to recognize when he should be suspicious. "This isn't Blockbuster. You can't just check them out."

"Yes, you're right. How about I watch them here? That wouldn't be a problem, would it?"

"Maybe I should check with Jack," he said.

"Good idea. Is he here? He'll tell you he wanted my help."

"No, he isn't here."

"Do you want to call him?" she asked, hoping to heaven that he was in the air.

"I doubt I can reach him. I guess I could arrange for you to watch the disks."

Five minutes later, armed with a visitor's badge clipped to her blouse, she followed Alec down a corridor to a sparsely furnished room. A technician came in carrying a DVD player, hooked it up, and then asked which of the disks she wanted to watch.

"The first three and the last three, please," she said.

Alec stayed in the room while she watched the wolves. He did paperwork, but every once in a while, he'd glance up and ask, "Find anything yet?"

"No, not yet."

She scanned the first disk and the last.

"Okay, I'm finished," she announced. "I don't need to see any more. Thank you, Alec."

He walked her back to the lobby. "Sophie, what were you looking for?"

She smiled. "Superman. See you later."

She turned toward the door just as Jack was walking in. He seemed as surprised to see her as she was to see him.

He tilted his head. "Hi."

"Hello." She kept going. "Good-bye."

She tried to walk past him, but he grabbed her arm. "We need to talk."

"Did you tell her to watch the videos?" Alec asked.

Jack was looking at Sophie. "No."

"I was sure you did," she said innocently.

"You didn't lie to a federal officer, did you, Sophie?" Jack asked.

Sophie took a quick look at her watch. "Oh dear. I'm late for a meeting." She bolted for the door. "So nice to see you again."

THIRTY-EIGHT

SOPHIE FLED THE BUILDING SO FAST SHE NEARLY RAN INTO A couple of elderly women carrying shopping bags.

Jack didn't go after her. Hands in his pockets, he watched her until she was out of sight, then turned around and headed to the elevator.

Alec couldn't resist. "Want to talk about it?"

"Hell, no."

Alec grinned. Jack was a careful man and, like most men, kept his emotions close to the vest. Relationships were not a comfortable topic of discussion, and he certainly wasn't going to talk about the woman he loved. Not now, not ever.

Alec recognized the signs. Jack's life had just become very complicated, and he was confused. Had his friend hit the misery stage yet? From the look on his face, Alec thought maybe he had. He'd definitely hit the stage where everyone else could see what he refused to acknowledge. Alec had been through it himself. He knew that it was only a matter of time before Jack fell.

Jack and Sophie. Now that was going to be an interesting combination.

Jack punched the elevator button. "Why did Sophie want to watch the videos? Did she tell you?"

Alec waited until the doors closed. "She said she had a theory, but she wasn't ready to talk about it."

"Wasn't ready? Why didn't you make her talk about it?"

"*Make her?* You're kidding, right?"

"You're an FBI agent—"

"Hey, it would take a team of agents working around the clock to get her to tell them what she had for lunch. And even then, she'd probably lie."

"If she's found something and she goes barreling in, she could get into trouble. Do you realize how many times she's been shot at? I'll tell you. Too damn many. I think I'll call Gil and put him back on Sophie."

"Good idea," Alec said. "You know Gil. He likes the extra money for poker, and he loves Sophie."

Jack waited until he reached his desk to tell Alec about his trip to Minneapolis and his conversation with Dr. Halpern.

"He's written a bunch of books and gotten awards, but he's a pretty unassuming guy," Jack said. "I can't imagine how he could stand being cooped up with three other men in Alaska all that time. I'm kind of surprised he didn't go postal."

"It's the quiet ones who do. I understand Marcus Lemming is the—excuse the pun—polar opposite. Evidently he doesn't mind telling you how great he is."

Jack and Alec went through the files of information that had been gathered on the case. Closing the last one, Jack pushed his chair back and stretched his legs. "According to the reports, Halpern and Lemming weren't at Inook when Harrington was killed. They claim they never heard of William Harrington. Eric was by himself, and they didn't know what he was doing. Lemming's due back in town tonight. I think I'll pay him a visit," Jack said.

*   *   *

JACK STOPPED HIS CAR in front of Marcus Lemming's home, a tiny 1960s tract house. The one-story, square structure looked naked sitting on the lot. There wasn't a tree or a shrub or a blade of grass anywhere near it. Weeds that had been scalped to ground level substituted for a lawn.

A scientist who spent most of his time in the Arctic probably didn't have time to care for a house, Jack thought, but he wondered how the neighbors with their manicured lawns and well-trimmed shrubs felt about him.

Alec had been right about Marcus Lemming: he was nothing like Kirk Halpern. A brawny man with a square jaw and a distrustful scowl opened the door. When Jack showed his ID and asked for a few minutes, Lemming stepped aside to let him in.

The interior of his home was almost as sparse as the exterior. The small living room had bare hardwood floors. A futon sat against one wall, and a desk and chair faced the window that overlooked the street. Another wall was covered entirely by bookcases, the shelves stuffed so full of volumes they bowed under the weight.

"What is it you want to know?" Lemming asked. "I've already told the other agents everything I can about Eric."

"How would you describe your relationship with him?" Jack asked.

"We got along well enough. We were great friends at the beginning, but it became obvious to all of us that Eric was jealous of me. I had already published several books and was asked to join the boards at two major institutes. Eric's résumé was—I hate to speak ill of the dead—but I'm afraid his résumé was rather pathetic. He actually went to a state school. He became very possessive of his own work, not wanting to share with the rest of us. He'd go off by himself at night and work on his notes and his videos. He seemed almost paranoid, as though he were afraid of someone stealing his ideas. I can assure you, Eric Carter didn't have anything that I would want or need to steal."

There wasn't an ounce of sympathy in Lemming's voice as he

continued to deride Carter's credentials. "I have no idea why he snapped like that. I think maybe the pressure got to him."

"So you didn't see the data he had compiled or the videos?"

"I saw a few of them. But like I said, toward the end he kept them to himself."

"Do you know what happened to his records?"

"The rest of us e-mailed our data home, and we boxed up our hard copies and shipped them. I couldn't tell you what Eric did."

"We found his notebooks and some disks, but it appears that the most recent ones are missing. Do you know anything about them?"

"Not a clue."

The more questions Jack asked, the more impatient Lemming became. When William Harrington's name was mentioned, a look of concern crossed his face. "I heard what happened," he said. "A polar bear . . ." He shook his head. "Horrible way to die. I can't imagine what he would have been doing out in the middle of nowhere like that."

After several questions were answered, Lemming hadn't told Jack anything he hadn't already read in the files. However, Jack began to notice a theme running through every statement Lemming made: Eric Carter was acting alone.

Why was he so insistent on this point? Why was it so important for him to distance himself? Those were questions Jack would keep to himself . . . for now.

Minutes later, back in his car and driving away from the scientist's home, Jack looked over his shoulder. Lemming was standing in the window.

THIRTY-NINE

J ACK HAD LOOKED GOOD, REALLY GOOD . . . AND TIRED, SO-
phie thought. But really, really good.

She had spent the afternoon on an assignment and had pushed Jack MacAlister out of her mind, but now he was creeping back in again.

She wondered what would have happened if she had thrown herself at him in the lobby of the FBI building. Would alarms go off?

Crazy thoughts. And it was all the big jerk's fault. She missed kissing him.

Feeling melancholy, she told herself to stop thinking about him. She had more important things to concentrate on. Like turkeys.

Jack hadn't even bothered to call her since they had returned from Alaska. Why not?

She was hurrying back to the newspaper. A deadline was loom-ing. She increased her pace until she was almost running. Not good in stiletto heels.

By the time she reached her office building, she was primed for a fight. She hoped she found Gary in her cubicle again. She'd have a reason to punch him. Let him sue. What did she care? She didn't have any money, so she wouldn't lose anything.

Mr. Bitterman spotted her making her way to her desk.

"Blond—" he shouted, but stopped himself before adding, "girl."

Sophie was pleased. Mr. Bitterman was trainable after all.

"Put your stuff away, Sophie, and come in here. I've got another assignment for you."

If the assignment was a follow-up on the turkey people, she thought she might just buy one—a frozen one—and clobber him over the head with it.

Okay, I've got to stop thinking like this. This job is turning me into a violent person, she thought.

Gary was huddled at his desk and didn't look up when she walked past. The day was getting better by the minute.

Pad in hand, Sophie went into Mr. Bitterman's office and shut the door.

"Did you notice I didn't call you Blond Girl?"

"Yes, sir, I did, and I appreciate it. Now maybe you could work on not whistling for me."

"All right," he said. "Now sit down and tell me what you found out at the FBI. Anything?"

"Sort of," she hedged. "I have this theory, but it's way out there. Are you sure you want to hear it?"

"Try me."

"I think that Dr. Eric Carter wasn't just watching the wolves. I think he was doing something to them. One wolf in particular, the alpha male. I can't prove it, though. The FBI could," she added. "Their scientists could get blood samples from the animals or examine the pack or—"

"What do you mean, 'doing something *to* the animals'?"

"I think Carter was altering them in some way."

"You're serious, aren't you?"

"It's crazy, isn't it?"

He nodded. "Did you tell Jack or Alec your theory?"

"No, I didn't." Before he could ask why, she said, "I don't mind you laughing at me, but I don't want them to."

"Let the FBI investigate this," he ordered.

She didn't argue. She had hit a dead end anyway. "Yes, sir. I've done as much as I can, and eventually the missing videos will be found, and they'll answer a lot of the questions."

"I don't want you to work on this anymore. Okay, Sophie?"

She nodded. "You said you had an assignment for me?"

The worry left his eyes. "That's right, I do. Promise me you'll hear me out before you start arguing."

"Yes . . . ?" she asked suspiciously.

"I'd like you to take over 'Kathy's Kitchen' column."

"Take over?"

"Kathy's opening a bakery downtown in the spring."

"And you need someone to fill in until you find a replacement?"

"No, I want you to take the position full-time. We'll call it 'Sophie's Kitchen.' "

She started to laugh, but stopped when he didn't join in.

"You're not joking."

"No, I'm not."

"Sir, I don't know how to cook. I couldn't possibly—"

"You'll get the hang of it. You've got five months to learn. If you want, I'll pay for a cooking class. Don't sell yourself short. You can do anything you put your mind to."

"But I . . . but . . ."

"Good, I'm glad you agree. I sent that story back to you to proof. Need you to do that right away."

"But I . . ."

IT WAS A GOOD THING she had a sense of humor, or she'd go looking for that bus again. First turkeys, then the kitchen. Could her life get any crazier?

Gary had a smirk on his face as he watched her walk by. Such a creep, she thought for the thousandth time. Out of sight, out of mind. Gary was forgotten once she started working. Mr. Bitterman wanted her to proof one of her stories, which was code for "Rewrite it, I hate it."

She was on the last paragraph when her phone rang. She didn't take her eyes off the computer screen as she answered. "Hello."

"Sophie Rose?" The voice was deep and gravelly. This was not a newspaper call. The man had not used her professional name.

"Yes," she answered hesitantly.

"I have something that you'll want to see," he said.

"Who is this?" she asked.

"I can't give you my name."

"Then I'm afraid this conversation is over," she answered.

She was about to hang up when the man said, "Wait. Please. Don't hang up. I need your help."

His pleading tone made her pause. "I'm listening."

"I have the tapes that will show you what Eric Carter was doing in Alaska."

That caught her attention.

"Where did you get them?" she asked.

"I can't say. All I can tell you is I had nothing to do with any of it. I didn't know what he was doing. It wasn't right, and I should never have gotten involved. I just need to get rid of them."

"Take them to the FBI," she said.

"I can't. They'll come after me."

"Bring them here to the newspaper then," she said.

"No, I can't." He sounded frantic now. "I'm not letting anybody else have them. I trust you. I read your article. You either take them off my hands, or I'll destroy them, and you'll never know what happened to William Harrington."

"Where are you?" she asked.

"Sixty-eighth and Prescott. Meet me there," he said. He added, "And come alone, or you won't be getting the tapes."

"No," Sophie said. "I'll choose the place."

"Okay, where?"

Sophie's mind raced through various spots, public places with lots of people. "Cosmo's," she said. She gave him the address.

"Be there at seven," he said, and then added, "You better be alone, or the deal's off." He hung up.

Sophie's watch said it was 6:15. If she hurried, she could get to Cosmo's early. On the way she'd call Jack and have him meet her there.

She didn't turn off her computer or tell Mr. Bitterman she was leaving. She grabbed her purse and hurried for the exit. On the street, she searched for a taxi. With rush hour in full swing, the odds of finding an empty one were slim to none. She'd have to take the El.

As she was running, she pulled her phone out of her purse to call Jack. The phone rang before she could flip it open. It was her father.

"How about I take you to dinner, Princess?" he asked. "I'm back in town, and I'm not a wanted man today. We can catch up face-to-face."

"That'd be great, Daddy," she said, "but I can't talk now."

"Where are you?" he asked. "You sound out of breath."

"I'm cutting through Nelson Park to catch the El," she said. "I'm meeting someone."

"It's getting dark. You have no business walking through a park in the dark. Why won't you let me buy you a car?"

"Not now, Daddy," she rushed. "I'll have to call you back later. I need to get hold of Jack right away. This is really important."

"Jack? Jack MacAlister?" he asked.

"Dad, I can't—"

He heard, "No . . . don't . . ." and then a scuffle.

And she was gone.

FORTY

JACK SAT AT THE CONFERENCE ROOM TABLE WITH THREE other agents and a stack of case files. Pittman walked in carrying three more files and took her place at the head of the table. Alec trailed in a minute later.

"You're late, Agent Buchanan," Pittman barked.

"Yes, I am." He didn't offer an excuse. She wouldn't have appreciated one anyway. He wasn't a child. He was late.

"We'll start with the Alaska file. Jack, you're up."

Jack gave an update on his interviews with Kirk Halpern and Marcus Lemming. "Both of them basically reiterated what was in the file. Halpern told me Lemming had the closest relationship with Carter. They spent a lot of time together. Lemming, on the other hand, would have you believe he couldn't stomach the guy. He blamed Carter for everything but the snow. He didn't particularly like the questions I asked, so he told me what he wanted me to know. He's an arrogant prick. He made a point of stressing that Carter wasn't as smart as he was. He sure wanted me to believe that Carter was keeping secrets. Protested a little too much, if you know what I mean. I think we should be tailing him."

There was a knock on the door, and Pittman's assistant, Jennifer, looked in.

"I don't want any interruptions," Pittman reminded her.

"A call just came for Agent MacAlister."

"Take a message. We're in the middle of something."

"It's Bobby Rose."

Everyone at the table turned to Jack.

The announcement took the wind out of Pittman. "Bobby Rose? Why would he be calling you, Agent MacAlister?"

Jack was already crossing the room to get to the phone when Jennifer said, "Mr. Rose insists it's urgent."

Something had happened to Sophie. Jack knew it before he answered. Bobby Rose would not be calling him otherwise.

"Put him on speaker phone," Pittman ordered.

"Line four," Jennifer said before pulling the door closed.

"MacAlister here."

"Sophie's missing. Someone took her."

"When?" he demanded. "What happened?"

"She was cutting through Nelson Park on her way to the El."

Pittman identified herself and asked, "How do you know she was taken?"

"I was talking to her on the phone." Fear made his voice hard. "She told me she was going to meet someone, and she needed to call you, Jack. She had to tell you something important."

"How long ago was this?" Alec asked the question.

"Five minutes at the most. She was saying good-bye, and suddenly she screamed . . . then she was gone."

"We'll pinpoint her location," Pittman said as she nodded to an agent.

"Where are you now, Mr. Rose?"

"I'm on my way to the park."

"We'll meet you there," Alec said.

"Listen to me, MacAlister. You find her. You hear me? You find her."

The second the call ended, Jack looked at Pittman. In a rage, he said, "That son of a bitch Lemming has her. I know it." He threw his chair out of his way and ran.

Pittman grabbed the phone and called for help as she began issuing orders to the others in the room.

Alec caught up with Jack in the parking garage. "I'm driving," he shouted.

Shaking with fury, Jack was trying not to think about what could be happening to Sophie, trying to concentrate on finding her.

Nelson Park wasn't far away, but by the time Alec and Jack arrived, the area was swarming with police. There was no sign of Sophie, and no one had seen anything.

"He has her, Alec. You know I'm right. I should have dragged him in. I should have—"

"There isn't any evidence."

"Screw evidence." He looked around at the crowd and the police. Other agents were arriving on the scene.

"We're close to Sophie's office. Maybe she left something behind. An address, a note, anything."

Jack was running to the car nodding. "We're losing time. The longer he has her—"

"We'll find her, we'll find her," Alec promised as he jumped into the driver's seat. "Why? Why would Lemming risk taking her? He knew we didn't have any evidence against him. He'd be in custody if we did. It doesn't make sense."

Alec slammed on the brakes in front of the newspaper offices and left the car double-parked with the lights flashing.

"I don't know what his reason is," Jack said.

Bitterman was turning the light off in his office and heading to the door when he saw Jack and Alec running at him. "What's happened?"

Alec quickly filled him in. Bitterman's face paled.

"Did she mention where she was going when she left here?" Alec asked.

"I assumed she was going home. She was supposed to turn in an article, but she left without finishing it. That's very unusual for Sophie."

"Did she say anything to you, anything at all about where she would be going or who she would be talking to?"

"We talked about work. She told me about the doctors up in Alaska. She thought they were doing something to those poor animals. I made her promise to stop snooping, and she agreed, said she'd let the FBI figure it out."

Bitterman led the way to her desk.

Gary jumped up when he saw the agents. "What's going on?" he asked.

"Sophie's missing."

Gary immediately looked down at his feet. "I wouldn't worry. She's probably shopping. She'll turn up."

Jack was tearing through Sophie's desk looking for anything that might shed some light on her whereabouts.

"She's not shopping," Bitterman told him in a near shout. "Someone took her."

"Oh . . . I see. I hope she's all right."

Jack spotted the bug on the back of Sophie's monitor. "What the . . ."

He looked at Alec and picked up Sophie's phone. He had it apart in seconds.

"Another bug," he said. "Short range."

Alec turned to Gary. Jack slowly advanced.

"You want to step out into the aisle?" Alec said.

"Why? I'm not finished working."

Jack wasn't going to waste time explaining. He grabbed Gary by his shirt and tossed him out of the way.

"What do we have here?" Alec asked, pointing to an earpiece underneath a box of paper clips inside the desk drawer.

Gary tried to back away. Alec blocked him from going any farther.

"You've been listening to her phone conversations, haven't you? You bugged her office, and you bugged Bitterman's office, too."

"No, no, I didn't—"

"It was you?" Bitterman demanded.

"What did you hear on Sophie's phone?" Alec asked.

Jack had Gary by the throat. "You listen to me, you perv. I'm not wasting time here. If you know something, you better tell me now. I'm going to count to five, and then I'm going to snap your neck. One . . . two . . . three . . ."

"Okay, okay. Some man called her and said he needed her help. He wanted to give her some videos she could take to the FBI. She told him to bring them here, but he wouldn't, so she was going to meet him."

"Where?"

"Cosmo's. He wanted her to meet him somewhere else, but she wouldn't."

"Where did he want to meet?" Alec asked.

"Sixty-eighth and Prescott."

"When I told you Sophie was missing, why didn't you speak up?" Bitterman demanded.

"Then you'd find out I was listening, and I'd get in trouble. I wasn't gonna hurt anybody. I was sure her father would call and maybe say something I could sell—"

Jack shoved him so hard, he fell across his desk.

Alec was running for the stairs talking on his cell phone, and Jack followed right behind.

Bitterman shouted, "What can I do to help?"

"Keep him here," Jack shouted. "Don't let him out of your sight, and if he remembers anything else, you call me."

"I don't know anything else," Gary screamed. "You can't make me stay . . ."

Bitterman picked up the phone and called security.

Jack and Alec flew down the stairs to the street. "I'll call Pittman," Jack said as Alec gunned the motor. "I don't know this city. Where's Sixty-eighth and Prescott?"

By now, Jack had Pittman on the phone and he repeated the question to her. She had a map spread out on the conference table but didn't have to use it.

"Old warehouses and storage units," she said. "It's a big area, Alec. You'll need help doing a sweep."

They got backup within minutes. Jack could hear sirens as police rushed toward them. "How far away are we?"

"Not far," Alec said. "She's stronger than she looks, Jack. If she can hold on . . ."

"Can't you drive any faster?"

Alec was speeding like a NASCAR driver on the final loop.

Pittman called back, and Alec put her on speaker. "They're setting up around the perimeter. More men on the way."

Police cars barricaded 68th Street. Alec slammed on the brakes, and Jack jumped out before the car came to a stop. He looked at his watch. She'd been gone almost an hour. Her chances decreased with every minute.

Hang on, Sophie.

FORTY-ONE

S OPHIE SLOWLY REGAINED CONSCIOUSNESS. SHE GROANED and tried to sit up. Falling back, she tried again, this time bracing her hands on the floor to balance herself. It was pitch black. She reached out to find a light switch, but there wasn't anything there. She touched the floor again. It was cold, hard . . . concrete?

Where was she?

She finally gained enough strength in her limbs to stand. She swayed back and forth but stayed upright. Her head was pounding, and she felt dazed and disoriented. Stretching her arms out in front of her, she took a tentative step. If she could find a window or door, she could let some light in.

Something blocked her. She pushed, heard a crash, reached out again, and felt cardboard. Sophie stood perfectly still. With deep, calming breaths, she tried to control the panic she felt welling up inside her.

Where was she?

She couldn't hear any noises, any traffic. Someone had hit her.

She could still feel the pain. She touched her face, felt stickiness. Blood from the blow?

Her memory was coming back. Daddy. She'd been talking to her father. Yes, she'd had her cell phone up to her ear, and suddenly there was excruciating pain . . . then darkness.

She had to find a door or a window and get outside. Oh, God, what if she was in a tunnel or a cave? What if she couldn't get out?

She tried to control her fear. She put her hands out again, feeling her way until she reached a wall. What was it? Cement blocks? She moved across the wall to a door. She felt a handle. She whimpered as she tried to turn it.

The door suddenly burst in on her, and she was thrown to the floor.

She screamed and scrambled to her feet. A glaring light was shoved in her face, blinding her. She put her hand up to block it and saw the outline of a man behind the light, but couldn't see who he was.

"Hello, Sophie. I'd like to introduce myself. I'm Dr. Marcus Lemming. Recognize my voice? We had such nice talks over the phone. Of course, I called myself Paul Larson then."

He put the flashlight on a cardboard box, propped it up, and stepped forward. He was holding a crowbar in his left hand down at his side.

"You've caused me a considerable amount of distress. Do you know why? You couldn't stop poking your nose in where it didn't belong. You had to keep searching . . . had to find out . . ."

He lashed out with his fist and hit her hard in the shoulder, knocking her into the wall. She crumpled to the floor. Before she could recover, he grabbed her arm, yanking her up.

"What do you know about the Alpha Project?"

She didn't answer fast enough.

"What did Harrington tell you?" Lemming demanded.

"Nothing," she said, her voice trembling. "He didn't . . ."

"Don't lie to me. What do you know?"

He slowly swung the crowbar back and forth. "How did you find out about this place? How did you know to come here?"

"I didn't know . . . I . . ."

"Liar," he shouted. "Did you find my journal? Is that how you found out about the project? No, you couldn't have," he answered his own question. "The journal's here."

He took another step closer. "Who told you?"

"No one . . . I didn't . . ."

He hit her with the crowbar, though he was careful not to kill her. He needed his answers first. The sharp edge had cut into her skin above her ear, and blood now poured down. She tried to focus. He was moving in the light, and there were shadows dancing along the wall. She thought she saw something moving in the corner. Was someone there? Had someone followed her? Daddy? Or Jack . . . did he call Jack? Please let it be Jack. She had to distract Lemming. Her mind raced. Hurry. *Hurry.*

"How did you know to come here?" he asked again.

The question made no sense. He was out of his mind, Sophie thought. Had he become delirious? "You know how I got here," she said. "You know."

He stopped, tilted his head, thinking about her answer. "I know? How could I . . ." He shook his head. "No, you're lying."

"If you kill me, they'll hunt you down."

"They'll never find me. I'll have fifty million dollars and a new identity." He pulled her to her knees. "I had great plans for you, but now I'll have to change them. Too bad you had to be so nosy. You're making me do this . . ."

FORTY-TWO

A LEC BUCHANAN WAS THE AGENT IN CHARGE. HE LEANED over the hood of his car. In front of him was a map of the area that one of the policemen had grabbed from his glove compartment. Two plainclothes detectives flanked his sides, and one aimed a flashlight toward the map, watching while Alec sectioned off zones for each team to search. The police and FBI agents were gathered in a vacant parking lot at the end of the huge complex, an industrial area of warehouses and storage units. Most workers had gone home for the night, so the streets were empty.

"This will take days," an officer complained in a whisper to his partner. He happened to look across the car at Agent MacAlister and immediately regretted the comment.

"What about Lemming's vehicle?" Alec asked a detective.

"Every cop in the city is searching for it. We'll find it."

"He could have parked his car inside one of these buildings."

A young policeman in uniform stepped forward and spoke to Alec. "Excuse me, sir, but I know this area. I think I can help." He pointed to the map. "Prescott ends here," he said. "The buildings to the east are boarded up. I know. I've had to drag kids out of there. The city's going to tear them down, but they haven't gotten around to it yet. There are several places a car could squeeze in . . . alleys, too. I'd start there and work my way east."

He pointed to another section. "This three-block area here is filled with self-storage units. Some have fences around them, others don't. I don't think he could hide a vehicle in there. He'd have to park on the street . . . or maybe in between the units."

Agents and policemen fanned out in every direction to circle the area and slowly move in. Alec made sure every cop in the city was on alert, but the warehouse district got priority. At the moment, it was the only lead he had.

Another agent, Hank Sawyer, took over so that Alec could search with Jack. They got into Alec's car and headed east. They drove through the broken gate of a wire fence and turned onto 70th Street.

"Wait a minute, wait a minute," Jack said. "He'd have a reason to go to one of the self-storage units. When the team searched his home and his office, they found computer files, but they didn't look for the hard copies. Kirk Halpern said there were hard copies shipped back. Lemming had to have stored them. Those missing discs could be here. Look where we are. No one's going to ask questions when you rent one of these. If he paid cash and used another name . . ."

"Why would he bring Sophie here?"

Jack shook his head, feeling at though he was grasping at straws, but desperate to have an answer. "He plans to pick up his stuff and get out of Chicago. Maybe he wants to get even with Sophie. Maybe she was getting too close . . . I don't know. One thing I'm sure of: if he has her and he plans to run, he won't take her with him."

Alec made the turn into a narrow alley between two tall buildings. With the headlights turned off, the car rolled forward at a snail's pace. Most of the streetlights were burned out or broken. Up ahead a bulb hanging off a post flickered and buzzed repeatedly. Emerging onto a street, they saw a police car four blocks away patrolling slowly, on the same mission.

"Stay in the alleys," Jack said. The night air was fogging up the windows. He rolled his window down to get a better view as they drove up and down the tight passages.

"Wait," Jack said suddenly. He stuck his head out the window and squinted.

Three alleys over, neatly tucked between two rusted Dumpsters, was a car. Alec pulled to a stop.

"That's it," Jack said. "That's Lemming's." He got out. "Call Sawyer. Tell him, no sirens, no lights." He slowly walked down the alley, studying the doors on the left, while Alec followed, concentrating on the units on the right. The rolling doors were big enough to drive a truck through, indicating the volume behind them was large. Next to each garage door was a side door. Everything was locked up tight.

Jack had almost reached the end of the row of doors when he saw a sliver of light peeking beneath the rubber weather stripping. He moved closer, straining to hear sounds.

A man's muffled voice was low and threatening, but Jack couldn't make out what he was saying. Then he heard a scream . . . Sophie's scream.

He shot the lock, kicked the door in, and raced inside, taking in the scene all at once: cardboard boxes stacked high, a flashlight propped on top, the beam directed at Sophie. She was on her knees on the floor. Lemming, in the shadows, stood over her holding a crowbar. He was swinging it down toward Sophie when Jack shot him.

Once wasn't enough. It was a solid hit to the chest, but Marcus Lemming didn't go down. He staggered back, gained his balance, and lunged at Sophie again. Running toward the man, Jack shot twice more as he grabbed Sophie's arm and dragged her behind him.

Finally, Lemming dropped, face smashed into the concrete floor, the crowbar still in his hands.

Jack knelt beside Sophie and saw the blood on the side of her face.

"Sophie, look at me. Open your eyes."

She struggled to focus. She saw Marcus, then Jack leaning over her. He took her in his arms and gently lifted her. She tucked her head under his chin and felt him shaking. It hurt to move, but she forced herself to turn her head just enough to press her lips to his ear. "Two," she whispered.

Jack understood. He looked up in time to see a shadow move between boxes against the back wall. With lightning speed, he threw himself on top of Sophie and fired. The shadow darted out and wildly returned fire. Jack emptied his clip and reached for another. Alec appeared in the doorway.

"Behind the boxes, left side," Jack shouted.

"I've got him. Get her out of here," Alec ordered. He fired once and moved in front of Jack.

They heard a click and knew the bastard's weapon was empty now.

"I surrender. I surrender. Don't shoot me. I'm dropping my gun and coming out. Don't shoot."

Hands in the air, Kirk Halpern stepped toward the light. The son of a bitch had a smile on his face.

FORTY-THREE

THE SCENE AT THE HOSPITAL WAS CHAOTIC. SOPHIE HAD
been taken down to radiology for tests and was now back in
the emergency room, parked in a bed behind a curtain
while she waited for the plastic surgeon to stitch her up. Regan and
Cordie stayed at her side. A nurse and an aide recognized Sophie
from her last visit, and both asked to take their dinner breaks.

Sophie had a blistering headache, but the doctor wouldn't give
her anything for the pain, not even an aspirin, until he heard the results of her tests.

"He's waiting to hear if you've got a concussion," Cordie explained.

"Is my father here?" Sophie asked. "I was talking to him on the
phone when it happened."

"He's on his way," Regan told her. "I heard he was giving the police a hard time over at the park. They found your phone by the
fountain, and there was blood on it. He was beside himself."

"Where are Jack and Alec?"

"They were here, but once they knew you were going to be
okay, they left."

"Thank God," she whispered.

"What do you mean, 'thank God'? We know how you feel about Jack," Cordie said.

"So does my father. I don't think it's a good idea for both of them to be in the same room."

Cordie patted her hand. "It will be fine," she said as she glanced across the bed at Regan, gave her a look, and shook her head.

Sophie pulled a blanket over her legs. "It's cold in here," she said.

"You've been through a trauma," Regan explained sympathetically. "Your body is reacting. Would you like another blanket?"

With tears in her eyes, Sophie said, "It was awful. I thought—"

"You can tell us tomorrow," Cordie said. "It's too upsetting for you right now." Trying to brighten the mood, she added, "Mr. Bitterman was relieved to hear you're doing okay. He's very fond of you."

"He's secretly such a softie."

"He said to tell you that Gary was arrested. He was hauled off in handcuffs."

"Why? What did he do?"

Sophie gasped several times as Cordie repeated the conversation she'd had with Bitterman.

"What a weasel," Regan said. Sophie didn't disagree.

An aide pulled the curtain back and stepped forward with a tray. She saw Sophie, stopped cold, and slowly backed out, pulling the curtain closed again.

"What was that all about?" Regan asked.

"The staff isn't very friendly here," Cordie whispered.

A phone rang. Alec was calling Regan to tell her he wouldn't be returning to the hospital. Dr. Halpern, whom Cordie had dubbed Dr. Frankenstein, was talking up a storm and didn't want an attorney. They were taking advantage of the situation and getting as much out of him as they could.

The plastic surgeon took his sweet time getting to the hospital, but he was very kind, and he worked quickly. After checking the wounds to her face, he cupped Sophie's chin in his hand and tilted her head, studying her.

"Beautiful skin," he said. "Flawless. Good bone structure. Perfect nose . . ."

"She isn't here for a facelift," Cordie said, exasperated.

The doctor smiled at her. "The three of you could play *Charlie's Angels.*" Turning back to Sophie, he said, "You won't need Botox for a long time . . . as long as you don't lead a stressful life. *I'll* need it some day. Plastic surgeons live with stress."

Sophie would have laughed if her head hadn't been aching so.

"You think you've got stress? How many bullets have you dodged today?" she asked.

The doctor could tell he was in dangerous territory, so he changed the subject. "You don't have a concussion," he told her, "so you get to go home and sleep in your own bed."

Sophie's father arrived at the hospital in time to drive her home. He suggested that he stay the night with her, but she refused. She'd already had the same argument with Regan and Cordie. She promised to go right to sleep after he left.

Sophie was exhausted and felt grimy. She was careful not to wet the bandage on her face as she showered. After slipping into her nightgown and brushing her teeth, she dropped into bed. Her exhaustion had wiped her out, but she wasn't sleepy yet, so she turned on the television and surfed the channels. She stopped on the cooking channel. She'd never watched it before. Jack liked the shows, though. What was he doing now? Had he finished with Halpern? She hoped he'd gotten answers. Would he call her tomorrow?

She fell asleep wishing she was in his arms and wondering if he was thinking about her.

FORTY-FOUR

J ACK COULDN'T STOP THINKING ABOUT SOPHIE, AND EVERY
half hour or so he would leave the interrogation room and call
for an update. He knew when she left the hospital, and he
knew when she arrived home.

He had to take breaks to get away from Kirk Halpern anyway,
and so did Alec. The doctor turned their stomachs. When the urge
to smash his face in became too strong, Jack would know it was time
to get up.

Halpern had sure fooled him. He had seemed like the mild-
mannered, scholarly type, sitting in his worn chair talking about his
deceased wife and praising Sophie for being so compassionate, but
now that his game was over, his true colors came rushing to the surface. He didn't have to pretend modesty any longer.

Halpern was smug and conceited, and he wanted them to know
how clever he had been. Gaining respect for his superior intellect
was obviously important to him. Alec and Jack played along, anything to keep him talking.

"You never know how stupid people are until you live with
them," Halpern said.

"Eric and Marcus thought their little secret, their little Alpha Project," he said mockingly, "was so safe, but figuring out what they were up to was hardly rocket science. After the first year, I knew they were plotting something. Any child can operate eavesdropping equipment, and breaking passwords and codes is so easy, I make it my hobby. You can get pretty bored with nothing to do but watch wolves."

He went into great detail about how he listened to conversations and snooped through their files.

"The cherry on top was that Marcus was keeping a journal the whole time. Hiding it under his mattress was a smart move, don't you think?" he asked sarcastically.

Jack asked him specific questions about the scientific discovery.

"Eric came up with the formula," Halpern said. "I think he may have already had it the first year we were at Inook together. It was by accident that he discovered what it could do and how adrenaline altered its effects.

"We've already discussed Ricky, Agent MacAlister. Don't you remember that I told you he was a mature alpha male? They started experimenting on him right away. Eric would tell Brandon and me that he needed to take blood, that he was checking for different microorganisms, but I knew what he was really doing. He was injecting the animal, and after a while, when Brandon and I branched off to study other packs and didn't show any interest, he didn't even bother to bring back vials of blood.

"I don't know how many injections Ricky was given, but I started noticing a slight change in the wolf. Of course, I pretended I didn't see anything, and Brandon was too self-absorbed to notice. After a while, Ricky was getting stronger and bigger." He chuckled as he added, "A wolf on steroids, only it wasn't a steroid he was getting. This was a wonder drug with incredible benefits and no side effects.

"Eric and Marcus continued their experiments on other animals when they went back to Chicago. They had set up a lab. It's all in the journal."

"How did Sophie Rose play into all of this?" Alec asked.

"When their prime subject, William Harrington, was lifted to the test site, they found out she knew him, and had, in fact, talked to him at length. She had e-mailed him before they shut down his website; she left messages on his phone. She even went to his apartment looking for him. They wanted people to think he'd left on a long trip . . . just in case. But she wouldn't leave it alone. Then when Harrington was killed, her card was found, and they got scared that she might know too much.

"Eric got really paranoid about her, so Marcus called her pretending to be some guy named Paul Larson, just to find out how much she knew. He might have left her alone, but she asked him about the Alpha Project." He shrugged. "They were in too deep. She could ruin the fifty-million-dollar deal he and Eric had made. She had to go."

As Jack and Alec delved for details, Halpern became more verbose. His answers turned into lectures.

"Now I'll explain how I lured Marcus to the storage facility. It was so simple really. I called him, all befuddled, and said that this reporter had contacted me saying she knew about some secret scientific study that was going on at our camp, and she said she had found out where the missing tapes were that would prove it. She was on her way to get them."

He stopped for a moment, a slight smile tilting the corners of his mouth as he remembered the call.

"I put him in such a panic, he couldn't wait to get off the phone and rush to his hidey hole. He never questioned how she could have found out."

"How did—" Alec began.

"Do not interrupt me," he snapped. His head twitched at his outburst, and he took a breath to calm himself before continuing.

"Luring the woman was a little chancy, but all I really needed to do was get her out in the open and isolate her, and I had her. I caught her in Nelson Park. I hit her hard. Didn't know my own strength, really." His gaze bounced back and forth from Alec to Jack. "She was out cold. I must admit, I didn't really care all that much about her, but when she called me at my home, I could tell she was getting close to the truth, closer than any of those agents who questioned me. I knew I had to get rid of Marcus, so why not two birds with one stone?"

"Why would you want to get rid of Marcus? Why not just turn him in to the authorities?" Alec asked.

Halpern studied his fingernails and smiled. "The money, of course."

"What money?" Jack asked.

"The fifty million. I knew Marcus would come after me when he found out that I had done a little wheeling and dealing of my own. His contact in Dubai was happy to get the formula and the research early. He didn't care who sold it to him." He sighed and looked off in the distance. "Fifty million. It's in a secure place, and it's all mine."

"You won't need money where you're going," Alec told him.

"But Agent Buchanan, what have I done?" he asked innocently. "I didn't kill anyone. If my punishment fits my crime, I'm sure I'll be a free man in no time at all." He paused to reconsider. "No, I'll be a free *rich* man in no time at all. Face it, gentlemen, I've outsmarted you. That money is in a safe place, and you'll never find it."

The interrogation went well into the night. When it was over, Jack and Alec handed in their preliminary reports and headed home.

Jack was beat. He needed some fresh air. He needed a shower. And he needed Sophie.

THE SOUND OF running water woke her. She rolled to her side and looked at the clock: 2:20. For a second she thought she was hearing rain, but then she heard something drop in her bathroom.

"Damn." It was a whisper, but loud enough for her to know that Jack was getting out of her shower.

The television was still on, but the remote was on the table on the opposite side of the bed. She never put it there. It was too far to reach.

Jack came out of the bathroom. He was yawning, and he wasn't wearing a stitch of clothing.

"Did I wake you, sweetheart?"

"Why are you here?"

He got into bed and reached for her. "You needed me here."

"I was sound asleep. I didn't need—"

"I needed to be here."

He grabbed the remote and turned off the television, then pulled her into his arms.

"How did you get into my apartment?"

"Shh. Go to sleep. You need your rest."

She was so happy he was there. She snuggled closer to him. "I'm changing the locks tomorrow."

"It won't matter. I'll still get in. You're not getting rid of me, Sophie."

She didn't know how to respond. He sounded serious, as though he really wanted to stay with her. Knowing who she was, he still wanted her. What was wrong with him? Why would he want her . . . except maybe for the sex. He surely wasn't staying for her cooking. Her mind began to drift.

His deep breathing told her he was asleep, yet when she tried to roll away, he tightened his hold.

SOPHIE WOKE UP MIDMORNING. Jack was stroking her back. She turned in his arms and kissed him.

"I love you, Jack."

"I love you, too."

"This can never go anywhere. You know that, don't you?"

"I'm marrying you, Sophie. That's what I know."

She kissed his chin, the base of his throat. "Daddy won't approve." Her hands slid down his chest and his stomach. She smiled at his indrawn breath. "You're a disappointment."

Jack growled low in his throat. She was driving him crazy.

"You know . . . FBI," she said.

He couldn't pay attention to what she was saying. She was stroking him, teasing, tormenting.

"He won't think you're good enough for me," she continued. "He's probably right."

Jack rolled her onto her back, braced himself on his elbows, and looked into her eyes. "No one will ever love you the way I do."

She wrapped her arms around his neck and pulled him toward her. "Prove it."

FORTY-FIVE

T HE ENGAGEMENT PARTY WAS HELD AT THE HAMILTON Hotel at Aiden's insistence.

There were over seventy guests. Jack's brothers were there. His father had died several years ago, and his mother was on her fourth or fifth honeymoon. Her sons couldn't keep track.

Jack was talking to Alec and Gil, but he never let Sophie out of his sight. She chatted with Mr. and Mrs. Bitterman and their daughter, who Sophie thought was lovely.

"Did you hear about the job our Sophie was offered? Big-time stuff," Mr. Bitterman told his wife. "It wasn't the only job offer. Isn't that right? It was after she wrote that story about William Harrington."

"I read that," Mrs. Bitterman said. "It was wonderful. 'The Forgotten Man.' "

"She turned them down," Mr. Bitterman said.

"I must be crazy, but I did," Sophie laughed. "I didn't want to change jobs after all. I just wanted to be asked, I guess."

"What will happen when your father is on the outs again with the police? You know it's coming."

"Jack says he'll take him in for questioning . . . if he can find him."

"You're okay with that?"

"Mr. Bitterman, you know my father. They can't hold him long. He'll negotiate his way out."

"Speak of the devil . . ."

Bobby Rose walked into the party. He was suave and debonair and, according to Mrs. Bitterman and her daughter, made the women feel giddy.

To Sophie, he was simply her father. He was heading for Jack, but guests surrounded him and delayed his getting to his target. Sophie excused herself and hurried to Jack's side.

Gil came to stand beside her. "How's your father handling this? His only daughter getting married."

"He's not happy about it."

"Oh, sure he is."

"No, he isn't," she insisted. "He doesn't like Jack."

"Now, Sophie, how do you know that?" Gil asked, thinking she was exaggerating.

"I know because he said, 'Sophie, I don't like Jack.' "

Alec choked on his drink. Gil looked nonplussed.

"It's okay," she said. "Jack isn't particularly fond of my father either, but they'll get along."

A few minutes later Bobby Rose faced the happy couple. He shook Jack's hand and kissed Sophie.

Mr. Bitterman joined them. "I was telling Mr. Rose that I had heard rumors that Kelly's Root Beer was going to reopen."

Bobby nodded. "It's a good investment." He winked at Sophie. "It might happen." He turned to Jack and said, "I read in the paper that Kirk Halpern is trying to make a deal."

"Not a chance," Jack said.

"Is it true he's hidden fifty million dollars?" Gil asked.

Jack nodded. "Yes. He says no one will ever find it."

Bobby Rose looked at his daughter and smiled. "Wanna bet?"

ABOUT THE AUTHOR

JULIE GARWOOD is the author of numerous *New York Times* bestsellers, including *Shadow Music, Shadow Dance, Slow Burn, Murder List, Killjoy, Mercy, Heartbreaker, Ransom,* and *Come the Spring.* There are more than thirty-six million copies of her books in print.

ABOUT THE TYPE

The text of this book was set in Janson, a typeface designed in about 1690 by Nicholas Kis, a Hungarian living in Amsterdam, and for many years mistakenly attributed to the Dutch printer Anton Janson. In 1919 the matrices became the property of the Stempel Foundry in Frankfurt. It is an old-style book face of excellent clarity and sharpness. Janson serifs are concave and splayed; the contrast between thick and thin strokes is marked.